RIDE
AND
DIE
AGAIN

RIDE AND DIE AGAIN

RIDGEMORE BOOK 2

LUCÍA ASHTA

Podium

All rights reserved. No part of this publication may be reproduced, stored in a retrieval system, or transmitted in any form or by any means electronic, mechanical, photocopying, recording, or otherwise without prior written permission from Podium Publishing.

This is a work of fiction. Names, characters, places, and incidents are either products of the author's imagination or used fictitiously. Any resemblance to actual events, locales, or persons, living, dead, or undead, is entirely coincidental.

Copyright © 2025 by Lucía Ashta

Cover design by Amanda Shaffer

ISBN: 978-1-0394-7855-8

Published in 2025 by Podium Publishing
www.podiumentertainment.com

For Nadia, Sonia, Catia, and James

RIDE
AND
DIE
AGAIN

1

That's Some Superhero Shit

I came to with a start, the fight surging awake with me. My heart thumped so hard it hurt, like it might bounce right out of my chest. I was lying down, and *hell no* I wasn't about to let a bunch of goons kill me and my friends while I lay around doing nothing to prevent it. Even as I struggled to wrench open my eyes—so freaking heavy—I forced my body to sit up, and fuck if I didn't hurt just about everywhere.

Hands pressed gingerly against my shoulders, holding me down. Before I trained my unfocused gaze on him, I recognized his touch.

Griffin.

Griffin was here.

A breath I didn't realize I was holding eased out of me.

"Shhhhh," he whispered, when he should have been screaming at the hired guns not to kill us.

Oh my God.

My mouth went slack as the shots rang through my memory. Five each for two of my friends—*my fucking family*. For a moment, I allowed my eyelids to drift closed—it was so much easier than trying to keep them open—and relived Layla shuddering as bullets tore through her torso, her body twisting and falling, suddenly lifeless; Hunt jolting as each bullet ripped through him, then crashing to the floor of the gymnasium and not moving again.

My heart ached even more, to the point of breaking. "Layyyylerrrr. Huuuunchtuh." Why wasn't my tongue working properly?

"Shhh," Griffin repeated, guiding me to lie back down. "They're alive. They'll be fine."

This time, when I got my eyes open, the face I loved more than any other was in better focus.

Griffin's eyes were heavy and dark, the hazel that brightened them at times subdued. His forehead was furrowed, his beautiful lips pinched, and scruff darkened his face.

He smiled at me, soft and sad, his eyes glistening. "Hey there, Joss. It's so fucking good to see you awake."

He closed his eyes for several seconds, holding back whatever else he was feeling, thinking, unwilling to say. When he opened them again, the moisture was gone and the hazel blazed. Breathing hard, he simply stared down at me for several moments.

"Whatttt happeeedd?" I slurred, focusing on my surroundings, sensing what I'd missed before: the scent of disinfected cleanliness, but not as acrid; soothing, dim incandescent lighting; calming classical music playing softly. I recognized the song, knew it well, but its title was beyond my reach.

Griffin released my shoulders, clasping my hand instead. "Magnum Chase had his people set the gym on fire. Then he sent armed soldiers in to kill us." He paused to unclench his jaw. "They killed all of you. After you"—he gulped, his Adam's apple bobbing—"died, Brady went apeshit and they shot him too. So then I couldn't do anything to them or I couldn't be sure they'd bring you back. If they killed me too, then they might've left us all dead."

His eyes were so tormented that I couldn't look away from the greens, golds, and browns popping in his irises. It was clear that restraining himself in order to ensure we all lived had been more difficult for him than dying a second time.

I squeezed his hand but the effort was pitiful. Just the same, he glanced at where our hands met and laced our fingers together. When my attention followed, I noticed a tube snaking from a vein in my arm to an IV stand from which fluid bags hung. I was in a hospital bed. A blood pressure cuff, currently deflated, adorned my other arm, connected to a machine that silently recorded my vitals.

"You're groggy and slurring 'cause they have you on a morphine drip. The slurring'll stop soon, if what happened with Hunt and Lay's any indication."

I snapped my gaze to his face, and he read my unspoken question.

"They're both awake. They've been awake. You . . ." He inhaled and exhaled deeply enough to make his chest visibly rise and fall. "You took longer."

"Why?" I croaked. My throat was parched. Rough.

Again, Griffin understood. He rose and crossed the room to a small, slim table holding a crystalline pitcher filled with water, matching glasses beside it.

The room was about the size of my bedroom, with recessed lighting revealing warm gray walls. An ample window with a seat framed a clear blue sky. Daytime, then. The floor was carpeted in a plush cream—who the hell put light carpet in a hospital? The furniture—a twin bed and two armchairs—looked comfortable. The chairs were upholstered in sleek leather. A floor-to-ceiling armoire occupied one corner of the room, its wood a deep, rich black. Vivid orchids in pots adorned either side of the deep window seat. Everything about the decor screamed expensive elegance.

Griffin slid a hand behind my back and helped me lean forward, bringing the glass to my lips. I drank several sips, swallowing roughly.

"They intubated you," he said, setting the glass down on a ledge. "That's why your throat feels like that. They did it to me too, when I died."

Quietly, I snorted. When the hell did our lives—and *deaths*—become so fucking absurd? It was our senior year in high school. We were supposed to be partying and living it up—not dying and resurrecting.

Inching the arm with the blood pressure cuff toward my forehead, I hesitated before running my fingers across the skin. Smooth as usual.

"What? I thought . . ." I cleared my throat. The words were starting to come more easily. "Last I remember, the guy was pointing a gun at my head."

But that wasn't actually the last thing I remembered . . .

. . . the desperation transformed Griffin's face when I told him I loved him . . .

I'd told the man who was supposed to be no more than a friend—never more than that—that I *loved* him. Sure, he could have interpreted my declaration as I had his: an expression of platonic love in a dire, terrible moment. Then again, maybe he now knew that I'd broken the most significant unspoken rule among us.

My crew was too important to me to risk it. I'd upset the balance between us all, even if I was the only one aware I'd done it.

I glanced up at him—at the man I loved and shouldn't—searching his face for clues. Had I screwed things up between us? Between all of us?

Ignorant of the new reason for my sudden tension, Griffin answered, "He ended up shooting you in the chest." Pain, as obvious as if its cause were physical, flared in his eyes. His lips twisted into a snarl. "I'm guessing 'cause they didn't want to leave a scar that couldn't be easily hidden behind clothing."

"Shit," I murmured, not sure which messed-up part out of all of them I was lamenting.

Griffin's hands curled into fists. "Five shots for each of you. Brady too. Though Brade didn't need to be defibrillated to be brought back this time."

"Really?" I tried to tilt upward.

Griffin piled the pillows under my head and shoulders before sitting beside me again. "Really." He frowned, though surely that was a good thing. "Seems the first time's the only time we need the extra juice."

"And now we've all . . . died . . . and come back," I said, trying the fact on for size.

"Yup."

"Damn."

"Yep. That about sums it up."

I scooted farther up on the pillows, hooked the neck of my pale cotton gown, and peeked under it. Bandages covered my entire torso. I needed to get a look at the skin beneath. Soon. I released the gown to pat my thigh, the one that had been wrapped in a cast and now wasn't.

Griffin nodded as if answering the question I was struggling to form. "The fractures are healed. They x-rayed the leg to confirm."

"Wow," I eventually said. "This is all . . . a lot."

"Yeah. It is." His lips pursed.

"So . . . this doesn't look like the same hospital you guys were in."

"That's 'cause it's not. We're in a private facility."

I arched my brows.

"Funded by Magnum Chase."

My eyes widened, dispelling any remnants of my earlier sluggishness. "Say what now?"

He scowled. "Trust me, I'm no happier about it. None of us are. But he forced my hand."

"I'll just bet he did."

"They took away the defibrillators. Told me I could take my chances with Ridgemore's EMTs. Convince them to attempt to revive the four of you even when you were so clearly dead. Hope they'd do it, then try to explain how the five of us are all now 'miracle kids.' How we recover from mortal wounds no one should be able to come back from."

My thoughts were coming faster now, sharper. "And putting ourselves at risk for some black, unmarked van with government plates to show up and cart us away."

"Exactly." He rubbed his neck; worry and lack of sleep darkened the skin beneath his eyes. "They wheeled in four stretchers and told me they had surgeons on standby, waiting to help my friends." He snorted.

"That asshole's got some balls on him," I muttered.

"He hasn't even shown his face yet. I thought he'd be up in our business the second we got here, but nope."

"I'm sure he'll make an appearance before long," I said, not bothering to conceal my bitterness. "So, where are the others?"

"Hunt woke up first. Well, long after Brady, who was only out for a few hours."

I whistled. "A few hours?"

He nodded, his dark hair shifting atop his head. The strands stood up in parts, suggesting he'd been running his fingers through them over and again.

"That's some superhero shit," I whispered with a mixture of reverence and astonishment. "What the fuck, Griff?"

"Yeah, trust me, I know. I'm the one who had to watch you all come back. Layla came to a couple hours later. It took them a while, but once Hunt and Lay were able to be wheeled around, they all came here to wait for you. But . . ."

"But what?"

"But you've been out for three days."

I blinked at him. "Seriously?"

He nodded, eyes heavy, revealing how exhausted he actually was. "They woke up that same day, that night. You . . . didn't."

He ran his fingers along the seam of his jeans, picking at it. "I haven't left your side except to do quick checks on the others."

Careful not to dislodge the IV needle, I placed my hand atop his. "I'm sorry."

He jerked his gaze up to mine. "What the hell do you have to be sorry for? It's the billionaire asshole who's gonna get every ounce of my wrath the second I lay eyes on him."

I rubbed my thumb across the back of his hand. "You thought I might not come back?"

He didn't respond at first, following the movement of my finger across his skin. Then, he nodded jerkily.

"It crossed my mind a few thousand times."

"That's what I'm sorry for," I said. "I remember all too well what it felt like to think I might've lost you. Shit, I won't ever forget it." More softly: "Though I hope I do. It was the worst moment of my life."

Wow. Way to diss Brady, Joss.

He'd died too. And then we hadn't yet known he'd come back to life, which made his death terrifyingly horrid. But believing I'd never see Griffin's smile again was worse even than seeing a stick of rebar the circumference of my arm spearing Brady's chest.

Griffin only nodded, seemingly lost in his own thoughts. Eventually, he squeezed my hand as if coming to some internal conclusion. "Layla said she couldn't stand another second of 'ick' and a hospital gown that showed her ass and left for her room to 'uncrustify.' Her words. Hunt and Brady went with her."

Finally, a spark of that usual playfulness lit his tired eyes. "I think Brade was gonna try to help her take a sponge bath."

I spit out a laugh before choking around my still-tender throat. After another sip of water, I smiled, aware the gesture felt somewhat forced. Wasn't it wrong to laugh and smile when things had been so terribly tragic recently? Even if they'd had a lively ending?

Griffin's smile was weary but real. "With how freaked out he's been, he might actually go through with it. You shoulda seen him, Joss—he was frantic with the thought of losing her. Hunt, too, obviously. But it's like Brady finally realized how lucky he is to have a twin."

I leaned my head back on the pillows, gazing up at the ceiling—painted a smooth, understated cream to match the carpet. "He *is* lucky." I looked back at Griff. "We're all lucky to have each other."

I'm lucky to have you. The admission hovered on my tongue, eager for me to share it aloud. I couldn't bring myself to do it. Not after what I'd said in the gym. Not after what I'd already done.

Griffin slid nearer and bent forward so his face was only inches away from mine. He gripped my fingers harder, sliding our joined hands onto his thigh.

This close, his eyes seemed to swirl, entrancing me.

My heart beat faster, and I was grateful the heart-rate monitor was silent, or else Griffin would know the effect he was having on me. I swallowed around my tender throat and became overly aware of my breaths—deep with anticipation.

My nerves jumped, overshadowing the otherwise overwhelming ache that weighed down my entire body, as if I'd been shot everywhere at once instead of just my chest. The desire to rub at my wounds was gone. There was only him.

"Joss," he said, and I licked my lips. He followed the path of my tongue, though I didn't think he noticed he did. Or maybe he did. I didn't actually know what he was thinking, and I desperately needed to.

"Joss, I . . ." he said, trailing off.

"Yes?"

His stare drifted toward the wall behind my bed before returning to mine. "Before you . . ." He sighed heavily. "This is never gonna get easier to talk about, is it?"

Since I didn't know what exactly the hell he was referring to, I didn't answer, hoping he'd continue all on his own instead, and that he'd hurry the hell up while he was at it.

Again, he sighed. "Before you died . . ." Anger suddenly shrouded his eyes. "No, that's not right either. Before that fucking sonofabitch *killed* you, fucking *murdered* you, and I don't care one single shit that he thought you'd come back. Before that, you said something to me. You said—"

"I remember."

His mouth twitched. He swallowed again.

Holy shit. Griffin Conway, who was smooth as silk and cool as ice, was fucking *nervous*.

Had I not been so interested in what he was going to say next, I might have drawn out the topic a bit, seen how long I could enjoy seeing him hopping around on proverbial hot coals.

But I was all but dying all over again to hear his next words.

His brows furrowed as his eyes seared their intensity into mine. "And you remember what I told you before I went over the cliff in Clyde?"

"Of course." My response was barely a whisper. Jitters wriggled beneath my skin, erasing everything about my circumstances but him.

"And what do you think?"

"About what you said?" I asked, tipping my head to one side in confusion. "Or about what I said?"

"Both."

"I know what I meant by what I said. I can only guess at what you meant." Never in my life had I been so obtuse with the man.

Our friendship had always been easy, blunt, straightforward. Fuck, had I already ruined that?

"And what did you mean by what you said to me?" he asked. "Did you mean that you love me as a friend or . . . ?"

There. It was out in the open. The fucker had put it all on me. Though, to be fair, he'd said the words to me first. Maybe this made us even.

His stare was unrelenting, and eventually I closed my eyes just to escape it for a moment while my insides melted and then clenched and then melted all over again.

Of course I knew my answer. How could I not, when now that I was being truthful with myself, I'd been in love with the man for months, probably even years? But once I confirmed my feelings, there'd be no going back. No more chance at claiming a platonic affection.

For fuck's sake, Joss, you just survived literal death. You've never been a coward before. Now's not the time to start being one.

Before I could chicken out, I snapped open my eyes and said, "I meant that I'm *in love* with you."

The declaration was softer than I'd wanted, as if at the last moment a part of me had tried not to lay out my already clenching heart on the bed between us, a pulsing, aching, bloody, pulpy mess.

His breath hitched before he released a long, loud exhale. "Oh my God, Joss, I—"

The door to the room swung open. Layla and Hunt hobbled in, leaning on walking sticks and taking steps that were slow, careful, gentle. Brady, only slightly less spritely than his usual self, entered behind them, closing the door.

I'd forever be happy to know all three of them were alive and well, but right then I wanted to scream at them to leave and come back in ten minutes. *Just ten measly minutes.* Even one would maybe have been enough.

But Griffin had already turned to face them, breaking the moment between us, when Layla called out in a slightly hoarse voice, "Holy fuckballs, Joss! You're finally awake. You about had us losing our shit when you wouldn't wake the fuck up."

Forcing myself to accept that Griffin would know exactly how I felt while I'd now have to wait to find out what he thought, I directed my attention to experiencing my genuine relief. It was there, for certain it was. Despite all odds, life had taken the nuttiest of turns for us all. And the five of us—my best friends, my crew, my family—had survived a small army's assault.

Every single one of us was gloriously alive.

Beaming up at them, I grinned. "So fucking happy to see your gorgeous faces, guys. We def have gotta stop doing this."

In slippers and scrubs, Layla and Hunt shuffled across the room, each claiming one of the armchairs and lowering themselves gingerly into them.

Brady plopped onto the guest bed, leaned over his thighs, and clasped his hands. "Now that everyone's awake, we've gotta talk. Shit's bad."

2

Starring in Our Very Own Shitshow

With a wince at the tug on my chest wounds, I pushed up farther onto my pillows so I could more easily see Brady, Hunt, and Layla. Griffin, well, I could scarcely take my eyes off him where he remained next to me on my bed.

That was going to be a problem—a freaking huge one. Lately it seemed we were racking up a whole long list of them.

My voice raspy, I told them all, "Given that every one of us has *died*—legit *died*—in the last few months, I'd say shit's more than bad."

Layla crossed and uncrossed her legs, trying to find a comfortable position atop the armchair. When she grimaced, I guessed she hadn't found one that didn't pull on her own healing injuries.

With a frown, she said, "If shit's not as bad as it gets, then I don't wanna find out how bad things *can* get. I'm calling us done, right now. Right the *hell* now."

In turn, she glared at each of us, even her brother. "No more dying. And I fucking mean that." As if we hadn't gotten the message—as if any of us actually wanted to die—she meted out another round of glares, this time punctuated by a stabby index finger jabbing the air between us. "No. More."

Hunt grunted out, "You got that right."

But Brady gazed at his sister with wistful eyes—I might have gone so far as to describe them as adoring eyes.

Griffin wasn't kidding. That was definitely new. After Brady had come back to life, it hadn't taken long for Layla to resume treating him just as she always had: like he was an annoyance she only tolerated because he was her twin. Who would have guessed Brady had a soft, mushy side to him?

"Are our parents freaking out?" I asked before chuffing darkly. "They've gotta be." I groaned. "They're gonna have a field day with all their *I-told-you-so*'s."

"I'm sure they're freaking out," Brady said, swinging his legs against the edge of the bed a few times. "Mom's probably got search parties out looking for us."

My muscles tensed, causing another painful tug along my torso. "Wait. How come they don't know where we are?"

Hunt scowled. "Because we can't call out. None of our phones work, and before you go looking for it, we even tried yours. Apparently, we're in a dead zone. Intentional, obviously."

Layla nodded, brushing her long bangs out of her eyes. "Every time a doctor or nurse comes to check on us, we bug the crap out of them with questions, obvi. But it's always the same answers."

Brady grunted, and then he, Layla, and Hunt quoted at the same time: "Mr. Chase will be here shortly to answer all your questions."

I felt my eyes widen. "Are we trapped here, then?"

Obviously restless, Layla let her head fall against the headrest of the armchair before immediately snapping it back up. "It's looking like it. Just for now, though."

"Yeah, 'cause we're getting out of here no matter whose asses we gotta kick to do it." Brady cracked his knuckles.

Hunt nodded, his dark eyes bright with his resolve. His jaw clenched before he waggled it to loosen it.

"Why haven't you guys tried to see if we can get out of here yet?" I asked, but even as I did so, I realized the explanation.

Griffin faced me, gazing down at me with an open, guileless expression I might have also described as adoring if I hadn't known better. He was just relieved I was alive, that was all. And why wouldn't he be? We'd all been friends forever and a day.

"We weren't gonna leave before we knew you were all right," Griffin said, his voice gruff. "As much as I might hate this asshole for everything he's done to us, and man do I have a hate-on for him, there's no doubt he's got the best medical care money can buy."

Brady harrumphed. "You and I came back just fine at Ridgemore Hospital."

Holding my eyes instead of turning to look at Brady, Griffin said, "True. But we all came back a lot faster than Joss. Who knows what might've happened at the hospital?"

"Why didn't I come back as fast as you guys?" I asked.

"No idea, girl," Layla said with a forced smile. "Maybe you were just enjoying some of that R and R we've been talking about. Maybe you just wanted a break from all this crap, so your subconscious kept you under."

I arched my brows. That right there was a major stretch.

Her shoulders slumped at my expression. "We don't know."

Brady snorted. "There's a whole lotta that going on. We don't know shit about shit."

Layla smirked bitterly. "At least we know that."

Griffin's gaze trailed my fingers as I gently pressed against the gown that covered my chest. "So what are the wounds looking like?"

Layla bounced in her seat as if she'd just remembered something, starting to behave like her usual self despite the grimace that followed the movement. I, however, doubted I'd be in the mood to so much as try bouncing anywhere for ages. My body felt like it'd gone several rounds with an angry, vengeful *real* ninja, not any of us and our wannabe skills.

"Oh my God! Brade tried to help give me a sponge bath." She snorted. "Can you believe the bozo? A *sponge bath*." She glanced at him, a modest dose of her usual mischief dancing across her face. "Admit it. I'm a total hottie. You've always known it. It was your chance to grope my fine-ass titties and you went for it."

Griffin, Hunt, and I glanced between the twins, waiting for their inevitable reactions.

As one, their faces screwed up into mutual disgust, making their similar features appear identical.

Brady's nose scrunched up into an accordion of lines. "Ew, Lay. Just . . . *ew*. Do you ever *think* before you speak? Seriously, man! That went too far."

Layla shuddered. "It totally did. My bad, dude." She didn't bother promising she'd start thinking before she spoke; we all knew there was no point. Layla was Layla, and Layla would do what Layla did, no matter how crass or twisted. I was oddly comforted by the fact that some things never changed, even if most other aspects of our lives were so different they bordered on unrecognizable.

When Brady and Layla seemed like they'd be continuing the grossed-out spiel for a while, I prompted, "So, our wounds?"

Hunt was usually as agile as an alley cat. Now he inched toward the edge of his seat before aiding himself up with his arms. But then he stood without the aid of the walking stick, steady on his feet, and lifted the top of his scrubs. Unlike me, his sculpted chest was free of gauze. The skin was pink in five round, puffy spots. If I hadn't known better, I'd say they looked like superficial cigar burns.

"Will they heal more?" I asked.

He shrugged, lowering his shirt. "We'll have to wait and see."

Brady scooted forward across the mattress, his feet dropping to the floor. Like the others, he wore scrubs. Presumably, the t-shirt he'd worn to the pep rally was also riddled with holes, his pants at the very least blood-spattered.

When he lifted his shirt, I gasped. Even Layla, who always had something to say—especially when no one wanted to hear it—stared at him, mouth agape.

In addition to the scar from the rebar, five angry welts dotted his muscled chest. They looked like swollen mosquito bites. And the rebar scar? Last time I'd seen it, the flesh had been a sad, shiny, puckered pink, the size of a lemon. Now? It was the size of a jawbreaker.

"How's that possible?" Layla whispered, when Layla never whispered.

He smirked. "What do you think? We're immortals, Lay."

"I don't know if I'd go that far," I said. Though, why wouldn't I? If we couldn't actually die, what *did* that make us?

And why was I the last to come back?

As if following my train of thought, Layla offered, "My scars look about like Hunt's. I'd show you, but then I'd be flashing my titties, and I don't wanna tempt my gross and pervy brother."

Brady huffed in exasperation, running a hand through dark blond hair that was currently styled with a fade that crested into a two-inch mohawk. Post resurrection number two, his mohawk sagged. "Oh for fuck's sake. You're the one who's gross and pervy! You go too far. Waaaaaay too far. You can't say that kind of shit! Not even as a joke. You've gotta stop!"

But Layla's eyes were sparkling, telling me she was enjoying herself, despite the shitshow we were currently starring in. She thrived on doing precisely what she wasn't supposed to. Brady telling her "can't" was her version of catnip. The girl got off on dancing the cha-cha along the line that demarcated the taboo.

"I've gotta get under the bandages to look," I said, more to myself than them. "See if I, you know, healed as well as you guys did. If I took that much longer than all of you to revive, who knows . . . At least my leg healed."

Layla grinned a shit-eating smile. "Sure. Flash them titties, Joss. I'm sure Griff won't mind."

My eyes widened until they bulged as I did my best to shoot death rays at her. "LAY-la!" I scolded harshly. Had the girl lost her ever-loving damn mind? Maybe dying had rattled some screws loose. Even for her, this was all a bit much. We'd always been extremely careful not to blur the lines of friendship—let alone incest, for that matter. Girl was being nuttier than a freaking squirrel.

Brady was shaking his head. "I swear Mom or Dad dropped you smack on your head when you were a baby. The shit that comes out of your mouth . . ."

Layla turned her entire body in her seat to glower at him. "If they dropped me, then you'd better believe they dropped you first."

"That doesn't even make sense."

"'Course it does. If you think I say crazy shit, then you say just as much crazy shit as I do."

By objective standards, no. No he didn't. But Hunt, Griffin, and I had long ago learned not to get in the middle of the two of them until they started throwing punches.

Regardless, I waded right in. "Come on, you two. We have really important stuff to figure out."

Brady crossed his arms over his chest and really settled into the glare-a-thon. Layla imitated his posture, making him snort and dip his head haughtily.

"Just 'cause you think you're hot shit doesn't make you any less of a steaming, stinky, wafting turd," Layla snapped.

They were rapidly devolving into the kind of insults we'd endured years ago.

To be fair, pretty much every one of our classmates at Ridgemore High probably did think Brady was hot shit, and not the smelly kind.

Brady's smirk grew, and Layla huffed, her cheeks growing pink as she became flustered. Letting Brady best her was top of her list of dreaded things, along with asparagus, which she inexplicably despised, nails across a chalkboard—understandable—and dying, which lost some of its dooming threat when its finality had grown so dubious.

"You know just as well as I do that Griff would eat up the sight of Joss's tits," Layla said combatively, as if somehow proving a point.

My breath froze in my lungs so abruptly that I couldn't tell if I'd been mid-inhale or exhale.

"What the *fuck*, Layla?" I growled. Then, before she could defend her statement, and she would—oh, she most definitely would—I added, "Could we *please* focus already? All of us but Griff literally just died. I don't know about you guys, but that's rattling the shit out of me. I'm not okay. Not okay at fucking all. We're possibly trapped with a filthy rich lunatic who had no problem setting a fucking school full of kids on fire, and who sent actual hitmen into said school after us, for fuck's sake. Our phones don't work, and I'm assuming there are no landlines." Hunt shook his head in confirmation. "Our parents are probably losing whatever was left of their sanity right now as you guys argue over . . . well, whatever the fuck it is you're actually arguing about!" I threw up my hands in case they'd missed my growing agitation, and winced when that movement pulled at my IV line and injuries. I was guessing my chest wounds weren't as far along in their recovery as my friends'.

Layla's eyes glistened as she redirected her glare at me. Right then, with how pink they suddenly were, her eyes appeared more blue than their usual gray. "Why do you think I'm spewing so much bullshit?" she asked in a high pitch.

"Because you usually do?" Brady suggested.

She whipped her glower over to him, but the next second it was back on me. "I'm losing my ever-loving shit over here too, you know. *What the fuck?* I mean, WHAT THE FUCK? *We all just got gunned down at school.* Gunned the fuck down. How . . . what . . . how does that even happen? What the fuck is happening with our lives?"

Her tone was getting increasingly squeaky. Hunt reached over to pat her forearm, and Brady's shoulders slumped.

"Not only did they kill me," she went on, "but they messed with the people I fucking love the shit out of. I am gonna murder the motherfucker responsible the very second I set eyes on him, and then I'm gonna pray he somehow comes back to life just so I can do it all over again. And then I'm gonna piss on him, boy style. I'm gonna stand right over him and splash all over his stupid face. And then maybe I'll set him on fire. I dunno. I'm still deciding on that last bit."

"Hell, yes," Brady growled. "That man's got no idea who he messed with."

"He messed with *family*," Hunt snarled in that stoically quiet way of his that carried so much strength despite a low volume. "*My family.*"

"I couldn't agree more," Griffin said in a rolling grumble of menace. "I had to watch you all die," he seethed. "Every single one of you. I had to watch it happen, knowing I couldn't stop it." He shook his head. "You were all lying there, dead, dead, dead, fucking dead, and I was the only one left. Just me. I will *never* forgive him for that. He's gonna pay in flesh."

"Right on," Brady said. "We'll make him pay together."

"Together," the remaining four of us chorused as if it had been planned.

"We're always in it all together, through thick and thin. Now, even through death," Griffin echoed before opening his mouth as if to say more. He stared off into space for several beats, then glanced over at me.

Oh no. His eyes were as intense as I'd ever seen them.

Turning from me, he looked from Brady to Hunt to Layla. "Actually, that's why I have to say something. Now that Lay brought it up in her special way." He chortled.

"Damn right," Layla interjected.

"There's something I've gotta tell you all."

No, no, no, no, no. He wasn't about to say something about him and me, was he? *No, no, no.* He couldn't mess things up, especially not now when we had a billionaire mofo to murder. Talk about some group bonding.

"Griff," I warned, unsure there was reason to. Though his expressions were as familiar to me as my own, maybe I was reading him wrong this time.

He kept his stare pinned on our friends and, without looking, reached behind him to grab my hand. He knew right where it was, and he laced his fingers through mine.

Although he'd touched me thousands upon thousands of times over our years growing up together, my hand zinged as if with pins and needles.

Then, like it wasn't going to blow up our world, in a steady voice he announced, "I'm in love with Joss."

3

Courtesy of Mr. Chase

My heart fluttering in outright elation, a greater high than even the morphine had delivered, Griffin's declaration—*I'm in love with Joss*—looped giddily through my mind multiple times before I realized everyone was silent in the face of it.

Too silent. Unnervingly silent.

My friends were so rarely quiet it could only mean one thing: my fear had been realized. Griffin and I falling in love had ruined everything. We were in the process of ripping our crew apart. We'd broken a cardinal rule of our friendship—don't date each other and make things weird—and now the only people in the entire world I could actually rely on were divided. The only people I truly loved with all my heart were no longer one indivisible unit. No longer a fully bonded *family*.

Fuuuuuuck. My buoyant heart shifted gears on a dime and now barreled toward a shattering I wasn't sure I'd survive. And at the very worst time possible: when we had real enemies hunting us. When our lives were being turned upside down so incredibly savagely. When even our parents had betrayed us, and we found ourselves all alone fighting for our ultimate survival.

Griff's declaration continued echoing in my mind, fulfilling a desire I'd had longer than I'd earlier admitted to myself. I sighed loudly. A devastated lament was already worming into my veins to circle my body along with the IV fluids.

"Why, Griff?" I asked softly. "Why'd you have to do this now of all times? You could've waited some more, till things were better. Easier at least."

He was squeezing my hand when Hunt's astute stare pinned both of us. "You've been hiding it from us?"

"Damn, guys," Layla added with a disappointed shake of her head, making my heart plummet along with my already churning stomach. "Seriously? After everything we've been through together, you're keeping secrets from us? About *this*, no less?"

Wanting to rip off the bandage all at once, I looked to Brady, who scowled at Griff and me so intensely that his nostrils flared. With jerky movements, he crossed his arms over his chest, his biceps bulging with tension from under his scrubs.

He didn't have to say anything for me to understand. They were all on the same page. Griffin and I were on a different one. What had once been a perfect book was now split in half, a beautiful story forever ruined, its beginning separated from its end. No more happy ending.

Griffin chuckled—fucking *chuckled*—and I whipped my head around to gawk at his profile. Had he lost his damn mind? Had resurrection after death messed with his head?

Rubbing my hand in what seemed like a gesture of comfort, he told the others (with yet another laugh, the crazy fucker), "It's not like that, guys. We're only just figuring it out ourselves. We told you practically before we told each other."

Layla narrowed her eyes, again shining an angry blue. "But you already told each other. And didn't tell us."

"Yeah, but not like you're thinking. I told her right before I went over the cliff in Clyde."

"That was weeks ago."

"It was, but I don't think Joss got it then. Not how I really meant it. We all love each other."

The others waited for more, so Griffin continued. "I probably wouldn't've even said it if I hadn't realized I was about to die. But it just kinda slipped out. Like I had to say it in case I never got another chance."

My subdued heartbeat accelerated once more.

"We didn't even talk about it after. Then, when Joss realized she was about to die in the gym, she said it to me. Told me she loved me. I wasn't sure if she meant it the way I wanted her to since we all do love each other—as friends, you know. But then when she woke up just now, I asked her about it. When she explained it's more than friends for her too, I told you guys right away."

"Even before you fucking told me," I grumbled, my thoughts slipping out unintentionally.

Layla's burning stare heated my face for several moments before she barked a laugh. "Damn, Joss. You're pouting. Didn't know you had it in you."

"What the hell're you talking about?" Brady said, uncrossing his arms and crossing his ankles as he continued to lean against the side of the bed. "She pouts all the time."

"I do not," I protested automatically.

"Do too," Brady said. "But apparently it does the trick for our boy."

Gingerly, Hunt leaned back in his armchair and spread his long legs out in front of him. He looked at Griff, then me, then Griff again. "All right."

"All right?" I asked, feeling my forehead scrunch.

"Yeah. All right."

My brow pinched. "All right what?"

He looked at me like I was the one who'd lost my damn mind. "Allright. What do you need me to spell out for you here?"

My chin dropped. "You don't have a problem with . . . ?" I glanced at the side of Griff's face, which was all I could see from where I lay. His features were even, steady. *Okay, then.* "With whatever this is between . . . ?" I'd barely even allowed myself to think about the two of us as a couple. I gulped, my throat still tender. "Between the two of us?"

Layla snorted. "Oh my God, this is gonna be so good. If Joss is this flustered just talking about it, can you imagine what she's gonna be like when they start doing it?" She rubbed her hands together, a devilish expression on her face. "Can't wait. This is gonna be so lit."

I shook my head to clear it, but my brow wouldn't unfurrow. "Wait. You guys are seriously okay with this? Like, for real?"

"Sure," Brady said lightly. "You're our peeps. Happy for you."

I shook my head again. But nope, what they were saying remained as unbelievable as before.

"Well," I started to say, before devolving into a stupefied, "Wow."

Layla laughed. "What? Did you think we'd crucify you for falling in love with each other?"

I met her eyes.

She frowned. "That's really what you think of us? That we wouldn't want you guys to be happy?"

"I know you guys want us to be happy. Of course you do. But, well, I thought it would mess with our friendship. That you guys would be mega pissed." More quietly, I added, "That it'd blow up everything most important to me."

"Nah, girl. We saw it coming."

My brows jumped up my forehead. My face had probably never been this animated. "You did? How? I didn't even see it coming."

She snorted. "Dude, we aren't blind you know. We see how you guys look at each other, especially when you think no one's paying attention."

"Yep," Hunt said.

A smirk tipping up one side of his mouth, Brady nodded. "Especially when we've been drinking or toking. You really drop your guard then."

"For real," Layla said. "I was just waiting for little cartoon hearts to pop up in your eyes."

"Why . . . why'd you never say anything?"

"Why should we? It was your business, not ours."

At that, we all laughed. Brady actually guffawed, saying, "Sticking your nose in other people's business is *your jam*, Lay."

"Is not." But a moment later even she laughed. "All right, fine, it is. But I love you guys." Her eyes jumped from me to Griff. "I didn't want to do anything to mess this up for you."

"Thanks, Lay," Griff said, cool as a crispy cucumber. "'Preciate that."

"Besides, it was worth it just to see Joss's face now. Fucking priceless."

"I thought I was gonna lose you all!"

"No way, man," Hunt said. "You can never lose us."

"That's right," Brady agreed.

"And you don't need me to tell you," Layla said. "You and me, we're sisters from other misters." She tipped her head. "Now that we're crossing lines though, maybe Hunt and I should start getting frisky with each other."

Hunt just laughed.

She swiveled toward him in her chair, arching a single brow in unspoken menace. Tartly, she asked, "Are you saying you don't wanna tap *this*?" With a sweep of her hand, she gestured to the length of her body.

He brought up both hands, palms facing her. "Oh no. I'm not saying any such thing. I wouldn't dare. All I'm saying is, I'm not fireproof, so I make it a point not to play with fire."

Layla was tilting her head one way then the next, as if deciding whether calling her *fire* was a good thing or not, while Hunt squirmed.

Out of all of us, he was the last to squirm.

"Just 'cause it seems we're likely to survive dying by fire doesn't make us fireproof. It just makes us 'dead' proof." He rubbed his chin as if considering the many ramifications of our apparent undying state.

Slowly, Layla rose to her feet, dismissed the walking stick, and shuffled toward my bed. "Come on, girl. I'll help you with your bandages. I won't go lesbo on you, promise, even though you do have some fine titties. Not as fine as mine, of course, but you win second prize."

She sat on the opposite side of the bed from Griffin, telling him, "Move. Better your first time seeing them isn't like this, and we need to figure out how well she's healing. Just in case, you know . . ."

Regrettably, I got the feeling we all understood precisely what she was referencing.

In case someone tried to kill us—yet again.

But before Layla could so much as lean toward me, the door swung open and in prowled two guards with guns raised, the same guards who, days ago, had taken off their gas masks and offered up the defibrillators with a casual, "Courtesy of Mr. Chase."

Griffin and Brady rocketed to standing, and Hunt was only seconds behind. Layla inched protectively closer to me while I eyed my IV drip line, considering how quickly I could yank it out, unfasten the blood pressure cuff, and get my feet under me.

Not fast enough. Definitely not faster than a bullet or five.

"Easy," cautioned the bastard with the blue eyes who'd pointed his gun at my face in the gym. "Take it easy."

Gun on a swivel, he kept the door at his back and stationed himself several feet away from Hunt, who was closest.

The second soldier slid out from behind him and lined himself up with a wall at his back, his gun also trained on us.

"Don't so much as move," Bastard continued. "I don't even want to see a muscle twitch or I'll shoot. You got me?"

Oh, we got him all right. I could practically feel the five of us vibrating. I had no doubt the guys were going to jump Bastard the very instant they got a clear opportunity.

Brady growled, then said, "You killed my friends. You killed my sister. You killed me." A vein bulged in his neck. Brady was one smooth move away from charging, Neanderthal style.

Our stares were fixed on the men with the guns, waiting. Anticipating. Calculating.

Whereas in the gym I'd experienced fear—for my friends and for myself—now I felt none of it. My desire for righteous justice, and yes, maybe also a fair helping of vengeance, was so strong as to crowd out everything else.

If Bastard and his fellow soldier managed to kill one of us, more likely than not we'd come back. If we managed to kill either of them, they wouldn't. Even though we found ourselves on the wrong end of the weapons, we still had a certain advantage over them.

Brady cracked his knuckles as if preparing to tear them limb from limb. Suddenly, I wanted that and, for a swift moment, I allowed myself to fantasize about leaping from this bed and snapping their stupid fucking necks, how satisfying it would be to break their spines.

"You will not move, got it?" Bastard pressed. "You'll stay right where you are."

We didn't respond beyond a rumble rising up Griffin's throat.

"You will do nothing to threaten Mr. Chase or you'll get a bullet to the chest."

Oh, so we were about to see the asshole himself, were we?

The smile that spread over my lips was spitting mean in a way it had never been before.

In a seductive purr, I said, "We can hardly wait."

Bastard was obviously a poor judge of character, facial cues, and voice intonation, because he called over his shoulder, "It's clear."

Quietly, so as not to draw attention to my movements, I eased open the Velcro on my cuff. Layla slid down my covers. When my feet slipped onto the floor, Brady and Griffin were already rushing Bastard, their arms reaching to tackle him to the carpet. Hunt made the most of those long legs of his, sprinting toward the second guy as if he'd never been killed and resurrected.

Shots rang out, too loud in the confined space, and I desperately searched for where they'd hit.

The men were locked in struggle and I couldn't tell if anyone had been hurt. Then Magnum Chase strode into the room as if he were as invincible as we were.

"It's in your best interest to stop and listen to what I have to say."

The men merely grunted, wrestling and rolling across the floor, smashing into the small table. The water pitcher and glasses came crashing down, shards flying in all directions. Chase looked on, unimpressed, unaffected. Impassive. Like an entitled psycho.

"I promise you *will want* to hear what I have to say."

I hated it, but he was right. I *did* want to hear what he had to say. Nearly as much as I wanted to murder him, I wanted to understand.

And apparently, so did the others. Griffin, Brady, and Hunt disentangled themselves from the soldiers, bloodied and breathing hard. Hunt was holding a gun.

4

Un-Bloody-Fucking-Likely

Before he got his feet fully under him, Bastard was jerking his pistol toward Hunt. The second guard did the same, aiming a small, backup gun at Hunt's head while he stalked toward Hunt's other side, his wary stare flicking from him to the rest of us crowded inside the room.

Hunt was as fast as a damn jungle cat. He stared down the barrel of the gun he'd somehow lifted from the guards, straight at Chase, who contemplated him blandly, just as if there were no pesky, lethal steel in the way.

Of everything that was going down, that unperturbed demeanor was perhaps the most unnerving.

I perched against the foot of my bed, Layla at my side, a hand squeezing Brady's arm in support. Blood already soaked the shoulder of his scrubs around a bullet hole.

Legs wide and ready to lunge, Griffin stood alone beside the armchairs. Cuts from the shattered crystal and glass dribbled blood along his bare forearms. His nostrils flared, his jaw clenched; he was seconds away from charging again.

Just the thought of him getting shot sent a surge of nerves racing across my body, leaving gooseflesh in their wake.

Bastard's eyes were pinched so ferociously that he looked one wrong move away from shitting his fancy, all-black, elite-soldier pants that had enough holsters and pockets to make me jelly. His finger vibrated on the trigger, begging for any reason at all to pull it.

"Don't you hurt him," Bastard warned Hunt, a subdued edge of panic revealing he considered the billionaire more than just an employer. Was it deluded hero worship? Or was there more to their bond?

"You can't stop me," Hunt said with a steady resolve that caused Bastard's left eye to twitch.

"Oh yes I can. I'll blow your head open like a ripe melon before you so much as—"

"There'll be no need for any of that, Jaggar," Magnum Chase said with a calm that belied the fact he was staring down the hollow end of a semi-automatic.

Chase either had balls the size of a prize-winning stud bull, or he knew something I didn't.

Jaggar didn't argue with Chase, chewing the inside of his cheeks instead.

Chase took another step into the room. Another step closer to the gun and Hunt's unwavering grip on it.

Jaggar openly bit his lip, his finger ever so slightly tightening around the trigger.

"Don't you dare pull that trigger," I snapped at him.

He whipped his head toward me, his gun remaining right where it was.

"I see you," I told him. "You want to do it. But you'd better not."

"Yeah," Layla said. "We'll come back from the dead and haunt your ass so hard that you'll turn that gun around and point it at yourself and *BOOOOM!* Pull the fucking trigger." She wiggled the fingers of her free hand in the air as if stars rained down from the sky. I couldn't decide why, but then Layla had never been weighed down by trivialities such as making sense.

"Jaggar won't be pulling any trigger," Chase said. "At least not today, not now. Neither will Raynar. Men, lower your weapons."

Raynar lowered his gun in obedience. Jaggar hesitated until Chase arched a perfectly groomed brow in his direction.

With a swallowed grunt, Jaggar unwrapped his finger from around the trigger—but kept it beside it at the ready—and lowered the gun to his side. With nearly as much menace, he kept his glare trained on Hunt, who kept his weapon trained on Chase.

With a docile, patient expression I wasn't buying, Chase stared back at Hunt, appearing to simply wait.

When moments drew out and still Hunt didn't fall into line, Chase said, "There's no need for violence between us."

"Your guys literally just *shot* me," Brady said, picking at the gaping hole in his shirt to peek beneath it.

"Actions cause *re*actions. You attacked my men, so they protected themselves."

"By shooting at a bunch of unarmed hospital patients?" Griffin growled with a scowl that was mega-sexy despite the circumstances. "*Trapped* hospital patients, I'm gonna add. You're keeping us here against our will."

Chase *tsked*. "You'll be free to go soon enough." He gazed upward, where two bullet holes pocked the otherwise smooth stretch of cream directly overhead. "Besides, the ceiling seems to have gotten the worst of it."

I wasn't buying his act.

Brady scoffed as if somehow shocked that the man who'd hunted us only to have us gunned down wasn't overly concerned Brady was once again injured. He sputtered, "You're a piece of work, you know that? You talk about taking responsibility for your actions while you behave fully fucking egregiously, believing you have impunity. Well, you motherfucking don't."

Finally, Chase glanced from Hunt to Brady. "It's lamentable that you're injured. It was a completely avoidable result, one I attempted to prevent by telling you that it's in your best interest to *listen* to me, not try to kill me."

I gaped at him, fumbling for words. "Are you for real right now?" is what ended up tumbling out. "You fucking *murdered* us. *Murr-durred*. If you think for one second we're going to—"

"Look, Joss," he interrupted, and Griffin growled. Again, Chase didn't flinch. He was either impervious to the very real threat we posed to him or he knew something we didn't. I still felt like roadkill warmed over, and yet I was considering dismembering the rich fuck, limb from expertly dressed limb.

"All of you, really," Chase went on, glancing at each one of us. "Despite our past or how we met"—Brady barked out an incredulous *hah*—"there's absolutely no reason we should be enemies. If you'll calm down enough to reason the situation through, I think you'll soon see we can all be on the same side."

"Un-bloody-fucking-likely," I snarled.

Chase looked from me to Hunt's gun, then back to me. "From all accounts, the lot of you are brilliant. Appearances apparently aren't everything."

"Since you look like a shitstain," Layla said, "for your sake let's hope not." She offered him her best mean-bitch fake smile, and the asshole actually chuckled.

Chase brought up a hand in what I thought might be surrender before he slid up the sleeve of his shirt to check a watch that sparkled with gold and diamonds. Apparently the man didn't believe in hiding his obscene wealth.

He dropped his arm to his side. "You don't get to where I am in life by wasting time. I have what I believe will be life-altering information to offer you, along with a proposal. Would you like to hear what I have to say, or would you like to keep playing games that waste time for all of us?"

"You call shooting me a game?" Brady snarled.

"No," Chase answered sharply. "I call it avoidable idiocy. The best surgeon in several states is ready to fix you up if you're finally ready to listen."

When still none of us agreed and Hunt showed no sign of moving the gun from where it pointed at the billionaire's forehead, Chase eventually sighed.

"I truly thought you'd all be smarter than this. You perform off-the-charts in every aptitude test known to man. You're playing with an incomplete deck of cards. Don't you want to check out the aces up my sleeves?" He flicked his fingers at his sides, but that was the end of his theatrics.

Unimpressive.

His brows rose a fraction of an inch, and his eyes danced. "Don't you want to know how far your parents' lies go?"

My muscles tensed. *Yes*, I very much wanted that.

"Though calling them your *parents* is quite the stretch."

Hunt tilted up his chin to study Chase over the gun's sight. "What do you mean?"

"Put the gun down and I'll tell you."

Hunt looked at the rest of us before scanning Jaggar and Raynar. Turning back toward Chase, he told him, "Tell them to pile up all their weapons on that table there"—the one that had once held the water and now lay overturned—"and sit in the armchairs. Then I'll put down my gun."

"That's *my* gun, actually," Raynar corrected.

Chase whipped his head toward his soldier. "I wouldn't remind anyone of that," he snapped.

Raynar swallowed and nodded with a jerk.

"All right," Chase started before Jaggar said, "Sir, no, you can't—"

Chase pinned Jaggar with a stare so ferocious that Jaggar visibly wilted beneath its intensity. "Are you questioning my judgment?" Chase asked with cold calm, and I doubted a question had ever sounded more dangerous.

"Of course not, sir. It's just that they're trained and—"

"You will disarm as Mr. Fletcher suggested and take your seats."

Jaggar and Raynar hopped to obey, though Jaggar was openly twitchy as he took in how Hunt didn't bother to lower his weapon as they placed theirs out of easy reach.

Chase stared down Hunt's barrel and waited. What felt like an entire minute passed before Hunt finally lowered his arm to his side. He continued to hold the gun.

"Get help for Brady. Griffin too. Then we'll talk."

"I'm fine," Griffin interjected. "No need."

But Chase went on as if he hadn't heard him. "I'll get them help now, but we don't wait to talk. There's too much on the line, and those thieves who call themselves your parents are looking for us as we speak."

"'Thieves?'" I echoed under my breath while Layla apparently squeezed Brady's arm hard enough for him to yelp and yank it away.

Our parents, mine especially, were definitely liars. But thieves?

If the billionaire had been dangling strands of sparkly diamonds or pretty, shiny blades, or the keys to a freaking Lambo, I wouldn't have been half as intrigued and tempted.

"What did our parents steal?" Hunt asked, a heartbeat before the words could slip from my own lips.

Chase didn't shy away from the question. He leaned forward onto his shiny, wing-tipped leather shoes to make eye contact with each of us in turn. "They stole industrial secrets, the results of years of experiments, invaluable data that didn't belong to them. Expensive equipment too, but that's not the important thing. They stole *biological material*. My property."

Meeting my stare head-on as if he anticipated that my mind would be blown wide open, he added, "They stole all of *you*."

5

The Devil You Know

From across the room, I blinked at Chase so many times that his polished, smooth-shaven face began to blur.

He saw us as *biological material*. We were *his property* that our parents supposedly stole.

That's why his eyes were glinting with avarice. The motherfucker actually appeared to believe he *owned* us.

Surely, he couldn't be that insane.

A memory of Jaggar pointing his gun at me moments before he pulled the trigger—on Chase's orders—flashed through my mind.

Never mind. Obviously Chase was precisely that insane. Not only did he think he owned us, but he thought that gave him the right to kill us, in order to . . . what? Provide him with more precious data?

When forced to confess, our parents *had* admitted they'd run from their "employer" and hidden us from said employer. They'd failed to mention that a narcissist considered us his possessions, but the rest added up well enough.

"Raynar," Chase said, slicing through my thoughts. "Go get the nurses."

With a quick glance at the discarded weapon, Raynar rose from the armchair and exited the room.

Once the door shut behind him, I told Chase, "No matter what you think of us, we aren't your fucking property. We aren't anybody's property."

"Seems like that should go without saying," Hunt inserted.

I huffed a bitter snort. "Totally. And taking us away from an obviously awful, incredibly toxic situation doesn't make our parents thieves."

It made them good parents, right? Maybe they'd redeem themselves after all.

Chase's lips parted to reveal expertly whitened and straightened teeth. "If they were your actual parents, your argument might have some merit. Perhaps. But they aren't."

Again, my eyes lost their focus as his words registered.

"Come again?" Layla whispered.

"Your *parents*"—the billionaire hooked manicured fingers into air quotes, his shiny watch catching the light—"aren't your parents. They *were* the lead researchers of my most important project. They *were* my employees, with no rights to any part of discoveries they made while in my employ. Their research was advanced under a work-for-hire arrangement. I'd explain what that means, but you're all smart enough to already know. I won't talk down to you."

Oh, so "talking down" to us was his main concern here? The balls on this asshole!

"You're the result of experiments conducted under my authority, funded by me. That means you're my property, and they took you. Plain and simple. That makes them thieves, and that also makes you mine to do with as I please."

Layla and I shot to standing, and even as I wobbled, a growl rumbled in my chest.

I wasn't the only one. The five of us sounded more like beasts than people. Even shot and bleeding, Brady clenched his teeth and narrowed his eyes at the nutter, about to attack.

Beyond grumbling their disapproval, Griffin and Hunt had gone still. That meant they were as dangerous and poised to take down a mofo as Brady, Layla, and me.

I was unsteady on my feet, and any attack I might attempt would likely result in my ass landing on the floor.

Didn't mean I wouldn't do it anyway.

This megalomaniac was too fucking much.

He didn't even care that Hunt was holding a gun! Did he believe he, too, was invincible? That he'd come back to life after Hunt shot him between the eyes? Maybe he did. But money couldn't buy a person a second chance at life, even if they had enough cash to fill an entire Olympic-sized swimming pool.

Chase chuckled—further proof there was something majorly wrong with him—while Jaggar cast what he must have thought were covert looks at his weapons, just out of reach.

"I'm not saying that's the kind of relationship I want us to have," Chase clarified, presumably as clarification of his *ownership claims*. "I'm just stating facts so you can understand the situation as it really is. The scientists who've charaded as your parents all these years have been lying to you your entire lives. I'm here to tell you the truth."

Layla snorted. "Yeah, I'll just bet you are."

Chase tipped his head in a way that said, "But I am!" Then the door opened and a nurse in plain gray scrubs marched into the room with no more than a glance at the standoff going down right in front of her. She was either remarkably well paid or had seen enough to know that she should keep her curiosity to herself. She flicked a glance at Griff, then Brady—triaging—before walking over to Brady first.

A second nurse entered, pushing a stainless-steel cart laden with scalpels, needles, and other surgical supplies. Behind her, an orderly with a broom swept the glass and crystal shards, cleaning them all up, before a surgeon waltzed in. Unlike the nurses and the orderly, his eyes widened at the scene. Even so, he didn't say anything, stalking across the room to examine Brady's wound as the nurse cut open his shirt.

"Well?" Layla prompted. "You said there was no time to wait to talk. So, talk."

"Yeah," Brady said, then hissed as disinfectant burned his wound. "Before one of us decides we'd rather pummel your ass than hear you out."

Chase positioned himself so he could lean against the patch of open wall beside the door and crossed his arms over his chest. "I wonder if this group aggression is a side effect of your unique makeup."

"Sure, why not?" Griffin barked, his sarcasm thick. "It couldn't be because none of us are fans of being fucking *owned*. Or of a manipulative asshole pulling strings to get us all *killed*. It couldn't be that, no."

The surgeon looked from Brady's gunshot to the rest of us, his eyes wide and startled.

Chase caught his stare with an intent one of his own, and the surgeon hastened to make a show of examining the back of Brady's shoulder and finding an exit wound. A clean shot through. That was something, at least.

The nurse injected Brady with a local anesthetic while Chase said, "First off: all of you, please, call me Magnum. I'd like us to be friends."

Brady and Layla snorted. Griffin and Hunt seemed to vibrate with pent-up ire. I wondered if maybe I was dreaming all of this, starting with Brady impaled upon unforgiving rebar at that party. The experience felt too bizarre to be real.

"We'll get there," Chase said.

"If you really think that, then you don't know the first thing about us," Hunt said.

Chase appraised him and the gun he still held, though loosely now. "Maybe it's you who don't know me."

"Whatever, dude. Get to talking."

Raynar carried in one of those ergonomic seats with knee, ankle, and elbow cushions instead of a back, and placed it in front of Chase. Without so much as a nod of thanks or acknowledgment, Chase slid onto the leather-and-polished-wood contraption, his posture perfect, and studied the five of us, his attention sliding off the others in the room as if they weren't even there.

"How much do you know about your past and your abilities?"

"Assume we know nothing," Griffin said, coming to sit beside me on the bed, Layla on my other side.

Chase nodded, his sharp eyes going distant for a few moments. "Across recorded history, and even before then, handed down from generation to generation in oral tradition, there have been legends, stories, and myths of immortal beings. The details vary greatly depending on the culture and its overarching belief system, but it boils down to the same thing: there are those who can outlive death. The topic has long fascinated me."

None of this was news, and yet I wouldn't hurry him along. Perhaps we'd finally get some answers.

"I tasked a team of promising young scientists with discovering a source of said immortality. I wanted to replicate it. To be able to create this ability in others."

In himself, he meant. The billionaire who had everything money could buy, and now wanted what it couldn't.

Typical. Nothing was ever sufficient for those lucky enough to have their every conceivable need met with ease and luxury.

"When my scientists managed to duplicate the conditions that brought about immortality in the lab, they repaid me by stealing every piece of information that would reveal how they'd done it. Including you."

"How? How'd they do it?" Hunt asked while tucking the gun into the waistband of his jeans, against his lower back. I knew from watching him practice the move: he could draw a weapon from that position faster than Jaggar could reach his.

"The answer to that question," Chase said, "is a trade secret. Once I secure your agreement to honor confidentiality, I may be willing to share more of the details with you."

"Wow," Layla sneered. "So fucking generous of you."

Chase slid his stare to her. "If you give me the chance, you'll find that I'm extremely generous. I can make things very good for all of you."

"I don't call being killed and shot at 'good,'" Brady retorted as the surgeon stitched him up. From what I'd observed from our too-frequent recent experiences with hospitals, surgeons usually left secondary doctors or nurses to do the stitching or stapling. But beneath Chase's watchful supervision, the surgeon didn't hesitate to do it himself.

Chase steepled his fingers atop the cushion. "I wouldn't call that good either. It's regrettable, but it became unavoidable when my former employees decided to break their agreements and set me back years by stealing from me. I assure you, moving forward, we *can* be friends, and I can make life better for each one of you than you've ever dreamed of."

Layla harrumphed from my left but didn't say what I was sure she was thinking because I was thinking it too: we couldn't trust the finely dressed snake as far as we could throw him.

Griffin clasped my hand as I said, "Just like you probably did for the Aquoians?"

He whipped his head to look at me. Deep and penetrating, his stare saw too much and revealed too little. In a clipped tone he hadn't used with us yet, he said, "I offered them the easy way. I offered them riches so great they could have radically improved the lives of their people for many generations to come. They could have bought back much of their land, perhaps even secured more of their rights with the amount of money I offered them."

"To think, money can't buy everything," I said, a taunt I instantly regretted.

His eyes hardened to brown, brutal flints. "As I told you already, we can be friends. Or we can . . . not. I think you'll all much prefer having me as a friend."

Then, without breaking eye contact with me, he asked, "Dr. Chadbourne, are you finished with your patient?"

"Yes, sir. But I've not yet treated the second."

"You're excused. All of you, leave now."

Not even Jaggar complained as he and Raynar collected and holstered their weapons, then hurried to join the others in leaving us alone with the man with more money than sense.

When the door clicked shut, Chase leaned forward onto his elbows. His stare remained as sharp as before. Finally, we were seeing more of what lived beneath that polished exterior.

"This storytelling isn't suiting us. Let me get down to the meat on the bone. I'm deeply invested in seeing the five of you thrive. I'm uniquely situated to help you understand yourselves, your powers, and to pretty much help you do whatever you want with your lives. With my support, there will be very little you can't do."

"And in exchange?" Griffin asked.

Chase didn't flinch at Griff's bluntness. "In exchange, I get to study you, observe you, help you."

"You want to become immortal yourself?" Hunt asked. He remained standing in the center of the room even while the rest of us sat. He tracked every one of Chase's movements for sign of a new threat.

"Wouldn't you?"

"I don't know. I wasn't given the choice."

"True. But I've given you a great gift."

"Maybe, maybe not," Brady said.

Meeting each of our stares in turn, Chase then said, "You may not like me now, but I think you'll soon see I'm the one who offers you the most benefits." He chuffed. "By far. You may be thinking now that you'll never trust me."

"We are," Brady said.

Chase shrugged, the crisp shoulders of his shirt rising to accentuate his total lack of concern. "Trust me or don't, time will reveal that, but realize, I'm the devil you know. I'm not hiding my motivations from you, and I won't hide information from you either, once we come to an agreement."

"So you keep mentioning," Layla said. "What about our parents?"

He leaned back, his hands coming to his thighs. "Again, not your parents. Not a single one of you were carried in the wombs of those you believe to be your mothers. I paid surrogates quite handsomely to do the job."

My mom's smiling face flashed into my mind. The many photos she and my dad had shown me of her with a swollen belly, him hugging her, and the two of them beaming as they celebrated the baby soon to come.

Me.

"Bullshit," I snarled.

"No. They might have stolen from me, but I have my resources. Of this, I have plenty of proof."

"Show us," Layla whispered, her volume alone suggesting her disbelief likely rivaled my own.

"I'll show you everything. I'll share the truth. It might not be pretty, and you might not like it, but I'll never lie to you."

None of us said anything. If we couldn't even trust our supposed parents, like hell were we going to just start trusting this guy.

A man who'd proven he had no qualms about justifying murders—ours and who knew how many others.

"What would you prefer? The liars and thieves who deceived you for your whole lives? Or me? At least with me, I don't claim to love any of you. I don't even like any of you yet; I only like what I can get from you. With me, you'll always know my motivations, which are predictable. Can you say the same about the scientists who stole their lab rats and pretended to be their parents?"

Brady whistled. "Man, you are one stone-cold sonofabitch, aren't you?"

"I am. And that alone makes me more trustworthy than them."

"Show us the proof," Layla said, "and then we'll see."

"I could. But I won't. I know how to play the game of leverage and I play it quite well. My many business associates can attest to that.

"At this moment, the people you believed to be your parents are scouring the area, searching for you. By now, they've probably figured out I'm behind the fire at the school and the disappearance of their precious 'children.'" He scoffed. "What a ruse. All to have continual access to up-to-date data. Before long, they'll find us. After all, I hired them because they're the best in their fields, which makes them at the very least smart enough to follow a few breadcrumbs. You agree to come with me and I give you the truth. All of it."

"And if we refuse?" Hunt asked while Griffin squeezed my hand.

Chase looked at Hunt, his face relaxed and unapologetic. "I take you anyway, by force, and then we don't get to be friends. And you don't learn the truth your *parents* will never give you because they don't want you to know what they've done. You won't like what you find out about them, I'll warn you."

With that, even though it was maybe stupid and definitely reckless, I was in.

"Where would you take us?"

"To a special school I've been building just for those like you."

"There are others like us?" Griffin asked softly.

Chase smiled genuinely for the first time. "There are. And their experiences are just as promising as yours."

With that, I suspected the rest of my friends were on board. Without exception, we were a bunch of curious fuckers.

We might not be able to be certain about much, but we did know a few things: our parents were most definitely liars—we just didn't know to what degree. We could likely survive most danger and be no worse off than we currently were. And I wanted to know how far this rabbit hole went with a fervor that kicked any reservations and desire for prudence swiftly in the ass.

"If we were to go with you," Hunt said, "would we still get to choose whether we stay or not?"

"You would. But I won't make it easy for you to go."

Truth.

Hunt looked at each of us. One by one, we nodded. I understood I might regret the decision even as I nodded to accept it. But if there was a better option, I didn't see it.

Hunt faced Chase. "Fine. But I keep the gun."

Chase laughed. "Of course. It won't make a difference."

Shit. We were so majorly fucked.

6

Not Entrapment, Enticement

The very instant Chase secured our hesitant agreement to check out this sketchy-sounding "special school" of his, his people swarmed into the room to get us ready to roll. Unease pricked along my skin as a nurse attempted to whisk everyone else away so she could prepare me for discharge. No surprise: none of my friends were willing to leave my side. Chase excused himself while Brady, Hunt, and Griffin looked away. The nurse removed the IV line and stripped me of my hospital gown and gauze. I discovered I now sported five angry pink scars the size of nickels across my chest—narrowly missing both my boobs. Fuck Chase hard for that, though at least my girls were safe. It wasn't much, but it was something. Layla helped me into a set of scrubs that matched theirs. Griffin alone wore street clothes, the sole one of us to not have a single bullet hole marring his beautiful skin.

The five of us crammed together on the long bench seat of Chase's limousine, leaving the billionaire alone on the equally sizable seat across from us. I barely dared to look away from him, though he was theoretically the one who was vulnerable here. We were the supposed immortals, not him, and although Hunt still carried a gun, Chase ordered Jaggar and Raynar to ride in the matching black Cadillac Escalade that tailed us. The medical staff rode along in another Escalade.

Our convoy resembled the standard bad guy parade in pretty much every movie I'd ever seen. According to Hollywood 101, this scene made Chase a drug lord, mob boss, or worse—the secret big bad who pulled everyone else's strings, letting them do the dirty work while he raked in the benefits.

"Where are you taking us?" Layla asked.

The windows were tinted but I could still make out the forested outskirts of Ridgemore as we swept past. We were headed in the direction of the Fischer House, which sat at the edge of town.

Chase crossed an ankle over his knee, his charcoal slacks sliding up to reveal a crisp argyle sock that looked as expensive as everything else about him. He tipped his head to one side and studied Layla. "I already told you where we're going."

"You told us we're going to some school. I want to know where said school is located."

"Yeah," Brady said, backing up his twin without hesitation now that we had a common enemy.

Chase arched a brow. "It's in Ridgemore, of course."

Confusion was pinching my forehead when Griffin asked, "Ridgemore? You said we had to hurry to get out of there so our parents wouldn't find us before we could learn the truth they wouldn't tell us."

"Again, not your parents." He swirled the crystal tumbler he held casually with the fingertips of one hand, ice clinking softly in amber-colored booze that probably cost more per shot than I could fathom. "And we had to get out of *there* because it wasn't fortified. None of them are soldiers, surely, but I don't underestimate my opponents, especially not when they believe themselves to be well motivated. Since Brady first died, I've been preparing for this moment."

An accusation burned on the tip of my tongue. I wanted to blame him for Brady falling atop that awful rebar, even though it had to have been an accident. There was no way he could have orchestrated Rich and Brady fighting, the balcony collapsing beneath them. It was random, an unpredictable tragedy.

Wasn't it?

Chase seemed to think his reach was endless . . .

"Were you responsible for Brady dying that night?" I asked.

The stares of my four best friends whipped to me before narrowing on Chase.

"Well, were you?" Hunt pressed when the man didn't respond quickly enough.

He sipped at his bourbon or scotch or whatever the fuck, then chuckled. "No, I didn't do that."

"It was your *nephew* who started it all," Griffin insisted.

Again, Chase snickered. "Yes, finally Richard proved useful." He drained his drink and leaned over to place the empty glass in a recessed cupholder built into the polished wood interior. "Had I been aware of your capabilities at that time, I likely *would* have engineered Brady's death. The death of one of you, anyhow."

I shouldn't have been surprised, and yet I flinched at the boldness of his admission. On either side of me, Griffin and Hunt tensed, their thighs rigid against mine.

Chase tapped his fingers on his knee. "But no, I didn't know. Not then. I'd been searching for you since you were first taken from me, but my former employees proved surprisingly adept at concealing you from me. It was only after Brady's death that I knew where to find you."

"So you could *kill* the rest of us," Brady snarled.

Chase merely met his accusatory glare without reaction. "As I told you, I'm the devil you know. Isn't this better than the endless lies?"

"That remains to be seen," I muttered bitterly.

A part of me wanted to grab my friends and jump from this car while it was still rolling. Were we being absolute morons right now? Were we truly better off playing along?

I had no fucking clue, and I absolutely hated that. But attempting to resist, only to be *forced* to cooperate by this man with unlimited resources, didn't seem any better.

"Kitty fucking Blanche led you right to us, didn't she?" Griffin asked, his question sharp as a blade.

"She's proven useful, yes."

"I'll just bet she has," Brady added, venom dripping from every word. "Did you spy on us with a drone?"

Chase looked at us, his expression open, his eyes unshuttered, as if he had not a fucking thing to hide. That was a *yes*, then. "I reward my people well for their loyalty. There are few better uses for my wealth."

"You can't buy us," Hunt said.

Fact.

"Maybe not. But I can prove to you that you're better off with me than with thieves and liars."

"At the school," Layla said.

"For now, yes."

"And where the fuck is it? How've you been preparing for this entrapment of all of us?"

"Not entrapment. Enticement, definitely."

I huffed but didn't bother arguing with the man's twisted morals.

"When I finally found Brady, and therefore all of you, my immediate priority was to break ground on the facility where you'd all train. Ridgemore had plenty of suitable properties, and I wanted you to be comfortable."

I snorted as Layla said, "You really expect us to believe our comfort played any part in your schemes?"

"No, I suppose I don't."

Hunt leaned forward. His still-healing wounds must have pulled along his torso because he winced and, more slowly, sat back again. "You wanted us out of that private medical facility or whatever it was."

Chase waited, his gaze held on Hunt.

"You thought our parents, or whoever they really are, would come for us, and that place wasn't fortified. But then you've apparently built an entire school for us and those like us within Ridgemore town limits. Makes no sense unless . . . unless you *want* our parents, whatever, to come for us now."

Chase grinned, and the gesture was so disarming that I found myself leaning into Griffin's side. Instantly, he wrapped an arm around my shoulders and pulled me closer. I settled into his warmth.

"Good," Chase said as the limo rolled past the turn that led to the Fischer House. Automatically, my eyes went to Brady, who shuddered. Layla's eyes grew haunted.

"I see you're as smart as I'd hoped," Chase went on. "Good. That will make everything easier. The people who deceived you into believing they're your parents—that's getting annoying fast. They're like 'The Artist Formerly Known As Prince.'" He chuckled at his own joke. No one else did.

"You could just refer to them by their names," Layla suggested with a huff of annoyance that could have been in response to myriad things.

"I could," Chase began, "but you and I know them by different names."

My eyes widened before I could stop them from revealing my shock. If our parents had truly lied about who they were and what they were to us, it shouldn't have been any more upsetting to learn they'd hidden their true identities from us as well. And yet, somehow, I hadn't imagined it. I couldn't think of them as anything but Monica and Reece Bryson, boring small-town nerd couple.

As the limo took a turn onto a road I'd never been down before, Chase studied us all. "I see you hadn't expected that. Maybe not as good at seeing the big picture as I'd hoped. Testing of the intellect can't portray a full spectrum of someone's complete intelligence."

"Fuck off," Layla bit out.

"My point made," Chase said, though I didn't see how. "They remain the best of the best in their fields, especially now that I've confirmed they continued their research of you all this time. There are no other scientists as uniquely qualified to understand the many facets of your immortality. Now that I have you, I can lure them in again. I have the leverage."

"Because they'll want their 'children' back," Layla suggested, but her tone was hopeful. Too fucking hopeful.

"Because they'll want their prized experiments. Because they know their research could win them several Nobel Prizes if they were able to make it public. People like them, they live for those accolades." He glanced out the window. "They'll come for you. Without a doubt, they'll come, and finally, after all these years, I can continue my research."

Staring out the glass, he almost sounded like he was talking to himself. "After all this time, every step brings me closer. I can practically taste it now."

While he salivated over our powers of resurrection, I exchanged looks with my friends in the resulting relative privacy. How many times had we heard our parents discuss the Nobel Prize like it was their combined life goal? Like it was nearly within their grasp, only just out of reach.

If what Chase said was true, then he was right. Our *parents* would come for us—for what we represented to them.

"This school . . ." Hunt drew out until Chase once again faced us. ". . . are you suggesting we finish out our senior year there?"

"I'm suggesting that once you see all it has to offer, you'll want it no other way."

"We'd live at the school?" Griffin asked, his heartbeat thumping beneath my ear, steadying me.

"Like royalty. You'd want for nothing."

"Except actual families," Brady said, surprising me with his nostalgic tone. Of all of us, he was the least likely to long for the family unit, the one most eager to escape Celia Rafferty's nightly family dinners—whoever the hell she actually was.

"You were never destined to have those," Chase said without apology, running light fingers along a precisely trimmed sideburn. "You were born into this world as experiments."

"Damn," Brady grunted, then whistled. "Cold motherfucker."

Chase's eyes whipped to his. "Yes. Just like you, I was destined to be how I am."

"What the hell does that mean?" Layla asked.

"It means we're nearly there."

I peered out the window beside Hunt. So far, all I could make out were thick old-growth trees against patches of azure sky.

Chase uncrossed his leg, placing both feet on the floorboard, preparing for arrival.

"If we do decide to live here," I said, pretending we had a choice, "I have a dog."

Gazing out the window, he answered, "A two-year-old pit bull male named Bobo. Yes, I know. All arrangements have been made at the house for him as well." As he turned his head toward me, I quickly schooled my features to hide my surprise. Was there anything about us this man didn't know? Fucking hell.

"When you're ready, I'll have him brought to the house for you."

"What house?" Layla asked.

"Though there's little that money can't buy, and though I've certainly hurried along the construction as much as possible by oiling the gears and arranging work crews around the clock, the school campus isn't quite finished. It's getting there, but there's still more to go. I had your house completed first. Again, I wanted you to be comfortable."

So much to process. I couldn't decide what was true anymore, what was even real. A part of me still expected to wake up from a very long dream that began with our arrival at the Fischer House party.

The limo slowed and turned onto a single-lane paved road, and suddenly an entire campus of buildings, connected by a web of single-lane streets, sprawled across my view.

"What the . . . ?" Brady mumbled. "How . . . how could you've built something like this without us knowing? You would've had to hire whole crews of construction workers, and people talk, especially in Ridgemore."

"Yes. The joys of small towns. I have no idea why my sister loves it here." His mouth twisted into a grimace. "I brought in my own crews, along with portable housing for them. You were busy with all your dying and coming back to life, and Kitty Blanche was very helpful in keeping everyone's focus off what I was doing."

"And on us," Griffin said through gritted teeth.

Chase frowned. "Her tenacious nature got in her own way."

"Meaning?" Layla asked.

"Meaning, since we'll be arriving in moments and I don't know how long it will take my former employees to locate their research subjects, I'll make one thing abundantly clear right now."

He glanced at his watch, pursed his lips, then looked back to all of us. "None of them are your parents. None of the women have ever even been pregnant. Well, except for the woman who now calls herself Monica Bryson, who got pregnant during an affair with the local sheriff, a Xander Jones. The pregnancy was terminated."

Despite everything, despite sufficient shocks to numb me, my jaw dropped open.

"No way," Layla whispered.

Griffin's biceps beneath my head tightened before he asked, "And the woman I believed was my mom?"

Chase laughed, and dread pooled in my gut. "'Mitzi Conway,' was it?"

Griffin didn't move, though his heartbeat sped up. I straightened and wrapped an arm around his waist, ignoring the tug of healing flesh across my chest.

"Mitzi never existed," Chase said.

"Never existed," Griffin repeated in a numb echo. "That . . . can't be."

"Explore the campus, your house, see what you think. Then we'll talk, you can ask your questions and I'll answer those I'm willing to answer."

"And my dad?" Hunt asked anyway.

Chase arched a brow. "The one who supposedly died in a car crash?"

His jaw clenched tightly, Hunt gave a single, sharp nod.

"The only thing real about him is that your biological sperm donor had Eastern Band Cherokee heritage. Everything else was a complete fabrication. You're not who or what you were led to believe. Not at all. You're something infinitely better."

The limo pulled to a stop. Seconds later, the door beside Chase was pulled open on silent hinges. He slid across the seat, and with a foot already on the ground, craned his neck around.

"Welcome to Ridgemore's Institute for the Advancement of Immortals." Then, he stepped out.

My friends and I gaped at the empty space he'd just occupied, for once entirely at a loss for what to say.

7

The Distasteful Business of Walking, Talking Lies

Magnum Chase's latest round of revelations detonated like a bomb inside the limo. It took my friends and I several speechless minutes to process the settling mushroom cloud. Not only had our supposed parents lied to us, they were actual *walking, talking lies* themselves. Assuming we believed the megalomaniac who'd murdered every single one of us, of course. Strangely, his "the devil you know" argument was working on me. No doubt he was a Hollywood 101 classic villain, down to the obscene wealth, perfect good looks, dubious moral compass, and penchant for monologues.

When the five of us eventually stumbled from the limo, Chase was gone—along with one of the Escalades. A woman stood waiting for us while consulting a tablet. An eight-seater cart—so shiny and crisp it had to be new—idled quietly beside her, a fresh driver behind the wheel. The other remained with the limousine.

The woman appeared to be in her mid-sixties, with a face that was fresh and only lightly lined, and a lithe body that suggested a lifetime of exercise. Her hair was a soft, silky silver that feathered around her face and shoulders in the way only expensive haircuts could achieve. But unlike Chase, who could have walked off the cover of *GQ* with his crisp business-casual clothes and impeccable grooming, she wore a brightly-flowered maxi skirt that revealed Birkenstock sandals beneath the ankle-length hem—no socks, thank the gods of fashion blunders—and a tailored navy-blue blazer that accentuated her slim frame.

She held up a finger to us while her eyes finished skimming across whatever was on her screen. Then her no-nonsense expression softened as she took us in.

Usually, we weren't prone to bunching together. Normally, no matter what the situation, despite our lifetime friendships, we usually stood apart as individuals. Thrived on it. But we'd never survived *our deaths* before having Chase go all *kaboomy* on us.

Griffin's arm looped around my waist, pulling me close. And Layla looped her arm through mine on the other side, hooking her left arm through Brady's. Hunt stood so close to Brady that their arms touched.

Stunned as we were, the message was clear: whatever we were about to face, whatever shit was going to keep coming at us, we were going to take it on together.

The woman tucked the tablet under her arm and frowned. "I see Magnum has had his usual effect on you. I'll have to have a word with him about that."

Moments before, I would have thought nothing else had the potential to surprise me this afternoon. But my eyebrows arched of their own will, and she chuffed.

"I've known Magnum since he was younger than you all," she offered by way of explanation. "I'm Frances Leeman, but don't you dare call me that, or worse"—she shuddered—"*ma'am*. You can call me Fanny." She smiled, and the sincerity of it lightened a weight that had been pressing on my chest without my awareness. I pulled in a deep breath, and Griffin tugged me even closer against his side.

"I'm Magnum's executive assistant. I realize this is likely an unsettling time for you, and I'm here to help and guide you. Whatever you need, whenever you need it, you come to me. I'll make sure you're taken care of. Think of me as your cool, fun aunt, the one you trust to hear you out without judgment. Believe me, not even Magnum Chase himself has always been this put-together. We're all allowed a few bumps in the road."

She studied us. "From the look of you all, I'm thinking this is more than a bump. More like a huge pothole."

"You can say that again," Layla muttered.

"Well, don't you worry yourselves any more than you need to. Everything's going to get better from here on out."

I chortled softly, resigned to the fact that our resistance wouldn't do much to help us now. "Are you aware that your boss *killed* us all?"

Again, Fanny frowned. "I am, yes. Very regrettable, that. Distasteful business."

As one, we all chuffed or snorted. Shaking his head, Griffin grumbled, "Distasteful business . . ."

"Yes, Griffin, *distasteful*. If it were up to me, none of that would have happened. But I don't get to make the decisions around here, Magnum does. My job right now is to make things better for you, now that Magnum has set us on the course he's chosen."

Oh-kay. So Fanny wasn't the enemy. Maybe she could even be an ally to a certain degree when *Magnum* was calling all the shots of any significance.

Fanny's astute attention zeroed in on Hunt. "I hear you're carrying. Do I need to be concerned about my safety or that of my team?"

Unblinking, Hunt stared back at her. "Not unless any of you plan on hurting my friends or me. In which case, I won't hesitate to shoot to kill."

She *tsked*. "Dear me, no. Think of me as your fairy godmother, one who hasn't yet sprouted wings, and not for lack of trying, let me tell you." She chuckled to herself, alone in her joke. The driver pretended not to hear a thing she said, his gaze pinned ahead down the winding road that appeared to lead farther onto the campus.

Oh-kay. So Fanny was a weird one. It only made me like her. Even my reaction to this disarming woman was probably part of Chase's plan. I had to remember: we were in the alpha wolf's den now. This campus, whatever it actually was, was Chase's territory.

Fanny hopped onto the open bench seat directly behind the driver and patted the empty spot beside her. "Come. I'll show you around. I think you'll begin to relax once you see the lovely campus Magnum has built for you all. And then, when you're ready, I'll take you to your new home, where you can get cleaned up and into fresh clothes, then eat and rest."

New home. The phrase knelled like a bell in my mind, its pitch not quite right. The Periwinkle Hill neighborhood still felt like home even though one fact had already become abundantly clear: neither I nor any of my crew had a true home to return to.

Whatever future we were going to have, and wherever we were going to have it, we'd be building it together.

The "school" consisted of seven buildings connected by a network of sidewalks. It was edged by dense forest on all sides. Manicured foliage accentuated every walkway, flowerbed, and hundreds of planters, though not even Chase's seemingly limitless funds could urge the plants to grow any faster than the starters most of them still were. The cluster of structures squatted in a shallow valley, the typical hills and mountains of Ridgemore hiding it from view. Unless someone was positioned just right—doing a fly-by or atop the peak of a neighboring mountain—I doubted anyone would know the institute existed. I suspected that was part of the location's appeal.

The three largest buildings were situated in the center. In the middle was the academic building, which put Ridgemore

High to shame with its gleaming surfaces, elegant minimalist design, and state-of-the-art tech with half a dozen classrooms, two student labs, and an auditorium. A physical training center that had me all but drooling stood to one side of the academic building. It had enough exercise equipment to accommodate an entire football, soccer, and baseball team at the same time during peak training season. It boasted a pool that was half-Olympic-sized (which made it far larger than any other swimming pool in Ridgemore), and hot tubs and saunas in both the women's and men's locker rooms. Best of all, it had a vast open space with high ceilings, climbing ropes hanging from them, and vertical obstacle courses. The floors were lined with sparring mats, and one entire wall was adorned with weapons of all sorts, from practice wooden swords and staffs to actual lethal katanas and nunchucks, plus a bunch of tools the lot of us, as obsessed with "ninja" training as we were, had never seen. Once our bodies finished recovering from being shot and killed, I guessed we'd be spending most of our free time here. If Chase was planning to offer us true ninja training, complete with competent instructors, then we might just be getting cozy with the damn devil. He'd killed us all, but at a facility like this we could train to never be prey to his ilk again. We could actually learn to master whatever power immortality granted us.

On the other side of the academic building sat a co-ed dormitory with an amazing recreation center that took up most of the ground floor. There were nooks with cushy couches; pool, foosball, and ping-pong tables; giant TVs and game consoles. I had to keep my jaw from dropping yet again when I spotted a three-lane bowling alley along the back length of the rec center. It was a co-ed's dream—assuming whoever was intended to use this room didn't have to die to get here like we did. When we'd asked Fanny if we were going to be living in the dorms, she'd assured us that *Magnum* had built something special just for us.

I was all for being special, fuck yes. But despite all this luxury, I wasn't sure I enjoyed being special to someone like Chase.

The laboratory facility for his scientists was almost as large as the training center, and I couldn't help but note how Fanny's tour of the structure was more superficial than any other campus building before it. Individual labs of all kinds and sizes lined multiple hallways, and when Fanny led us into the elevator, a sensor in the keypad required her key-pass to access any level beyond the ground floor. Above ground, the building appeared to have three levels. Of course, I couldn't be sure, but my love of books and movies told me a baddy like Chase would totally have a few levels of underground secret labs. That'd be where all the really bad shit happened. If he'd had no problem openly gunning down a bunch of teenagers, at a busy high school no less, I didn't want to begin to ponder what kind of activities he might deem worth hiding. I really didn't.

Rounding out the campus was a dormitory for the scientists and other employees, who apparently wouldn't be leaving the campus either (there was a dining hall and a store for snacks and small, miscellaneous items—no payment required for any of it), and an administration building. Chase's office comprised the entire top floor of the three-story admin building, but Fanny didn't take us up there.

Across all of it, the branding that was ubiquitous in every other educational or corporate building I'd ever been in was glaringly absent. If Chase hadn't announced this was an institute for the advancement of immortals, we wouldn't have known it. Evidently, huge amounts of money did succeed in buying quite a lot of secrecy, even in a town like Ridgemore, which was as fond of its gossip as any other standard small town.

Fanny had informed us that our tour was over and we were heading to our new "home" when her tablet pinged. Her mouth pinched when she glanced at it. Given that so far she was the closest thing to an ally we had here, I didn't like her reaction.

While replying to the message, she told the driver, "Don, change of plans. One final stop before we head to the house: the office."

Don, who was a middle-aged man with a military haircut and bearing, swerved into an immediate U-turn and then sped up, driving us back in the direction we'd come from.

When Fanny looked up at us, for the first time her smile was forced, and that was after she'd admitted to knowing Chase had *murdered* us.

"Where are we going now?" Hunt asked.

"To see Magnum. He has something he wants to show you before we call it a day."

The sun was getting lower in the sky, and my empty stomach had been loudly reminding me I hadn't eaten since I'd died—at the hands of this guy. As often as I could, I reminded myself of the kind of person we were dealing with here. We might not be prisoners, but he'd also admitted he wouldn't let us go willingly.

"That sounds ominous," Layla told Fanny.

Fanny shifted on her seat, crossing her ankles. "Yes, well, with Magnum, things often appear that way. You'll get used to it."

Would we, though? And if we did, how could that possibly be a good thing?

"Any more questions while we drive there?" Fanny asked, putting more effort into her smile.

"Yeah," Griffin said. "Who else will be here with us?"

"The staff, obviously. But as to fellow students, you're the first to arrive. You're Magnum's priority."

She consulted her tablet again.

"And what kind of student does *Magnum* anticipate bringing here?" Griffin pressed.

She looked up. "Others like you, obviously."

"How many others like us are there?" Brady asked.

"Not many. None exactly like you, anyhow. But Magnum is resourceful. I'm sure he'll find what he needs. Eventually, anyway."

"I'm just sure he will," I muttered.

When she only returned to her tablet, far less forthcoming with this line of questioning, I said, "The campus looks pretty complete from what we saw. What's missing?"

"Security, definitely the security." She nodded for emphasis. "And then small details, lots of those too. But don't you worry, Magnum won't let anyone get to you."

"Oh, we're not worried about that," I quipped. "He's the one we've been trying to get away from."

Fanny stared at me for a beat, blinked, then finally said, "A piece of advice?"

"Sure, why not?"

"It's far easier to go along with him."

"You do recall he *killed* us, right?" Layla asked.

"Yes, but you came back, and he knew you would. Heed my warning. Fight him and it won't go well for you."

"It's already gone about as bad as it can for us," Brady said.

"No, Brady, it hasn't. Trust me on this. Go along with him and you'll get something good out of it. Don't, and . . . well, just go along with him."

"Oh, we're here! That was quick, Don," she said in a high pitch I didn't like.

"Don't wanna keep the bossman waiting," replied Don, his back ramrod straight behind the wheel.

"No, we certainly don't," Fanny said, hopping from the cart with an agility I was loving in the older woman. Her tablet once again tucked under her arm, she gestured with both hands for us to hurry.

It only made the five of us slow down to a crawl.

Fanny narrowed her eyes at us.

"What?" Layla said. "We're all injured. Your boss fucking had us shot."

"Five times each," Brady emphasized.

Our steps slowed even further.

By the time we reached the top floor, the formerly self-proclaimed "cool, fun aunt" was impatiently tapping a foot, the heel of her Birk flapping. She used her key-pass to access the top floor, and the elevator doors whooshed open onto an "office" that was as much focused on luxury comforts as functionality.

Magnum was lounging in his own private hot tub, a waterproof computer console of some sort to one side of him, on the other a tray with a tumbler containing two fingers of amber and a one-person antipasto tray. His shoulders and chest were sculpted, tan, and smooth, free of any body hair. A woman behind him was hastily packing up a massage table.

"There you are," he said by way of greeting.

"Their injuries prevented us from arriving sooner," Fanny said, her voice terse.

Chase's astute gaze alighted on us. "I can only imagine."

I couldn't decide what he meant by that, only that I probably wouldn't like it. I scowled at him.

"How did you enjoy your tour of the campus?" he asked us as the masseuse exited through a side door. I caught sight of a stairwell before the door shut behind her.

"'Enjoy' isn't the word I'd use," Griffin said. "We reserve that for life situations we enter into willingly."

"I understand. We still have much to discuss. I'll uphold my end of the bargain and share what I can with you before you have to make your decision."

"I didn't realize it was a 'bargain' to be strongarmed with the choice of coming either willingly or by force,'" Hunt added.

Chase simply said, "I have someone I think you'll be interested in meeting before you see your new home. I didn't expect her to be in today, but she's very dedicated to her work.

"Tracy," he called out, raising his voice to carry. "Will you please come out here?"

Another door opened, and when I saw who emerged, I instinctively clutched Griffin's arm.

Everything about "Tracy" was gut-wrenchingly familiar. On lean legs I'd admired in dozens of photos of Orson and his wife from before she abandoned them, Griffin's deadbeat mom stalked across the open space between the hot tub and a large desk that bordered a wall of windows.

Griffin's arm trembled beneath mine, and I clasped him all the harder. Layla shored up his other side, and Hunt and Brady bunched behind him, offering silent support.

"I believe you know Tracy as 'Mitzi,'" Chase said, his intelligent stare eating up our reactions. "And as you can see, she's very much accounted for."

8

Not Even a Hundred of Their Sincerest Apologies Will Be Enough

As the five of us gawked at her, *Tracy* looked back at us, her eyes soft and compassionate. When she smiled gently, it was the exact same smile I'd observed dozens of times in the photo of her and Orson that sat in a silver frame on the bookcase by the TV: the couple entwined in each other's arms, Griffin's mom sitting across his dad's lap, a gray couch the backdrop to the selfie. The jilted husband kept photos of the woman all over the house. According to him, she was the love of his life, and he'd never stop loving her, no matter that she'd abandoned him and their three-year-old son when they'd needed her most.

"Fuck," Griffin breathed so that no one but me and maybe Layla heard.

After a glance at Chase, and a nod of encouragement from him, Tracy closed the distance between us until she stood across from the huddle of us, within arm's reach. She wore a pristine white lab coat, currently unbuttoned to reveal a silk blouse and pencil skirt beneath, all the better to show those sculpted legs of hers. I'd heard Orson mention how beautiful her legs were on several occasions. The woman did have perfect legs, their long, lean lines accentuated by the four-inch heels she wore.

Her gaze softened further as it settled on Griffin. "Hi, Griffin. Magnum tells me you've been led to believe I was your mother."

Griffin gaped at her, his jaw slack, and said nothing.

"I can only imagine how difficult it must be to find out that's not true, and then to see me in person like this."

Again, no comment from Griffin, but he managed to close his mouth, and the trembling was slowing down. Griffin had always been strong. I knew he'd be working furiously to pull himself together.

"When Tobias and I used to work together, we dated for a time. I've seen some of the pictures he's been displaying of us, and they're from the time we were together—though many of them have been doctored. I've never been pregnant, and yet there are images of me with a swollen belly that are remarkably convincing. Even I would've believed I carried a pregnancy to term." With a dark chuckle, she shook her head in what looked like disbelief.

Griffin cleared his throat. Even so, his question came out as a croak. "My dad . . . Orson, I mean, his name is . . . Tobias?"

Tracy nodded. Her mouth, painted in a conservative raspberry, curved downward in empathy. "Tobias Andrew Dole. For a while, he tried to get me to call him TAD, based on his initials. He thought it sounded cooler, but it never took." She grimaced.

"I told you I had plenty of proof," Chase said.

He observed all of us from his seat in the hot tub. Both Tracy and Fanny behaved as if Chase doing business from there was a common sight. If I were a man with more money than time, I suppose I'd be inclined to conduct my business from a hot tub too.

"If you agree to study here," said Chase, "to work with me, I'll show you all the evidence you can handle."

Oh boy. It was on the tip of my tongue to ask for the real names of my fake-ass parents, but I wasn't sure I wanted to take that on yet. I was still reeling from seeing my friends die, thinking I might be a goner, and then waking up to all of this. Give a girl a minute to catch her breath, dammit!

But soon, very soon, I'd need to know. I had to know their real names so I could properly cuss them out. I'd want to know it all.

Tracy studied me next. I returned the favor. Her slim, athletic frame was a close enough match to Griffin, but the rest of her? Not so much. Her hair was a rich, wavy auburn. Her skin was pale, her eyes a flat brown, and her cheeks round despite a thin face. She even had freckles. Griffin, with his olive-hued skin, dark hair, and chiseled features, didn't even look related to her. And now I understood precisely why we all lacked features in common with our *parents*.

Hunt sidled up behind me so that his face popped up above mine and asked Tracy, "Were you also involved in these experiments that, uh, created us, I guess?"

Tracy glanced at Chase, who shook his head at her silent question and sat up straighter in the tub, exposing more of his torso. From what I could see, the dude even had six-pack abs, and I didn't think it was possible to purchase those. The man had to work for them just like the rest of us.

"You'll have your answers soon enough," Chase told us. "I wanted you to meet Tracy since she was conveniently here. She's still in the process of moving over from the other lab to this one."

In answer to the question that immediately sparked in my mind, Chase continued, "Though my head researchers disappeared on me with everything we'd worked so hard to achieve, we kept going. We persevered. Didn't we, Tracy?"

Tracy scowled, apparently as put out by the betrayal of our *parents* as Chase was. "That we did, Magnum. That we most certainly did. I can't wait to see Tobias again." And then the pleasant, almost gentle-looking woman bared her teeth. When her face scrunched up, it revealed lines around her eyes and bracketing her mouth that I hadn't noticed before.

"He owes more than just these kids a major apology," she insisted.

Chase smiled, the expression reaching his eyes only to chill them to ice despite the warmth of the water he was sitting in. "Not even a hundred of their sincerest apologies will be enough."

"Are you planning on killing them?" Layla asked, and I started at the question I hadn't even contemplated.

Chase didn't. "I haven't decided yet. It depends on how useful I find them. They have a whole hell of a lot to make up for."

Well, at least the man was predictably blunt, I had to give him that.

"They most definitely do," Tracy chimed in. The woman I'd mistakenly believed to be soft didn't balk at the thought of her employer murdering a bunch of scientists.

I glanced at Fanny. Her expression was steady, blank. In that moment, she reminded me of a mix between a seasoned Judi Dench and a Helen Mirren, when playing their most kickass roles. She'd seen it all already and didn't shirk from whatever life was going to throw her way next.

To us, Chase added, "You'll be seeing lots more of Tracy. When you decide to stay here, you'll be working with her closely." *When,* not *if.* "Now, Fanny, please take them to their new house. They look exhausted."

No, we looked shot at, pissed the fuck off, and like our brains were on overload. After all that, once the smoke drifting from our ears settled, then we probably looked as tired as we felt.

"I think you'll find we gave a lot of thought to your space," Chase said. "I hope you like it."

Then he turned toward his computer monitor, waking it from sleep mode. *Dismissed.*

Without another glance at their boss, Tracy and Fanny walked toward the elevator, expecting us to follow.

Without anything better to do, we did.

Don pulled up in front of "our new house" just as the sun was about to set, and immediately scanned our surroundings. Above the tree canopies that enveloped the structure, their branches soaring toward it, the sky was slowly tingeing a beautifully riotous pink.

With her usual agility, Fanny jumped from the cart, her long skirt flaring for a second. My friends and I were slower to follow. This time, it had less to do with our steady healing and more with the building that no reasonable person would ever describe as just a house.

"This is a fucking *mansion*," Layla said with a whistle, this tendency of hers so similar to Brady's, reminding me they were twins.

Fanny chuckled fondly, as if her boss was just so dang cute. "Yes, I'd also describe it as such. Magnum doesn't do anything halfway."

"We're starting to get that," Layla responded, her head tilted back to take in the cantilevered roof that jutted strikingly out over the entrance, and the glass wall that lined the entire front wall.

Like the buildings on the rest of the campus, the mansion consisted of sleek lines and sharp angles, all elegantly understated and . . . perfect. The modern style reminded me of the designs of Frank Lloyd Wright and Ray D. Crites, two of my favorite architects, both long gone now.

Straight boards of dark wood sheathed the exterior walls, beautifully complementing the rest of the long lines and angles, and all that open glass.

Layla chuckled at my obvious appreciation as she shored up beside me. "Uh-oh. Nerd alert, nerd alert."

Griffin stepped to my other side, his arm a breath away from touching mine. Hunt and Brady joined us in staring at the place.

"It's not just Joss," Hunt said. "I really don't wanna say it, but this place is . . ."

"Freaking. Awesome," I said on a gush, not even attempting to hide how impressed I was. At least Chase wasn't here to witness my reaction, though no doubt Fanny would dutifully relay our reactions later.

She raised her tablet, her fingers racing across it. Okay, never mind. She was tattling in real time.

When she finished and her tablet was back beneath her arm, she smiled. "It's even better inside. Come on."

Jaw as slack as when I'd seen Griffin's long-absent "mother" appear in Chase's office, I didn't hesitate to follow.

"I think you'll enjoy exploring the place on your own," Fanny called over her shoulder, "so I'll just show you some highlights before I leave you to it."

We followed her up a path that wove around the house and led to a garage beneath the structure.

"Be still my beating heart," Brady said.

I couldn't help a snort. "Didn't think I'd ever hear you say *that*, Brade."

"Neither did I."

"Don't blame you though," I added as I took in the car silhouettes visible through the large wall of glass despite the failing daylight.

"Magnum thought you'd appreciate this," Fanny said as she bent over another keypad, pressing her thumb to it. "The house is keyed to the five of you. All you need to do to enter is press your thumbprint to any of the sensors."

Layla crossed her arms over the chest of her scrubs and frowned. "Of course you have them on file already."

Fanny didn't so much as blink. "We have every piece of data the scientists collected on you."

So when "the scientists" spied on me and my friends, going so far as to tap our private spaces and phones, Chase now had all that info too. *Fucking splendid.*

Fanny pushed on the metal frame of the glass wall and the entire door spun on a hinge in the center.

Despite myself, I *ooh*ed. Griffin stayed beside me as Brady, Hunt, and Layla rushed in. Only when I advanced did he enter too.

"Clyde," he whispered reverently. And there it was, his 1976 Ford Mustang Cobra II coupe, its body and sleek silver paintjob still damaged from when he'd gone over the cliff.

Bonnie was parked beside Clyde, the 2014 Shelby GT500 as pretty as ever, her deep-impact blue shimmering beneath the warm, incandescent lights that came on automatically when Fanny opened the door.

My unfinished 1999 SVT Cobra coupe, which I'd named Cleo, sat up on blocks, alongside two other Mustangs that had amazing bones despite their current rust-bucket statuses.

There was a Mustang for each of us, even Layla, who was supposed to share Bonnie with Brady, though we all knew Bonnie was more his than hers.

And the garage wasn't just for parking the beauties either. There were two fully loaded state-of-the-art bays, equipped with lifts, for working on our cars. There was even a contained paint booth off to one side. Five carts, each laden with brand-new tools for each of us, were tucked into a recessed niche in the wall that was clearly designed especially for them.

Slowly, I turned to look at Fanny, who was waiting with a smug smile. "Magnum also asked me to inform you that if you need anything else for your cars—parts, anything, no cost is too great—you just ask me, and I'll make sure it's delivered ASAP."

"He's really not messing around, is he?" Brady asked.

"He never is."

"He really thinks he can buy us that easily," Hunt commented.

"Like I said earlier," Fanny said, "Magnum gets his way regardless. It behooves you to make it easy on yourselves."

"And you feel good about working for a man like that?" I asked.

Fanny's smile dropped. "Magnum is many things, not all obvious to those who don't know him well."

"And you know him well?"

"Very."

"So you approve of him killing us to get us here?" Layla pressed.

"Everyone does questionable things. That doesn't inform the entire picture of what they're about, who they are, why they do the things they do."

Layla opened her mouth, no doubt to question that remarkably dubious standard of hers, but Fanny beat her to it.

"Now that you've seen the garage, I'll show you the rest of the house." Her tone was flat. Like, *How dare we criticize the perfect little murderer?*

"No thanks," Brady said, some of his former awe remaining despite the fresh reminder of why we were standing in this truly outstanding garage. "I'm gonna live right here with Bonnie. I won't even ask how he got her here; I'm just happy to see her."

A hint of her previous amusement danced across Fanny's face. "Then perhaps I'll leave you here to make your own way upstairs."

Half of us still taking in the cars, we nodded.

"The fridge is fully stocked. When you go to your classes, training, or checkups, staff will come in to clean and tidy up, and a chef will prepare your meals. If you have any specific requests, send them to me, and I'll make sure Magnum gets them."

"Oh-kay," I said. This was all so over the top, I was finding fewer words than usual.

Fanny's gaze alighted on me. "Do any of you need a nurse to come check you out?"

"Not at the moment."

"If that changes, day or night, you let me know. You'll find clothes to match your personal styling in each of your wardrobes, along with everything else we could think of. Joss, when you're ready for your dog—"

"I'll let you know." No way was I bringing Bobo here till I was convinced he was safer here than with the traitors. So far, it was a close call. At least here he'd be with me. But he'd also be in the den of a killer who did nothing to hide his glaring lack of qualms.

"What about our phones?" Layla asked. "How are we supposed to get in touch with you?"

"You may have your phones tomorrow. But your communications will be limited to messaging only, and your texts will be assessed before they're allowed out. In the meantime, you can reach me by pressing the 'information' button on any of the keypads, and I'll be here tomorrow afternoon at 2:00 p.m. I imagine you'll need some extra rest to recover from your ordeal."

Layla growled, her nostrils flaring. "That's some fucking bullshit."

"It's for your safety as much as ours."

"I highly doubt that," Griffin said on an incredulous snort. "What does everyone think about us disappearing like this? When they were all loaded up into the ambulances"—he glanced at the four of us—"no one saw us, but surely they noticed something went down."

All business now, Fanny smiled sharply before letting it drop. "Everything's been taken care of. The gymnasium of Ridgemore High burned to the ground, but Magnum is generously building an even better facility to replace it."

"Super fucking generous of him, yeah," I said.

Fanny's eyes flashed with irritation. "You'll find that Magnum has a good reason for everything he does, and he doesn't leave messes behind. Everywhere he goes, he leaves things better than he found them."

"Sure," Hunt said dismissively. "What about our friends? Where do they think we are?"

Or the sheriff, whom I told about our ability to come back to life in order to get him to defibrillate Griffin? Or the EMTs who were there to witness Griff and Brady's resurrections? Or the surgeons and hospital staff who wouldn't stop blathering about the "miracle kids"?

"They think you're being treated for smoke inhalation and currently unable to receive visitors," Fanny said. "After that, you'll be transferring to an elite private school abroad that is much better suited to educate geniuses with your abilities. When Magnum discovered five students with your test scores were at the same school as his nephew, he took interest. He's offered to fund your education for your final year, to give you the best opportunities in life by placing you in the best 'gifted' program in the world."

I gulped. They really were orchestrating our entire lives without our input. "And what of our former parents?" I asked, picking up on the defeat in my own voice and not liking it. I straightened my shoulders against it.

Fanny stalked to the door, and with her hand already on the frame, turned back toward us. "What do they matter? They've done nothing but betray you."

When none of us had anything to say to dispute that depressing conclusion, she walked out, closing the door behind her.

After several seconds of quiet, I exchanged looks with my friends. "Well then. I guess . . . welcome home, motherfuckers."

9

I Think I'm a Facilities Ho

After Don sped away with Fanny in tow, heading back in the direction of the campus buildings, and I finally found myself alone with the only people in the entire world I truly trusted, the events of the past few days settled across my shoulders like a thousand-pound barbell. No longer panicked about the immediate fate of my crew, I allowed myself to feel some of the terror and loss, and then the whirlwind of relief, that began with Brady's original death. As I did, absolutely every single part of my body turned leaden. I thought I'd sink to the floor and join Brady in sleeping next to Bonnie just so I wouldn't have to move for at least the next twelve hours. I had nothing left to give, and now that I paused, I recognized I was still woozy from whatever drugs they'd pumped through my system.

But when my similarly grim-faced friends headed off to check out the rest of the place, my curiosity pushed me to trudge upstairs after them, even though there was no way that whatever Chase had provided with the rest of the house would do anything to buoy my spirits.

Oh, how wrong I was. Turned out maybe I couldn't be outright bought, but I could most definitely be . . . encouraged.

A koi pond—yep, a fucking *koi pond*, filled with beautiful swimming fish—occupied a large basin at the bottom of a staircase that spiraled up and around it. A wall that led from the garage to the main floor—and then continued up to a second-story loft—streamed with a continual sheet of water that fed the basin. The trickling flow of water instantly soothed some of my ragged edges.

Beyond it was a large terrace with stunning views of the surrounding mountains and forest. To the other side, descending several steps, were a recessed indoor swimming pool, a hot tub, and a surrounding lounge area.

When I made it into what I guessed might be a living room—a large open area that reached all the way up to the second story—and found a large fireplace with a huge seating area around it, and a kitchen with gleaming stainless steel and marble everywhere past it, I halted right where I stood.

"Guys," I said. "I can't believe I'm gonna say this, but I think I'm a facilities ho."

From the other side of a wall I hadn't yet explored, Layla's voice trailed out. "If you're a facilities ho, then so am I. I could live here for the rest of my life and not mind one fucking bit. This bedroom's beyond gorgeous."

From somewhere else I couldn't see, Brady whooped, and I heard Hunt respond, though I couldn't make out what they were celebrating. Griffin walked on, exploring the place, never leaving my side for long.

By the time every space was accounted for, we'd discovered a bedroom for every one of us—each with an ensuite bathroom that included a deep-soaking tub, a view, and a walk-in closet already loaded with clothes and shoes—a theater and gaming room on the other side of the garage, and an art and music studio that occupied most of the loft area. The billionaire had spared no expense.

We pulled out a veritable smorgasbord of gourmet food from the fridge and pantry and spread it out on a wooden dining table that retained the slab's organic edges. Though we were still underage as far as the local drinking laws went, the fridge was stocked with some of our favorite local microbrews.

I loaded my plate with hummus, baba ghanoush, olives, cheeses, and fresh bread, shoved some into my mouth, sighed in relief, and leaned back in my chair with a beer in my hand. I took a long sip and studied my friends, who were stuffing their faces as eagerly as I was.

"So, what do we think about everything?"

Brady looked up from his plate while shoveling in a chip heaped with chunky homemade salsa. Shit, that looked good. I reached to add some to my plate.

"I think we're super fucked," he said around a mouthful.

As one, we all nodded. Then Griffin added, "So fucked. This is bad, guys. So fucking bad."

"It's bad," Brady said, "but still somehow so good." He groaned around a bite of what looked like an Italian sub. "So fucking good. I could eat a horse."

"Think they're listening to what we say?" I asked.

"Definitely," Hunt said, his eyes on me while he drank his beer. "I looked for cameras but didn't see any. Though"—he glanced at the blatantly obvious sophistication all around us—"I doubt we'd spot them if they didn't want us to. This place is . . . well, it's something."

"It's something, all right," Layla said happily, munching on some Greek pasta salad. Damn, that looked good too. I reached for that bowl as well.

"They can probably hear us through the keypad panels," Griffin said, scooping some salsa onto a pita chip, "if nothing else."

I narrowed my eyes at the nearest one, recessed into the wall beside the refrigerator. "For sure. So we have to keep that in mind." I laughed bitterly. "But hey, at least that part won't be that different from 'living at home with our *parents.*'" I hooked air quotes on that mega charade before licking some hummus off a finger.

Hunt leaned back in his chair too. "I know we saw 'Mitzi' with our own eyes, and my brain gets that she's a woman named Tracy and not actually Griff's mom, but still . . . " He shook his head. "It's like it just won't compute. I keep thinking of my mom—Alexis or whatever—as, well, my mom. It's messing with my head."

"Yeah, bro," Brady said around yet another mouthful. Knowing the guy, he'd likely eat for an hour straight before he'd have his fill. "I feel the same way. I'm kinda freaked about learning all their real names 'cause I already know it's gonna feel weird as fuck."

"Better to know than not," Layla said, snagging a slice of the Italian sub. "I can't even with them. They're lucky they're not here right now 'cause I legit might murder the both of them." She shook her head. "Celia with all her little obligatory family dinners. What a fucking shitshow. I keep thinking about it, and I *still* can't believe they lied to all of us. It's just. . ." She shook her head some more until she finally gave up on trying to summarize the mess that was our lives and bit savagely into her sub.

"My dad never even existed," Hunt added with a flick to the turquoise stone dangling from a silver hoop in his earlobe, the earring he so often wore. Supposedly, it had belonged to his deceased father. "Like, who the hell did this belong to, then?"

Layla snorted and popped a pita chip into her mouth. "Alexis probably bought it at a random stand on the rez."

"You give her too much credit," Griffin said. "She probably ordered it online."

"True," Brady said. "They even order the TP online. Everything gets shipped. Alexis for sure didn't get it from anyplace special at all."

Hunt sighed, drank from his beer before setting down the bottle, then unclasped the earring and tossed it onto the table. It slid to rest beside the bowl of olives. "To think that was one of my prized possessions."

I harrumphed. "To think we were carried by surrogates."

"At this point I'm glad," Griffin said, and I looked over at him. He sat in the chair beside me. "I half expected one of them to tell us we were test tube babies, developed in some sort of incubator till we reached viability."

I swallowed my bite of sharp cheddar cheese and it stuck a bit on the way down. "Well, I don't think the disclosures are over, not by a long shot."

"Agreed," Hunt said. "But whatever Magnum's told us so far, I think it's been the truth."

"Funny," I said, "I've been thinking of him as 'Chase.' Didn't want to give in to him by calling him what he wants."

Hunt shrugged. "Pretty sure the guy's got us by the balls regardless."

My shoulders slumped and I bent over my food. "Yeah. He's definitely trying to buy the shit out of us." Even so, I couldn't help but gaze admiringly at the living room beyond the dining room, each space more beautiful than the next.

"He's succeeding," Brady said, spearing a noodle from Layla's plate. She growled at him and dragged her plate closer. "I'd practically give my left nut to live in a place like this. Did you see the garage?"

"Yeah, Brade," Layla said, "we all saw it."

I laughed. "Never thought I'd see the day when Brady Rafferty *swooned*."

Unconcerned, Brady just reached for more tortilla chips and salsa. "I'm not ashamed to say it. I've found my price." He looked around pointedly. "*This*, this is my price. Shit, he even got Lay and Hunt their own cars. And Mustangs too! Man's a fucking manipulative boss. Sure, he's a murderous asshole of the utmost degree, but he's still a boss when it comes to knowing what to give us to keep us happy." Munching on a bite, he grinned. "Now I get Bonnie all to myself. No more sharing with the stinky sister. Bonnie's fucking thrilled."

"Hey," Layla protested. "She likes me too."

"'Course she does. But she *loves* me."

I rolled my eyes, scarcely believing Brady and Layla were already back to going at it. "Guys, not that long ago, all of us but Griff were dead."

My statement hung in the air like a smell too pungent to ignore.

Brady sobered instantly. "Yeah. I've died twice now. Never thought I'd be saying that shit, that's for damn sure."

"I never, and I do mean *never*," Griffin said so vehemently that we all stared at him, "want to go through that again. Seeing them kill you all, not sure if you were gonna come back or not, it was the very worst moment of my life. Next to Brady dying the first time, the worst. Never . . ."

"Well, it's not like we were fans either, Griff," Layla said.

He shook his head once, sharply. "I would rather die a hundred times than have to stand by and watch and be able to do nothing to stop it from happening. You guys . . ." He grimaced. "I just . . . I *can't* do that again."

Layla reached across the table to squeeze his hand. But I just stared at him, remembering what it had felt like to hear Clyde's tires sliding off the cliff, knowing Griffin was likely still inside the car.

"You won't have to," Layla assured him. "You won't ever have to go through that again."

"You can't know that."

It took me a long moment to realize the words came from me. But they were true. "Magnum is going overboard buttering us up. And we've already seen he's got no qualms whatsoever about doing whatever he wants to us, whenever he wants. Who's to say part of us being at this school of his doesn't mean he thinks he'll get to kill us again and again just to see what happens? I mean, he hasn't exactly hidden his intentions. All he cares about is getting immortality for himself. This place is probably one big lab experiment to him."

"It definitely is," Hunt said. "No doubt about it. He all but admitted it already."

Brady, all serious now, pushed away his plate. "At least we know that though. He keeps telling us he's the devil we know. Well, he is. Better than our lying scum parents, whom I can't get myself to stop calling 'parents' and it's pissing me right the fuck off."

"I know. Me too," Layla groaned. "We have no homes to go back to. No way am I going back to Celia and Porter, whatever their names actually are. Are you guys willing to go 'home'?"

"No," Griffin, Hunt, Brady, and I replied at once.

"Exactly," Layla continued. "Yeah, we could head out into the world and make our own way. I know we could do it. Together, we totally could. We'd all have to work, but we could cover our expenses easily with the five of us working. But then how would we find out about us? Now that I know some of what we're capable of, *I need to fucking know everything.*"

"I need to know too," Brady said.

"Ditto," Hunt added.

"I'd like to meet some of these other students, too," I admitted. "Are there really more people out there like us? And what are they like?"

"The campus isn't huge," Griffin said, "but it's big enough. Magnum's definitely expecting at least a few dozen students by the end of it."

Brady's eyes gleamed. "That's gonna be cool as shit. A school of fucking *immortals*." He whistled and let the impact of that notion settle around us all. "Plus, did you guys see the training center? I got a semi just looking at the place."

"Ew, Brade," Layla complained, but I chuckled and pointed at myself.

"Like I said, *facilities ho*, right here. Talk about some ninja training. I'll bet Magnum'll even have some sweet instructors lined up for us."

"And if he doesn't," Brady said, growing more enthusiastic by the second, "we can ask for them."

"That'll be cool," Griffin conceded begrudgingly.

Brady pulled his plate back toward him, a grin tugging at his lips. "The way I see it, we're already fucked as fucked gets. You heard the guy, he's already not gonna let us leave the easy way. Our options already suck. Add in that our *parents* aren't really our parents, that we have no allies beyond us, and things get even more dire."

His smile fell. "We can fight like hell now, he sets his goons on us, we die all over again, and this whole process starts over. Or, we just go with it, for now. We learn everything we possibly can about ourselves, our powers, immortality, whatever, everything about everyone else like us, what it all means, and then we can always leave later if we want."

"I doubt leaving anytime soon is on Magnum's agenda," I said.

Brady shrugged, but the flippant attitude was gone. "It'll be as much an option then as it is now. And by then, we'll know more about what we can do."

"That part's true," Layla agreed. "We'll prob be more powerful then too, or whatever. I mean, it can't get much worse than it is now, right? The more we know, the better." She scowled and gnawed on a chunk of cheese. "I hope, anyhow."

"At least we'll live like royalty in the meantime," Brady said. "Not great, of course not. But at least better. He could've locked us up in cells like true lab rats, the miserable fuckers. From what we've seen, he'd totally do it, too. So I say we do as Fanny suggested. We play nice for now so he does too."

He glanced around at the rest of us. We had no better plan to offer.

"In that case," Griffin said, "I'll be taking the bedroom next to Joss." He swiveled in his seat to fully face me. "Now that I know how you feel about me, I'm not leaving your side. No one's gonna take you away from me again."

A sudden surge of warmth spread throughout my body to tingle in my extremities. No matter how many times I'd allowed myself to imagine what it might be like to actually openly *love* Griffin, and to have him love me as more than just friends in return, I found myself with nothing ready to say.

Layla chuckled. "Oh man. This is gonna be a blast. *Flustered Joss* is my new fave."

"Shut up, Lay," I grumbled, but the others laughed.

Everyone but Griffin.

His eyes warmed to a bright hazel as they took in mine.

How would I ever sleep with him in the room next to mine? Talk about some wet dream potential.

My gaze fell to his full lips. I didn't even realize I'd done it until those lips tipped into a smile that was the sexiest I'd ever seen.

My stare flicked up to his, and his grin spread.

Then, he winked at me.

That warmth heated by several degrees.

Man, oh man.

I was fucked in so many ways.

10

Cuddle Puddle!

After eating, we'd intended to test out some of the incredible amenities our new quarters offered. However, we soon admitted defeat. Even Griffin, the only one not sporting five new scars ringing his chest, was exhausted. Apparently he really meant it when he said he would have preferred to die a hundred deaths than to have witnessed ours. His trauma dragged along his face, drawing his beautiful lips into a constant grimace. His eyes, usually sharp and alert, were often distant, as if he kept catching himself lost in a loop of awful memories.

It was happening to me, too. All those shots echoed through my mind, startling me all over again every time I heard them. Visions of Layla and Hunt dropping to the floor followed. My nerves were fried, and in the absence of all the adrenaline that had flooded my system, even my legs wobbled as I plodded around the unfamiliar house.

By 9:00 p.m., I dragged myself into bed with wet hair, just grateful I'd found the energy to shower. No one wanted to break in their new bed with *eau de dead on a school gymnasium floor*.

I thought achingly of Bobo, who usually slept at the foot of my bed. On the days I pampered him, which were often, he slept on the bed itself. I wondered how he was faring without me and if he'd already realized I was never coming back. He was a smart boy, very sensitive to his surroundings and to whatever was going on with me. I resolved to retrieve him tomorrow. If we were staying here for a significant length of time, I wouldn't trust his care to Monica and Reece, whoever they truly were. I'd never trust either of them ever again. In a time when I wasn't certain of much, I was certain of that.

The intoxicating lull of sleep was already tugging me under when the door opened and closed quietly. The part of me that realized I was now in constant danger tried to jostle me to alertness. But I was still recovering, and the morphine and whatever other drugs still lingered in my system, making me groggy. Besides, my crew was in the house with me. My eyelids fluttered in an attempt to remain open and failed.

"Hmmmmm," I hummed groggily a moment before I recognized *him*. His presence was different from anyone else's—somehow more mine than any of my other friends.

"Griff?" I mumbled into my pillow.

"Yeah, it's me." His voice was soft and alluring as a dream. "Do you mind if I sleep in here with you tonight?"

That got my eyes open. He stood at the edge of the bed, gazing down at me. He wore a t-shirt and boxers, his feet already bare.

"I don't want to be without you right now," he whispered so gently that I questioned if perhaps I was already dreaming. That was an unusually vulnerable admission for him.

"You wanna sleep in the bed with me?" I asked, unsure whether it was fact gathering or an invitation.

"I do."

I shifted from my side onto my back to stare up at him. The room was dark, but enough diffuse moonlight filtered through the closed blinds that I could make out the outline of his body.

We'd slept together countless times over the years growing up together. But our other friends had always been there too. There was a room at Hunt's house we'd dubbed the "sleepover room" since it was large enough to accommodate five twin mattresses.

But the rest of our friends weren't here this time as a buffer—and Griffin and I had admitted we loved each other.

We'd also all died, and despite our apparent immortality I'd never been so keenly aware of how fleeting life could be. Our resilience didn't guarantee a tomorrow, especially not with someone like Magnum Chase involved at every turn.

Apparently I was taking too long to answer. Griffin took a step backward.

"Never mind," he said, his voice gruffer now, "it was a stupid idea." He turned toward the door, padding away from me on silent footfalls. "You need your rest. I'll check on you tomorrow."

I pushed up onto my elbows. "Griff . . ."

He stopped and turned back toward me. "Yeah?"

My heart squeezed at how hopeful he sounded. Griffin had a soft side but he didn't often reveal it, not even to me.

"I don't want to be away from you now either," I admitted, drawing down the covers in welcome.

Unmoving, he stared at me for so long that I asked, "Is something wrong?"

Slowly, he shook his head and finally stalked toward me. "No. I mean, yeah, a ton of shit's wrong, obviously. But not between you and me."

Breathless, I waited for him to continue, hoping he'd confess to more.

He didn't. He did, however, tug off his shirt and toss it onto a lounge chair that occupied a corner of the room beside a reading lamp.

At the sight of his trim, muscled outline in nothing more than his boxer shorts, I became acutely aware of my own attire. Without the energy to properly explore the many new clothes awaiting me, I'd slipped into a sheer camisole and panties—that was it.

I was still debating whether I should get up to look for something additional to wear when he climbed into the bed and drew the covers up over us. Instantly, like a dumbass, I went rigid—as if we hadn't touched a million times before—but I was suddenly unsure where any of my body parts were supposed to go.

The heat from all that incredible bare skin of his radiated into me, making him seem too close and not close enough all at once.

His hand brushed against mine, and his fingers threaded through my own across the space between us.

When I *still* didn't relax, he tensed, his hand squeezing mine. "Is this too much? I can sleep on the floor if you prefer."

He tugged his fingers away as if about to get up, but then I finally got my brain to stop reacting so intently to the feel of his naked skin so near my own.

I tightened my hold on his hand. "No," I said a bit too forcefully. Softer, I added, "No, please stay. I just . . . it's weird to have you in my bed now that I . . . think of you differently. Doesn't mean I want you to go, though. I just need a minute to adjust."

It wasn't as if I hadn't thought of what it'd be like to have Griffin in bed with me before. I'd fantasized about his hands, mouth, and body all over mine, his body *inside* mine, enough that I was close to being able to call it a damn hobby lately. But then, before, he hadn't known I thought about him like that.

I hadn't known he thought about me like that.

Fuck. Has Griffin jerked off while fantasizing about me?!

"I don't know what I was thinking," he said in reaction to . . . whatever I was doing while fantasizing about him fantasizing about me. *Shit.* "This is too much for tonight. It's been a long, fucked-up, crazy day for all of us, and you're still healing."

I shook my head, my damp hair rubbing along my pillow, no doubt getting it wet. "No, Griff, stay. I really do want you here. I want to get used to this."

"Sleeping with me?" he asked with a hint of surprise.

"Well, I mean . . . yeah?"

What sparse light filtered in through the closed blinds wasn't enough to illuminate the planes of his face that I knew by heart. I *felt* his smile more than I saw it.

He rolled onto his side to face me, his pleased grin palpable even in the darkness. "You want to get used to sharing a bed with me?"

The smug bastard was fishing for more admissions. "I just said it, didn't I?"

He chuckled at my sudden attitude. I wasn't fond of putting myself out there first. We both knew it.

"Well, good," he said. "I'd like that too. We have a lot of new things to try out and get used to."

I wasn't one to blush or to flush. I was about as much of a shrinking violet as Layla was. But fuck if I wasn't blushing furiously now and thankful for the cover of darkness.

When a deep, sexy laugh rumbled through Griff's chest, I knew I wasn't fooling him.

"We know each other too well," I grumbled, turning away from him with a pout I didn't entirely understand.

He slid across the bed so that his body curved around mine, little more than a few inches of air between us. "That's only going to make everything between us that much more amazing. I know it will."

I harrumphed without a single good reason I could discover, and he chuckled. Then his fingers alighted on my waist, tracing gentle circles across the skin between my camisole and the lace waist of my cotton bikini panties.

"Are you still hurting?" he asked.

"Mmmmmmm, from what?" His fingers were light as a feather across my skin, but his touch was sending tingles weaving through tissue and muscle till I could feel him all over me.

His fingers paused before starting up again. "Um, from the five fucking bullets you took to the chest just three fucking days ago?"

"Oh, right." I'd never thought of myself as a dreamy romantic before, and maybe it was the drugs or that I'd been half asleep, but being here with him made all that ugliness seem so far away. As if it were part of someone else's life, not mine.

"I can barely feel any of that now," I said. "The scars are shrinking, and the skin doesn't even tug or itch anymore."

"I don't want to hurt you," Griffin added, his touch growing even softer, like the brush of a comforting breeze.

"You won't."

"I never want to. I'll never, ever mean to." He was referring to more than just the physical. "I really meant it when I said it, you know."

I inched back toward him so that the heat of his body slid across mine. The lengths of our bodies were nearly touching.

"Meant what?" I asked. Now look who was fishing.

"That I love you. That I'm *in love* with you."

I sucked in a gasp. To hear him say it again, and like this . . .

Slowly, so slowly, so that his fingers slid across my stomach as I turned, I faced him. "Say it again," I breathed, scooting closer so that when he draped his arm over my waist our bodies were flush, my breasts splayed against his chest, nothing but a wisp of cotton separating our bare flesh.

He traced his hand up my back, across my shoulders, and over to my neck. Gently, he pulled my face to his. So we'd fit together better, I hooked a leg over his hip.

Softly, he growled, like he wasn't ready for that kind of touch, that kind of proximity. Like he'd thought we'd work up to that. And surely we should have. There was so much newness to explore together before we let ourselves have sex. Because once we started having sex, I knew we'd never want to stop. I, at least, would need to remain in this bed with him for at least twelve hours a day, every day. Fuck Magnum Chase and all this immortality business.

His lips resting on mine, he whispered, "I love you, Joss Bryson." He groaned. "Or whatever the hell your last name really is."

Not even the fresh reminder that our entire lives were stupid façades could ruin this moment for me.

"And I love you, Griffin Conway—or whatever."

I giggled. Like we weren't currently living in the eye of the most massive shitstorm of our lives. I'd never been one to giggle. This man was upending my life already and we were only just getting started.

With his lips still against mine, he said softly, "We need to take this slow."

"I know."

"We have to," he murmured. "I can't let myself have you all at once, no matter how badly I've wanted you. No matter how much I want you, I need to drag it out."

"Mmmmm-hmmm," I said, the vibration of the sound tingling our joined lips.

"If it's too much, too fast, tell me to stop."

A breathy laugh. "Good luck with that, mister. Since when am I the picture of restraint?"

He groaned, and when I adjusted my hips I discovered him erect, his hard dick pressed against my stomach.

Totally wanton and unabashed, I groaned too.

"Ignore that," he grumbled. "He can wait. He *will* wait, dammit."

"Mmmmmmmm," slid out of me as I ground my core against him. A part of me wanted to take it snail-level slow with him. But my body clearly had other ideas.

"Joss, don't—"

I swallowed his protests whole as I kissed him the way I'd dreamed of kissing him in so many of my fantasies. He hesitated for only a millisecond before his tongue slid across mine, and we both moaned together. With my leg, I pulled him more tightly against me and clawed at his shoulder, sliding into his hair, tangling and tugging. I wanted to touch him everywhere at once.

"Holy shit," he murmured against my mouth. "Fuck..." Then he legit growled before spinning me onto my back, his legs coming to rest between mine. Instantly, I wrapped my thighs around his hips and pulled him against me. His cock throbbed against the rapidly dampening crotch of my underwear.

"Joss, fuck," he panted, kissing me as if he were a dying man, dragging his lips across my neck. Already, my nipples were hard points, doing their damnedest to lure his mouth to them.

"Fuck. Fuck. Fuuuck," he chanted down across my collarbones, and I bathed in the delight of so easily bringing him to incoherency.

Knowing it would push him over the edge, with the sultriest voice in my arsenal, I rasped, "Just wait till you feel what it's like to be inside me."

I loved living on the edge—and beyond it.

"Ohmyholyfuckingfuckfuck," he grumbled. "You're gonna fucking kill me, aren't you?"

"At least you'll come back to life," I said on a chuckle, as if joking about our recent life-and-death issues was completely normal. Then again, I'd never been normal. And hadn't Griffin admitted to feeling the exact same way just before he drove off the cliff near Raven's Lagoon?

Neither one of us was normal, and that was *before* we discovered we were probably immortal.

Roughly, he yanked down the neckline of my camisole and hooked it under a breast. I was expecting—nay, fucking *needing*—his tongue and teeth on it, like *stat*, when he pressed up onto a hand just to . . . stare, apparently.

"I need the lights on," he grumbled. "I need to see you." He actually tried to loosen the grip of my legs to get up.

"Unh-unh," I murmured. "There'll be plenty of time for that later."

"You have no idea how long I've wanted to see you like this." He pushed up onto his other hand as well. "Wait, fuck, is that a shitty thing to admit to? We were supposed to be just friends all this time, and I went and—"

"I went and fell for you too, you know," I interjected. "And the others are apparently okay with it."

"Yeah, they actually are."

"So then, what are we waiting for?" Though it was dark, he was still staring at my boob. "Do you have nighttime vision you never told me about or something?"

He snorted and laughed a deep rumble, but he didn't look away from the plump outline of my full breast. "No, I wish—fuck do I ever wish. I've just been picturing your titties in my head for so long, and now that they're right here in front of my face, I need to fucking see them. I need to see if I imagined them just right. I know they're totally perfect."

"They totally are." I wove my hands around his head, threading through his hair, preparing to bring it down to my straining nipple with a snarky comment about him doing his studying later, when—

Knuckles rapped at the door—a quick *knock-knock*—and the door cracked open.

Griffin scrambled off me so fast it was like our parents had caught us in the act. He was already lying beside me, both our chests heaving, when I quickly jerked my cami back into place and pulled the covers over both of us.

"Hey, Joss?" Layla's tentative voice called through the gap in the door.

"Yeah?" I said, wanting to kick myself for sounding so breathy.

But Layla only pushed the door open all the way. "Oh good. I was worried you'd be asleep already. Is Griff with you?"

"Yep." Anything more than monosyllables would give me away.

She turned to speak to Brady or Hunt, whoever was waiting behind her on the other side of the door. "They're both in here."

Then she, Brady, *and* Hunt waltzed into my room. Layla jumped on the other side of the king bed and hollered, "Cuddle puddle!"

While Brady and Hunt were dragging twin mattresses in behind them, Layla bent down to whisper in my ear, "It's been a lot lately. They don't want to admit it, but the guys need a sleepover."

I might *love* love Griffin, and I might be lying there wet for his hard-on still within easy reach, but I loved Layla, Brady, and Hunt too.

I could all too easily understand their need for the bonding sleepovers we hadn't shared in too long.

When life was shit, we drew even closer together. Crew forever.

So I did the only thing I could do when Hunt, ever observant, hesitated at the sight of Griffin already beside me in the bed. I echoed Layla's call and shouted, "Cuddle puddle!"

11

It Reeks of Stardom

I stirred from a sleep so deep I couldn't immediately tell what was happening. The room was dim, and I was cozy. Here—I remembered—I was safe.

Warmth pressed along my back. Probably Bobo. He knew he was supposed to remain at the foot of the bed, but my sweet boy liked snuggles. As much as I focused on consistency in his training, this was one area where I was lenient. I liked snuggling my pittie too much.

A muffled slapping sounded somewhere beyond the room, and some*one* groaned beside me. It definitely wasn't my dog.

My eyelids fluttered open and I found myself staring at Layla's face. Her head rested on the pillow beside mine, her eyes squinched tightly closed as if she too were struggling against waking.

The previous night came flooding back. We were in our new house, Magnum's mansion. Griffin in the bed with me. Oh God . . . *our hands and mouths all over each other, his body against mine, yearning for his* . . . Then, our friends.

Although I'd been nearly asleep when Griffin entered, after Brady and Hunt stretched out on the mattresses on the floor we got to talking. At first, it had been about the serious stuff, the fears and admissions that were easier to eke out in the relative anonymity of darkness. We'd all been secretly freaked out about pretty much everything that had gone down since the Fischer House party. But then we'd fallen into old, comforting patterns, and we'd stayed up reminiscing and laughing until the middle of the night, when our frayed nerves and exhaustion had finally claimed us all.

"Shit, someone's in the house," Brady mumbled from beside the bed.

"Fuck," Hunt responded, suddenly sharp, and Griffin—not Bobo—who'd fallen asleep on the other side of me, tugged my body closer, pushing up onto his elbow and partially leaning over me, as if preparing to shield my body with his.

"Hello! It's me, Fanny," Magnum's assistant called out.

Either Brady or Hunt groaned. Layla's eyes squinted open as she groggily wiped at a bit of drool in the corner of her mouth. And Griffin relaxed some, settling back down onto his side. I inched my hips back into the perfect spoon of his body—

To feel the stiff length of his dick now pressed against my ass. I had to swallow a moan as my body instantly wanted to respond to him. With Layla staring at me now, I couldn't let on. For one, she'd never let Griff or me live it down—the morning she'd woken up in bed with Griff's stiffy. I could practically hear her theatrics already.

Soft footfalls grew nearer, and then, with no more warning than Layla had given us the night before, Fanny rapped twice on the door before swinging it open.

"Whoa, lady," Brady scolded while Hunt shot to his feet atop the mattress. He wobbled for a second before crouching into a fighting stance, hands up.

Griffin only ran his strong hand along the length of my bare thigh, as if wanting to extend this closeness as much as possible before it came to its jarring end.

With Layla propped up onto an elbow to glare at Fanny, I wiggled my ass against his hardness.

His breath hitched. The change was quiet, but I delighted in the effect I had on him. God, I hadn't planned on letting myself be all over him quite so fast. I hadn't had much chance to imagine what our relationship would look like moving forward, but surely I would have guessed it would be gradual. Not friends to lovers in like three-point-six seconds.

His roving hand splayed across my bare stomach, the camisole's hem twisted up by my boobs. His fingertips trailed a line of fire up my torso until a single one brushed against the bottom swell of my breast, light as a feather but hot enough to brand me.

"What are you doing in here?" Layla accused Fanny when it probably should have been me since it was my room.

"I told you I'd be here at 2:00 p.m.," she replied without a hint of apology as she openly studied us.

"It's not two already," Layla mumbled. "Is it?" She glanced around us, but without our phones or a clock in here, we had no idea.

"It is, young lady." Fanny pressed her lips together. "You've already slept half the day away."

Groaning at Fanny's judgmental tone, I craned my neck to glare at her. "Well, excuse the hell out of us for needing the extra rest to recover after all we've been through. Maybe if you or your precious Magnum were the ones who kept having to die and come back to life again you'd care to be more understanding."

I registered what I said. My life was officially bonkers.

I expected her to react like either of my faux parents would when confronted by my "smart mouth," and instantly get on my case all the more. But Fanny's scowl softened into what almost passed as a smile, though not quite. "Yes, I suppose that much is true. You certainly have been through a lot over the last several months."

Hunt lowered his hands and looked around the room, finally settling on the lounge chair in the corner. He moved Griffin's discarded shirt onto the armrest before sinking into the seat.

"Had we known you'd all sleep in the same room," Fanny said, "Magnum might've saved himself some trouble in building you such a spacious home."

Brady kept his blanket over his legs but sat up, his back resting against the side of my bed. "We don't usually sleep together."

From where I lay I couldn't make out his face, but I could easily picture his expression all the same. Brows low, eyes slightly narrowed, lips pursed in a silent *fuck you*.

"Like we said," I added in a cold tone, "we've been through some *shit*."

"Yes, well, now it's time to get your *shit* together, isn't it?"

She sidestepped a mattress to access the panel embedded in the bedside table. With a tap of her fingers, the blinds began to rise.

Griffin, Layla, Brady, and I all groaned at the sudden brightness. Hunt merely stared at Fanny with a too-placid expression that reminded me of a cat biding its time for the eventual *fuck you* that would come.

If Fanny thought behaving like a mother would endear her to us, she couldn't have been more wrong.

She strode back to the door, calling over her shoulder: "Magnum is expecting us, and he shouldn't be made to wait. You have fifteen minutes before we leave. Don't waste precious time cleaning up after yourselves. Staff will be coming in every day when the house is empty. Be dressed and ready or I'm taking you however you are."

"What about breakfast?" Brady asked.

"The breakfast hour passed long ago, young man. If you wanted it, you should have been up in time for it. Magnum didn't invite you here to—"

"*Invite?*" The five of us growled in unison, with differing levels of incredulity.

Undeterred, she plowed on: "You aren't here to behave as spoiled rock stars. You're here to . . . well, I'm sure Magnum will have more to say on that when we meet him."

Halfway out the door, she turned back around toward us to clap her hands, like a fucking schoolmarm. I winced at the harsh volume.

"Come now! No time to dilly-dally. I for one am hoping every one of you will squeeze in a shower before we head out. It reeks of . . ." Her nose scrunched up. ". . . *stardom* in here."

Then she stalked off.

"What the fuck does she mean by *that*?" Layla muttered.

"Who the hell knows?" Brady grumbled. "Maybe she used to be a groupie or a roadie before she decided a life trailing after a rich asshole was more her style. Got up and personal with some stank 'stars.'"

"I don't trust her," Hunt said.

Griffin's hand trailed back down my bare stomach to settle across the dip of my waist. "Neither do I. But I don't think she's going to try to kill us, at least."

"Maybe not," Hunt said. "But Magnum has a whole team on standby she could delegate that fun task to."

Layla sighed loudly, snaking a leg out from under the covers and sliding toward the edge of the bed. "Well, I guess we'd better get moving. Even though a part of me doesn't want to just 'cause she told us to, I'm gonna hit the shower. After sleeping with these two lovebirds, I need a cold one."

She glanced at Griff and me, and I plastered a look of total innocence on my face, the one that had many times convinced my teachers.

Her eyes widened and she chuffed an incredulous snort. "If you're pulling out the 'I'm a Goody Two-shoes' look, it's way worse than I was guessing." Her eyes bulged. "Oh. Em. Gee. Are the two of you naked under there?! I didn't even think to look last night before I climbed in with you! Was I part of a threesome without even knowing it? 'Cause if so, I'll be super pissed. I've never had one before and I def need to be present for that bucket lister."

"No, we're not naked," I snapped. "Obviously we're not. Jeez. I can't believe you'd think that of us, that we'd do that to our best friends. Come on." I pulled at the strap to my camisole with a sharp *duh* tug. "Why would you even think that of us? Like we'd share a bed with you while getting it on . . ."

But it was like Layla wasn't hearing me—or she knew us too well.

She gripped the covers and tried to tug them down to expose us. While we *were* both dressed, it wasn't by much, and Griffin was still hard.

I clutched the covers like my life depended on it. Surprisingly, Griffin didn't, like now that we were out to our friends he had nothing to hide.

Well, no one was about to see his stiffy before I laid eyes on it first.

Layla rolled her eyes. "Seriously, guys? You horny fuckers . . ."

"Hey. It's not like that," Griffin protested but as usual, she barreled right on.

"Now I need to rub one out in the shower before I'm ready to face the day. Horniness!" She stabbed the air with a finger in some kind of imagined victory. "That's what Fanny was scenting like a freaking hound dog. I can smell it now, and it's making me horny too. Thanks a lot, you two."

"Lay," Brady breathed on a shocked gasp, though he couldn't actually be stunned. She was his twin after all, and Layla was just . . . like this. "What the fuck? Can you give it a rest with all your word vomit already?"

She grinned and stood, her feet next to the head of his mattress. "Nope. No fucking way am I gonna change a single little thing about myself to suit anyone else."

Brady leaned forward and whispered, "Remember, they're probably listening to everything we say right now."

"I really hope they are." She raised her voice. "Because they're a bunch of limp-dick cocksuckers, gunning down a bunch of highschoolers like they did."

She stopped by the door, mischief lighting up her face as she glanced at Brady, and I already knew a dig was coming.

So did he. He stood.

"At least you're already used to jerking off with your parents listening. No big change there. I think you might even like it."

She ducked out the door, and Brady charged after her.

"I'm gonna kill you, Lay!"

I would have laughed at their antics—a slice of normalcy, no matter how over the top—but his statement hit a little too close to my already sensitive nerves.

Hunt pushed his mattress against one wall and stalked out without a word, closing the door behind him.

Then it was just Griffin and me.

Suddenly, every place where his skin touched mine tingled like an electric shock was racing through it. His chest, his thighs, his arms, his hands, they pressed against me. Only the thin fabric of our underwear separated our extra-fun, saucy bits. The room, the bed, they simultaneously became too big and too small. He was everywhere, his body wrapped around mine, and yet not touching me enough.

He kissed my bare shoulder, drawing out the lingering press of his lips before flopping back onto the bed with an exasperated sigh. "Well . . ." he announced.

When nothing more arrived, I turned onto my other side to face him. "Well, what?"

He gazed up at the ceiling. "Given that we slept with Layla, and it's *Layla* we're talking about, that wasn't *too* bad."

"It wasn't great."

He dropped his gaze down to me, a smile stretching those plump lips of his, the ones I wanted to spend the rest of the day kissing. Now that I knew what they felt like pressed against mine, exploring my mouth, I wanted so much more of them.

"With Lay, it could've been loads worse though," he said.

"That's very true," I answered, staring at his lips and not bothering to hide the fact.

He turned back onto his side but this time didn't touch me, as if the temptation to keep going would be too great if he did. "I'm about to die I want so much more of you."

I grimaced. "I think we're gonna have to re-examine a lot of our usual expressions after everything that's happened."

"Nah. Lay might say some *shit*, and boy does she ever, but she was right about that. We don't have to change who we are. We shouldn't."

"It's gonna change us. All of this, everything, it will. But go on. With what you were saying."

He chuckled and stared into my eyes, holding there. "If we'd been able to keep going last night . . . fuck, I have no doubt it would've been beyond amazing and I would've loved every single fucking moment of it. But since last night went down the way it did, I think I'm glad now."

I arched my brow. "You're glad."

"Yeah. 'Cause I don't want to rush a thing with you. I've waited this long to have you. I literally had to die and watch you die to get where I believed it'd be okay to take that risk with the friendship between us and with the others. Now that we're here, now that we both know where we're at, I want to savor every tiny little bit of it. Of you."

I chuffed and smiled, probably a bit dreamily. "Nice idea and all, Griff. But not sure how that's gonna end up working out with the two of us. I'm not particularly patient once I get going, you know that."

He blinked, then grinned. "Yeah, I do. So we'll see how it goes. I'm already having to force myself not to touch you 'cause I don't know if I could get myself to stop even with fucking Fanny counting down out there."

So I was right.

Excited flutters drifted through my chest.

He inched only his head forward and pressed the gentlest of kisses against my lips. Not chaste. No, not a chance. But one that felt like a tender promise. Of what, I wasn't sure, but I liked it, whatever it meant.

Against my lips, he murmured, "You're my dream girl, Joss. I'm never letting you go."

And then, long before I was ready for him to leave, he climbed out of the bed and grabbed his shirt. I watched him as he tugged it on and arranged it to conceal the partial tent he was still pitching.

"Dream girl," he emphasized, beaming the happiest grin I'd seen from him in years, then he slipped out the door.

Fanny chose that exact moment to holler, "Five minutes!"

But even her forceful countdown couldn't snuff out the elation bubbling up my stomach and through my chest. It was like I was filled to the brim with fizzy champagne.

Finally with a moment of privacy to myself, I grinned my happiest too. I pressed a pillow over my face, kicked my legs against the mattress, and squealed as if I were still starry-eyed and naïve enough to believe love was a force so great it could overcome absolutely anything and everything.

I squealed once more, then tossed aside the pillow to scoot out of bed. No way was I letting Fanny drag me anywhere wearing what little I was.

Love was a powerful force, of course it was. Love was *everything*. My love, not just for Griffin, but for all my friends, was sufficient to move the proverbial mountain. No doubt about that, none at all.

But love also only made the losses that much more painful. Unbearable. Devastating.

Hell if that motivation didn't give me every reason I needed to fight and keep on fighting—no matter what or whom we faced.

Death might be staring us all in the face right now, but we'd never had more reason to live.

12

Unarmed but Extremely Dangerous

"You're late," Fanny snapped at us the moment we stalked into the lobby of the admin building, where she'd obviously been pacing while waiting for us.

Gone was the "cool, fun aunt" she'd claimed to be just the day before. Pursing her lips, she scanned us with unabashed judgment. Apparently we were found wanting, though we'd had no choice but to wear the clothes they'd picked out for us. Most of them I might have chosen myself. It was eerie, realizing how closely they must have observed us to know even the insignificant details, like what shade of eyeliner and what brand of tampons I preferred. Had they rifled through our personal stuff? Probably. It's not like there were lines they weren't willing to cross. They'd made that much crystal freaking clear.

"We can't actually be late," Brady objected. "We're only, like, a couple minutes behind you."

Fanny narrowed her eyes at him before spinning on the sole of her Birks and powerwalking away, calling over her shoulder, "We talk while we walk. Follow me."

"Ordering us around like we're toddlers," Layla grumbled under her breath, but when the rest of us trailed after Fanny, so did she.

We passed several large yet elegantly understated desks, all unmanned, before Fanny jabbed the button to call the elevator.

"I only agreed to let you take your own car instead of riding in the buggy with me," she said, "because I thought you'd be coming straight here."

As one unit, we bristled. But since this was at least a little bit about Bonnie, Brady spoke first.

"First off, we don't need your permission or anyone else's to drive *our* cars. And second, we literally only drove to the end of the road and then came straight here. So back off already, will ya?"

The elevator panel indicated the elevator was nearly at our floor.

"I know exactly what you did," Fanny said as she inched toward the still closed doors, as if seconds really did matter. "You drove to the gate to see if you'd be able to drive on out of here."

It was exactly what we'd done. We'd all piled into Bonnie, the only one of our cars that was currently operational, and driven to the exit to see what kind of security measures awaited us there.

Though much of the campus was currently empty, the gatehouse hadn't been. And the guard inside had seemed aware we were heading his way. He'd been standing with a phone to his ear, most likely reporting our every move. The boom gate had remained down, but then we hadn't pulled up beside him to ask him to raise it. We had, however, studied him as closely as he had us. He was no regular rent-a-cop guard. He wore tactical gear and was armed to the teeth.

The elevator doors whooshed open and Fanny all but jumped in, waving to hurry us along even though not a single one of us was particularly slow. We were all fully recovered from our injuries, even me. The bullet holes across my chest had shrunk. The scars now suggested I'd been shot with nothing more significant than a BB gun.

"Well," Layla told Fanny as the doors shut, "can you blame us? We were gunned down at *school*, taken out of there in secret. We come to in private hospital rooms and then we're transported to a secret campus. You don't think we've got questions? That we're entitled to have them? *Fuck*, to get some answers?"

Fanny hiked the omnipresent tablet she always carried farther up under her arm. She should wear some sort of carrier strapped to her chest if it was so freaking vital to her existence.

"Magnum will answer all your questions. He already told you he would."

I snorted. "And we're supposed to trust his word? Him, the man who ordered us all *killed*? Fanny, you've got some major Magnum worship going on, we can all see that, but you can't be this dense."

She bristled and whirled on me as the doors were about to open behind her. "You're a bunch of children who don't understand the gift you've been given. You're too inexperienced to understand the long-reaching impact of your immortality. With Magnum's guidance, you'll change the world. *The world!*"

She stalked out, emerging into an unfamiliar, ample hallway. My anger simmered beneath my skin such that I almost didn't follow her out. When my friends similarly hesitated, I knew she'd rubbed them the wrong way too.

But Fanny only kept talking as if we were on her heels—like good little children.

"With your immortality, Magnum will bring about a world without illness, without grief, without suffering."

Again, I snorted, and Griffin clasped my hand and commented under his breath, "She's really been chugging the Kool-Aid, hasn't she?"

"Right," Layla said. "Like Magnum's only out to do this—whatever exactly *this* is—for others." She laughed, and at the sound, Fanny spun toward us with a flare of her maxi skirt.

"Hey," Layla said, hands up for a second. "We're just saying. Magnum's sold you a tainted bag of goods, lady, and you're buying it all up."

"Yeah, you're in like a cult," Brady chimed in.

"You will treat Magnum with respect," Fanny seethed, actually seethed, her teeth showing.

"We'll do so if he ever earns it," Hunt said, the statement cutting and as unapologetic as Fanny was being.

"He's already earned it—"

Griffin led us toward her, lowering his head to her height to hold her stare. "Would you like us to kill you, see if you come back, and then ask you if you respect us? 'Cause we'll do it." He smiled, and I even found that cold, menacing grin of his sexy as fuck.

Brady shored up behind Griffin. "Fuck yeah we will. Unlike what you seem to think of us, we aren't weak little children for any of you to toy around with."

In fact, since the infamous Fischer House party, we'd all turned eighteen, but hadn't been in the mood to celebrate much. Our birthdays were grouped close together, a fact I'd never before found suspicious since I'd never once guessed we were created as an elaborate lab experiment—go figure.

Fanny tilted up her chin to level a stare that swung between Griffin and Brady, as if the two of them were the only potential threats. Obviously, their research hadn't taught them everything about us, then. "Don't you dare threaten me."

"We're not," Griffin said with another smile that didn't light up his eyes. "Since you seem unable to conceive of what it's like to be us, I was painting a picture for you."

She scowled so intensely that marionette lines bracketed her chin. Without another word, she spun again, with another flare of her flowered skirt, and stomped down the hallway—like a petulant child, I couldn't help but realize with a chuff.

Layla shook her head as she walked after her. "This shit's nuts. Totally bonkers."

I was silently agreeing with her while following. Griffin's hand still linked with mine, we ambled down another long hallway. Offices lined it on both sides, all empty; the lighting in the building was apparently being kept dim until it had greater occupancy.

When we took the next left, Griffin and I nearly bumped into Layla, who stood stock still, staring at the spacious room straight ahead at the end of the hall. The walls were entirely glass, putting the occupants on full display.

Magnum was there, at the head—of course—of a long, oval, wooden table that was so highly polished it reflected the recessed lights overhead. Several other men and women sat at his end of the conference table, unknown faces except for Tracy, whom my brain still registered as "Mitzi Conway."

And at the foot of the table, occupying every seat but the empty one at the end, were our lying, thieving, spying, manipulative, deceitful faux parents. Every single fucking one of them.

Griffin's fingers squeezed and released mine, squeezed and released—I didn't think he realized he was doing it. My jaw clenched so hard that I noticed, and when Brady and Hunt lined up behind me, I swore I could feel the tension radiating off their bodies. It felt so hot that it had to be more than their body heat.

I bent my head to either side, cracking my neck, wrestling with the urge to charge at these people who'd made us believe they were our families—though I wasn't certain what I'd do once I reached them.

My mind and my heart still registered them immediately as "trustworthy." How incredibly fucking wrong both were. I needed some major deprogramming, stat.

Fanny was taking a seat near Magnum when Brady's breathing, close to my ear, accelerated and deepened until it reminded me of a bull about to attack.

"I see you've noticed: some old members of my team have joined us today," Magnum called out through the open door. He leaned back in his leather chair, rested his elbows on the armrests, and steepled his fingers. "Please, come in, join us."

When not one of us took so much as a baby step toward the bunch of scheming, conniving, murdering assholes, he added, "You'll be completely safe, I give you my word."

"Does that assurance only cover this meeting?" Griffin asked, sounding as bitter as I felt. "Or are you promising we'll actually make it through the entire day without one of your lackeys shooting us?"

Several of the men and women who sat between Magnum and our faux parents winced. Magnum, Fanny, Tracy, and our liar *parents* did not. I guessed they either didn't regret their methods, or they'd long ago come to terms with them.

Magnum smiled charismatically, his face politician-handsome, and I itched with the urge to rip his mouth from his face. "Let's just go ahead and say the entire day, how about that?"

"Dandy, just fucking dandy," Layla said with as much sarcasm as I'd maybe ever heard her use. She prowled into the room, light-footed in her Vans, and I thought maybe I'd never felt danger wafting off her quite so intensely either.

The rest of us didn't hesitate to follow. Whatever it was, we'd never let her face it alone.

With unnecessary force, she yanked out one of the five empty chairs waiting for us, and wheeled it over to the interior wall of glass, where she parked her ass in it. Her message was clear: she wanted to be as far away from our scheming *parents* as possible. The four of us did the same, lining up our chairs next to hers. Then we waited.

"Very well," Magnum said, but Monica-who-wasn't-really-Monica stood and brought a hand to her chest.

She wagged her head in artful regret, real tears welling in her eyes. "We're so glad to see you all doing well. We were so terribly worried . . ."

I blinked at her theatrics, my jaw only clenching harder. Griffin spun his chair slightly in my direction, though I wasn't sure he even realized he constantly did these things to show me silent support.

"Sit down, Lynne," Magnum ordered, and I felt my eyes widen despite my resolve not to reveal precisely how upsetting this entire situation was.

Griffin, Brady, Layla, and Hunt glanced at me. I pretended not to notice while I schooled my features into impassivity. Right then, in front of all these people—all strangers in the end—I didn't want anyone to notice how much this revelation was rocking my world like a magnitude 8.0 earthquake. I was feeling *shook* to my foundations.

"You're not here for that and you know it," Magnum continued, stern in a way that suggested disobedience was a grave offense. "You'll sit back down and remain quiet unless called on, or you'll leave."

"But Magnum," *Lynne* protested. "These are our *children*. We worried they might actually be dead—"

"They are *not* your children."

"We raised them! They're as much our children as if—"

Magnum leaned forward and *Lynne*—fucking *Lynne*—trailed off. "What's it gonna be, Lynne? Will you and your traitorous cohort be part of this meeting to discuss their futures or not? Nothing says you have to be a part of their futures at all."

The liar, who'd droned on over the years about the importance of integrity and honesty, stared back at the man while her throat bobbed. But finally she sat, immediately pointing her chair so she could direct that stare at us.

Great, just freaking fabulous. I pinned my attention on Magnum just to avoid hers.

"As you can see," he told us, "the men and women who pretended to be your parents after stealing my research have agreed to join us again, under strict conditions of course."

I waited for him to share what those conditions were. He didn't.

"Those present whom you have not yet met will be your instructors."

"Should we choose to stay," Hunt inserted.

Magnum leaned back in his chair to smile magnanimously. "Of course. I was hoping you'd already decided to make your new home here."

"It's not too late," my faux dad said, his eyes blazing intently as he took in the five of us. "You can still come home."

Magnum frowned, but before he could intervene again, I said, "Where you, whatever your real name is, and *Lynne* live isn't my home. Apparently, it never was. Pretty sure my friends feel the same about their 'homes.' So drop it and let us focus on a real path forward. 'Cause it ain't with any of you."

"That's right," Layla added.

Brady said, "For sure."

Griffin and Hunt looked ready to murder a faux parent or two and didn't need to say a word.

Magnum narrowed his eyes at his former researchers. "Keep your mouths shut or you'll be removed. You know I mean it."

Apparently, they did. They sat back in their seats like obedient boys and girls.

What a total mindfuck.

Magnum turned his full attention toward us, anyone in the way ducking to one side or adjusting their chairs to give him a better view.

"You've indicated that you'd like to know exactly what's expected of you before you agree to remain here on campus and participate in what I have lined up for you. So here's what you need to know.

"There will be three main components to your time here, beyond your rest and relaxation time of course, during which you can do almost whatever you want. You're adults, and I never intended to 'parent' you.

"Academics will pick up where you left off at Ridgemore High or, if you'd rather, you can undertake personally tailored academic study programs that will actually challenge you and teach you topics you find interesting and rewarding. Based on your testing, I doubt any one of you have been challenged at that school for a very long time."

None of us denied it.

"The men and women sitting here at the table with us are, collectively, superb minds. Between them, I'm certain they can teach you a variety of topics that will fascinate you. If you want to learn something and no one here is qualified to teach you, I'll recruit whomever you want. No one says *no* to me for long."

No one in the entire room attempted to deny that. Though we were the newest to the dastardly ways of billionaire mastermind Magnum Chase, the fact that he got his way was already abundantly evident.

"Each one of you can already test out of high school and receive the equivalent of a high school diploma, however much good that will do you. What I'm offering is advanced university-level studies."

I snuck a glance at Hunt, whose eyes glittered with his restrained excitement. Dude *loved* to learn, even more than the rest of us, and we were all closet nerds.

"That includes fine art and mechanics," Magnum added, eyeing Layla and Brady especially.

"Next is the physical aspect of your time here. As much as you work your minds, you'll be expected to work your bodies. I believe you all share a love for martial arts and the like?"

Reluctantly, I joined my friends in nodding, doing my best to subdue my enthusiasm at the idea of finally getting to progress our fighting skills to the next level.

"I've assembled three of the finest instructors and sensei of martial arts and 'ninja skills' in the world."

My cheek twitched at his use of the phrase "ninja skills." That was how my friends and I discussed our abilities and goals when we believed we were alone and speaking in privacy.

Unable to help myself, I glanced at *Lynne* and whoever-dad. Lynne's face was guilt free, but my faux dad's was laden with it. I could see the truth of it there: Magnum had access to every transcript of every "private" conversation my friends and I had ever shared near one of their hidden wiretaps.

Magnum looked to two men and one woman who sat in a row along the opposite side of the table from us. Though they looked remarkably different in appearance from one another, and they sat at complete ease, I suspected each of them could kill everyone in this room without breaking a sweat. They put off that vibe—unarmed but extremely dangerous. Their bodies were lethal weapons.

Instantly, I wanted to train with them. Griffin also sat up straighter. Magnum sure knew how to lure us in, the observant cocksucker. First the mansion and the cars, now the badass ninja teachers? I was practically swooning on the inside.

"Finally, there's the study of your immortality, both by yourselves and by us. I'll expect you to learn everything there is to discover about your power, including if there's more of it, and I'll expect my team and I to learn about it right along with you."

"Meaning?" Brady asked.

"Meaning, we'll test your limits and together we'll learn all there is to know about what you can and can't do."

"Does that mean you're planning on killing us to see how we come back?" Hunt asked, and a foreboding shiver raced up my spine.

Magnum didn't shy away from Hunt's accusing stare. "Yes."

I gulped.

"But you'll have every possible support," Magnum added. "Of all kinds. I'll have the best medical personnel on standby to aid you and make the process as seamless and painless as possible."

"The process of us dying and coming back to life, repeatedly," Layla deadpanned.

"Yes." The *devil we know* held our murderous stares without flinching. "But this isn't about causing you pain. In fact, I'd very much prefer it if you didn't experience pain."

"You can't be serious," faux Porter Rafferty exclaimed. "They're children!"

"They're eighteen years old, all of them," Magnum said with a calm I wasn't experiencing. "They never were your children to begin with, and now they are adults."

He snapped his fingers. I was looking around, trying to figure out at what or whom he was snapping, when Jaggar, Raynar, and two other soldiers outfitted in paramilitary gear jogged in.

Wordlessly, they lined up beside our faux parents, the lot of whom stood, some with shoulders slumped in defeat, others glaring at Magnum and the soldiers. Faux Alexis was looking longingly at Hunt, her eyes wide and pleading. The soldiers led them from the room without incident, as if everyone there knew how pointless it would be to resist.

Their easy acquiescence only made the fight inside me brew more insistently.

Magnum continued as if there'd been no interruption. "We'll test your immortality and I'll expect you to submit to regular physical checkups so we can track your progress."

"How long do you expect us to stay here?" Hunt asked.

"To start, the rest of what would have been your final school year at Ridgemore High. You'll live in luxury, with your every need and desire met."

"So long as we die on the regular," Layla said with a snort. "Right."

"Right. It's not ideal, I understand that. But the gift you all possess is extraordinary, beyond extraordinary. And so are each and every one of you. I intend to draw out and examine every bit of that uniqueness you each possess, to marvel at it, to bow at its feet."

Oh-kay then.

"And after the school year is up?" Griffin asked. "Come June?"

"You can leave. But I'll be doing my very best to convince you to stay. I'll make you an offer that will be very difficult to refuse."

That sounded like both a promise and a threat.

"And if we decide to leave now?" I asked, though he'd already told us the answer to this question. I just didn't like it—not one bit.

"I'm not prepared to let that happen."

"Which means you'll order your goons to shoot us again," Brady said.

"Most likely."

"Basically you're saying our options as you see them are death, or death, or more death," I said.

"Yes."

I dragged my attention across every other person sitting at that table. A few of them twitched with discomfort at hearing our situation distilled so succinctly, but not many. Whatever Magnum had done to buy their loyalty, he'd succeeded.

"In all the wide world we live in," Magnum said, his eyes becoming a tad dreamy, "there's not one other like the five of you."

"What about the other students you said would be coming?" Brady asked.

"None exactly like you, none as wholly remarkable. Most are young adults like yourselves with a variety of abilities that defy logic and the laws of science. Many of them are extremely resistant to death. Still very useful, but not the same. I have some of my best people out scouting, tracking rumors and legends, chasing down leads. So while there will be other students, for the foreseeable future you'll be my superstars. And if others with your particular skills arrive"—his eyes glittered with greed—"then it will only enhance our ability to comprehend your immortality. The more data we have, the faster we'll advance."

He leaned his elbows onto the table and watched us. "So? What do you say? Are you in?"

My friends and I exchanged long, loaded looks. On their faces I saw reflected my own panic at being trapped in the situation as effectively as if our prison were walled in with bars. I wasn't deluded into thinking police of any sort would help when Magnum probably could erase any problem with sufficient bribes and violence. But in my friends I also recognized the excitement that was building inside me.

If we stayed here, one way or another we'd get answers. Yes, the way we got them would majorly suck and would likely be extremely terrifying. I for sure wasn't ready to face down death as a regular occurrence.

But *I needed to know.*

I needed to understand myself and the four other people I loved most in this world.

I needed answers more than I needed safety, something we wouldn't have even if we told Magnum to fuck the hell off right now. He'd hunt us, as he was hunting these other kids with desirable science-bending abilities, until he had us back in his clutches again. He wasn't even denying it.

I needed to understand what I was fighting for, and how hard we actually needed to fight to survive this hellish situation.

I needed to know what we were capable of—and what we weren't.

"So you're decided?" Magnum asked.

After another look at the others, I saw that we were, and that Magnum was a fucking ace at reading us. *Fewer advantages for him, not more, please.*

"For now," Griffin said. "But we'll only agree to take it one day at a time."

From beside him, I nodded.

"These four people mean the world to me," he added. "They're everything. There's no one I won't murder to protect them, and I do mean *no one*. If I were you, I'd keep that in mind. We're agreeing, but only so long as it suits us. We don't like something you do or how you do it, we'll let you know, and you may not like how we choose to do the informing."

Given our hands were almost literally tied, it was a bit of hot air. But I knew Griff—and the rest of us—well enough to know it wasn't entirely posturing. Yes, we were up Shit Creek—big time—and we'd never had a paddle to begin with. That didn't mean we couldn't find a way to forge a better path for ourselves, one and all, no matter how much blood-spilling it required.

Magnum's smile was victorious, as if Griffin hadn't just threatened his life. "Excellent. Then we'll begin getting you set up tomorrow. Think of it as orientation. Actual classes will begin the day after that. And Joss, you'll find Bobo waiting for you at home."

At the thought of bringing my sweet pittie into this fray, my stomach dropped. But then again, there were no better options. He wouldn't be better off without me; our bond was too strong.

Before Magnum could tie this meeting up in a neat bow or dismiss us as if we were his underlings, I stood. My friends did too, and as one unit we stalked from the room.

I wasn't able to pull in a full breath till we were all squarely inside Bonnie with the doors locked—as if that would do a damn thing to keep out the monster in a suit with enough money to act like a god.

13

Who's to Say What Is and Isn't Real Anymore?

Knowing Bobo was waiting for me, Brady drove us straight home. Of course, that decision was made all the easier by the fact that we couldn't leave the campus anyway, and the rest of it was a ghost town.

For now, our surroundings were new and exciting. But how long could that last? How long till the bars of our prison started to squeeze?

Bobo must have recognized the hum of Bonnie's engine; before Brady pulled up to the garage I heard his whine-bark through the open windows.

"Where is he?" I asked, panic riding my question at the thought of Magnum's people having their hands on my dog. I wore my hair loose down my back today, and as I flung my head in every direction searching for him through the rear windows, the long sheets of chestnut-tipped violet slid along my back. "Where? I don't see him."

My friends were searching for him too.

"If that asshole's done a single thing to hurt him . . ." I swore, still looking.

"Then we'll help you string him up by the balls," Hunt said, concern pinching his usually stoic features. He loved Bobo almost as much as I did.

"I'll pull out his toenails," Layla offered, before announcing, "There!" Her relief was palpable as she pointed. "I think I see the end of a crate behind the koi pond. Maybe they left him there so he could entertain himself watching the fish till we got back."

"Only if Magnum thought it'd win him brownie points," I said. "That man sees too much."

"Way too much," Griffin muttered from beside me. I sat in the middle between him and Layla. "It's majorly unnerving."

The moment Brady shifted into neutral and yanked on the emergency brake, I was pushing Griffin and Layla to hurry both along. Bobo's whining and barking had grown louder.

I tumbled out of the car behind Griff, then raced for the staircase and the koi pond beneath it. Sure enough, there was a large kennel—with my sweet pittie inside it.

His whining intensified as his tail wagged so hard it thumped repeatedly against the wire of his cage. His cone-of-shame and cast were gone.

"There you are," I cooed as I crouched in front of him. "Such a sweet boy, yes you are."

The latch was stuck, but after some wiggling—and more desperate whining—Bobo was released. He raced from the crate and lunged at me, knocking me onto my butt. His front paws landed on my chest; I tumbled onto my back, laughing, all too ready to excuse him all the *no-no*'s I'd trained out of him. He showered me with kisses, leaving a slobbering mess along my face and neck.

"Yes, yes, I've missed you too. I've missed you so much."

The entire back half of his body wiggled, seeming out of sync with the non-stop wagging of his tail. I tried to hug him to me but he wouldn't remain still. So I surrendered to accepting his loving—and the sure knowledge that I'd have to scrub off all the slobber once he was finished.

"My poor baby, you must've been really scared," I mumbled into his neck as he continued his ministrations. "I've never seen you so excited to see me. I'm so happy to see you're okay. I was worried about you too."

Bobo dragged his tongue along my cheek; I hurried to clamp my mouth shut. Once he was snuffling along my chest, I whispered, "I love you too."

Then, as if his stare were drawing mine, I looked up and straight into Griffin's eyes. The hazel was bright, the colors seeming to intensify as I tried to decide which of all the colors was more predominant in them: the green, gold, or brown.

Hands in the pockets of his jeans, he was looking at me like he wanted his turn to roll around on the floor with me after Bobo.

I smiled up at him and he blinked, as if suddenly coming to after being lost in deep thoughts.

Bobo somewhat stiffly bent his front legs and appeared ready to settle in on top of my chest. I laughed, my breath constrained already by the weight of him. After running my hands along the length of his back a few times, I patted it.

"Come on, boy. You're gonna have to get up. You weigh sixty pounds!"

Bobo only rested his snout against my neck.

"This probably isn't good for your leg."

Bobo rubbed his nose along my neck as if to insist, *I'm fine.*

Hunt lowered himself to the polished concrete beside us, crossed his legs, and made kissing noises. At the familiar sound, Bobo's head jerked up. When he saw who waited for him with open arms, he scrabbled off my chest, scratching the shit out of me, and covered the few feet separating us in one leap, nearly knocking down Hunt, who *oomph*ed but remained upright while he started doling out pets and lovings.

"I guess he's feeling well enough, then," I said with a chuckle, drawing up to sit across from them while Bobo made his rounds. When every single one of us was covered in wet dog kisses and he'd peed in the yard, we led him inside. Bobo tore through the entire place at full speed, his claws scrabbling and sliding on the tiled and wooden floors, bumping into walls and corners in his eagerness to take it all in at once. He climbed the stairs to the loft two at a time. When he was finally finished, he lapped up the water that was already poured for him in a stand with two stainless-steel bowls etched with his name, then hopped onto the couch next to me, his head in my lap, preparing to nap.

The others dropped into seats around us.

"Damn," Layla said with a smile. "Guess bringing him here with us was the right move, huh?"

I rubbed behind his ears. Hunt, who sat on Bobo's other side, ran a hand along the length of his shiny black back.

"I hope so," I said. "But it makes me hella nervous. It's bad enough having all of you guys here with me at the mercy of some guy with more money than restraint. I just don't know."

I allowed my head to flop back onto the couch behind me. "What are we gonna do, guys?"

Griffin slid closer on my other side, and I leaned my head on his shoulder.

"We survive," he said. "That's what we do. We do what we have to, and we all get out of this alive."

"After we all die again and again, of course," Brady said from the other side of the large marble coffee table between the L couches, resting his socked feet up on it.

Griffin grimaced. "Yeah." Then, "I still can't figure out how we've found ourselves here. Just a few months ago our biggest concern was getting our parents off our backs with all their pressuring us to go to college. Now look at us."

"Yeah. Without parents," Hunt muttered with a frown.

"Good riddance," Layla said from between Hunt and Brady, but her eyes were sad. "I can't stop wondering what Celia's and Porter's names really are."

"Me neither," Brady said.

"Lynne," I said with a disbelieving shake of my head that dragged my hair across Griffin's shoulder. "Can you believe Monica's name is *Lynne*?" I shuddered. "Feels *so* freaking weird."

Layla kicked up her feet too. "And that she screwed Wade's dad?" She shook her head. Her hair was currently blond with frosted pink highlights. "And Xander Jones got her pregnant? Shit, I sure didn't see that coming. Not in a million years. I wonder if Reece, whatever, knew it was going on. Like, were he and Lynne"—her upper lip curled as if the unfamiliar name were sour—"were they ever even a couple? Or was all of that a show too?"

I exhaled loudly, though it did nothing to relieve all the worries jostling for position in my chest cavity. "She got an *abortion*. Wade and I coulda been stepsiblings. Can you imagine that?"

Hunt frowned. "You would've had to really be Lynne's for that to happen."

My shoulders slumped. "Right. I keep forgetting. It's like so crazy shocking that they aren't really our parents and they lied to us all that time; I can hardly stop thinking about it. But then, somehow I forget, and think of them as my parents like always."

"I'm having the same problem," Griffin said. "Every time I see Tracy, it's like a knife to the gut."

I nuzzled my face along his shoulder in support before realizing I was probably wiping Bobo slobber all over him. He just laced our fingers together, a gesture that was becoming common with him.

"And my dad, Orson. His name is *Tobias*?" He wagged his head along the back of the couch. "Tobias Andrew Dole." He said it like he was testing out the words, his lips puckering just as Layla's had. "I never even had a mom."

Layla huffed. "Well, in fact, turns out none of us fucking did."

"All that shit about my dad," Hunt added. "I really believed Alexis was forever mourning him." He shook his head, continuing to pet Bobo everywhere but the recently healed leg despite his anguish. "Just a sperm donor."

"And to think now we're gonna have to work with them," Brady said. "Not sure I can stomach it. I might punch one of them straight in their ugly mugs."

None of our faux parents were actually ugly. But their insides sure were looking questionable at the moment.

Layla crossed her feet at the ankles and her hands over her stomach. "Before we get to really crying in our Wheaties, gotta say I'm pumped as all get out about the other students. What kind of yummy paranormals is Magnum gonna give me?" She rubbed her hands together with a slightly manic grin. "Maybe some muscled-up wolf shifters who have to shed their clothes on the regular? Mmmmmm. I could handle standing around with some fine buck-naked shifters, that's for sure. Or maybe some sexy-as-sin vampies? I'm thinking I could get into that whole bloodsucking thing. I can see how it'd be a turn-on in the right circumstances."

Brady scoffed at her, giving her the stink-eye. "Seriously, Lay, you're too much sometimes! You know that just 'cause those kinds of creatures are in all the books you like to read doesn't mean they're actually real, right? You get the meaning of *fic-shun?*"

Layla only smiled more, her eyes taking on a dreamy cast. "We can die and come back to life, Brade. Who's to say what is and isn't real anymore? If we'd had this talk at the start of summer, you would've thought immortals didn't exist."

"So would you've."

"Yeah, probably. But now?" She shrugged. "So who's to say what'll show up at the school? All I know is there'd better be some hotties for me."

"Is that really all you can think about?" Brady accused. "We've got some major, major problems."

"Of course not. But tell me you aren't gonna get jelly when Joss and Griff start fucking their brains out and we're stuck here staring at the walls."

"No one says we're gonna be fucking our brains out," I said right away, but then quieted. We probably *would* end up having sex, and after the taste I'd already gotten of Griffin, I could see the temptation of going at it like rabbits.

"See?" Layla pointed at my face. "No matter what Joss says, she just all but admitted it."

"What? How?" I asked, though even I could feel my cheeks flushing. What was up with all the flustering lately? It so wasn't me. Keeping my face snugly tucked against his shoulder, I was careful not to glance up at Griffin.

Brady jerked to sit up straight, his expression thunderous, though I didn't think his ire was truly directed at Layla. "I'm just a *tad bit* more concerned about the fact that we just agreed to let a maniac kill us, pretty much as many times as he wants, while he puts us on display and prods us to see how we tick. I'm the only one of us who's died twice. Lemme tell you, this is one area where I was hoping the third time wouldn't be the charm. Even when we come back, the dying bit still feels like dying."

"Yeah, it does," I answered miserably. "What are we gonna do, guys? I know I keep asking, but we've gotta have some better options."

Seconds passed before Hunt said, "I've been racking my brain over it. I agree, there's gotta be a better option than basically submitting to being guinea pigs. But"—he breathed in then out while scratching behind Bobo's ears—"the only two options I currently see are us doing it 'willingly'"—he hooked his fingers in air quotes—"or the even less fun way."

Even more miserably, I muttered, "There's gotta be another way."

For long moments, the silence was interrupted only by Bobo's deep, relaxed breathing. He was close to falling asleep.

Finally, Hunt added, "We're severely outmatched in experience and resources here. And right now, I don't see a single way around it, not when we have no one to lean on but ourselves."

After that sank in for a bit, I grimaced. "Hey, at least we have each other though, right? We've gotten through all sorts of shit together before. We'll do it again."

Griffin squeezed my hand. "That's right. We've got this. We always do."

The others nodded, but surely they were thinking the same thing I was. Sure, we were stronger together. No doubt. And yes, we'd gotten through some shit over the years, all made easier since we had each other's backs.

But we'd never been up against a challenge this significant or this dire. We'd never faced down a force as strong and indefatigable as Magnum Chase. The stakes had never before been this high or this terrifying.

"It's us against the world, guys," Layla said. "No different from before. We've just got to kick ass a little harder, that's all."

"Yeah, of course," I replied on autopilot. I desperately wanted to believe it, but I didn't. From the dour looks on my friends' faces, not one of them did either.

Magnum coveted the power we had. And yet we'd never felt less powerful.

14

The Dealio Sucks,
Yada Yada Yada, But...

I was already lying awake in my bed when the alarm went off at 7:00 a.m. the next morning. Despite our initial excitement at the amenities our new house offered, we'd dispersed early the night before to be alone with our own thoughts. I'd soaked in the deep tub of my ensuite bathroom until the skin of my fingers shriveled. I'd examined the problem of our newfound immortality and the iron hold Magnum had on us from every angle I could think of with no new results. I'd finally succumbed to sleep, to get away from my burdened thoughts as much as to rest.

Now, Bobo lay beside me, his tongue lolling out of his mouth and his feet in the air. I woke him with some belly rubs before sliding out of bed and getting ready for the day.

What exactly did one wear for their first day at, uh... supernatural school? Would I be dying today? Did I need to think about blood getting on my clothes?

"God," I muttered aloud to myself, "I can't believe I'm considering that."

When I trudged out to the kitchen—Bobo prancing happily beside me—I discovered my friends already there, their expressions equally haunted.

Griffin silently pressed a kiss to my cheek before popping an everything bagel into the toaster, possibly for me since those were my favorite.

"Wow, look at us," Layla harrumphed as she clutched a mug of coffee in both hands. "We're depressing."

Brady poured himself a glass of what appeared to be fresh orange juice. "It's not us who's depressing. It's everything else." With a full glass, he gestured to the elegant extravagance that surrounded us.

Layla snorted. When he snapped his incredulous gaze to her, she asked, "What? It's kinda funny is all. This place is amazing."

"Yeah, but—"

She waved dismissively. "Yeah, yeah, yeah, we all know. Let's not beat a dead horse, 'kay? I think we need to turn this all around."

"How so?" Brady asked, pouring himself a second glass. Dude could chug.

Layla's brows rose and she seemed to force a peppy smile onto her face. "Let's flip this thing around. We're here anyway. We know the dealio. It sucks, yada yada yada, *but* . . ." She leaned her waist against the marble island. "There's also some sweet cool stuff here."

Brady opened his mouth. She cut him off with another dismissing wave.

"I get it, Brade. We all get it. But if we make the best of the things we can make the best of, then maybe we can at least have a little fun while we're busy having the not fun part."

Brady walked by with a bowl of cereal; she snagged a frosted shredded wheat biscuit and popped it in her mouth while he spun on her with murder on his face. She didn't even really like shredded wheat, but she did love bugging the ever-loving crap out of her brother.

With a grin, she chomped away happily and noisily while Brady fumed and stomped to the far end of the dining table from her to enjoy his cereal in relative safety.

Layla swallowed and smirked. "I say let's show them by having a freaking blast."

"Not sure how that's gonna 'show them,' genius," Brady grumped.

"Why yes I am, thanks for finally recognizing my brilliance, brother. Took you long enough. And we show them by at least taking away any control they have over our reactions."

Griffin slid a plate in front of me; it held a toasted everything bagel slathered with cream cheese. I smiled up at him. "Thanks, Griff. You're the sweetest."

"No, he's buttering you up to get some later," Layla said. "Or in this case, cream cheesing you up."

I ignored her. Sometimes it was the better option. Griffin doting on me every so often wasn't anything new.

Griffin popped another bagel in the toaster. "We can't control what happens to us. That much has been blatantly proven over the last several months. But we can control how we react, what we do in the face of the challenges." He glanced at Layla. "I can get on board with that."

"Me too," Hunt said. "Only 'cause moping around for the next who-knows-how-long might actually drive me crazy."

Bobo jumped back in through the doggie door in the kitchen and ran to his bowl stand; he looked at me expectantly when he found it empty. I started to push my chair back, but Hunt shook his head.

"I got it."

I smiled at him as he scooped some food into the bowl. "Thanks for being such a good Bobo daddy, Hunt. He loves it."

Hunt hmmphed and tossed the empty can into a sleek stainless-steel bin. "It's my pleasure. He's the only one who's always been real with us."

Around a mouthful of cereal, Brady said, "What's that say about us? That we can only trust our dog? Not even our *parents*."

Our dog. I smiled on Bobo's behalf and licked some cream cheese off my finger until I caught Griffin's stare following the path of my tongue. Heat flushed my insides and I forced myself not to look at him so Layla wouldn't get on our case all over again.

Layla *tsk*ed at Brady instead, jabbing her finger in his direction. "Nope. None of that. I already told you."

He snorted. "And what? You think I'm just gonna do what you say? Like that's ever gonna happen. I'm not your bitch, Lay."

"Then quit acting like one."

Brady's spoon clunked against his bowl right as the buggy pulled up into the driveway.

Brady stood, jabbing his finger right back at Layla. "You're lucky we got interrupted."

"Oh, really? 'Cause what, Brade? What? You've got me shivering in my boots."

"Girl," I said with a shake of my head, "you're wearing sneaks." I chuckled. "Maybe give him a break while we get this all sorted."

"The day I give Brady a break is the day I'm freaking dead."

Apparently hearing her own words, she frowned.

Brady swept past her, heading toward the front door on this level—a sliding barn-door style I freaking loved. Over his shoulder, he called, "Someday, you're gonna learn to think before you speak, or you're gonna end up swallowing your feet whole. And we both know your feet stink to high heaven."

Before the twins could fall into even more squabbling, Fanny called out, "Knock, knock," on the other side of the door. Brady turned toward us just to roll his eyes before sliding it open.

In yet another floral maxi skirt and blazer, Fanny stalked past him and into the kitchen-dining area we currently occupied.

"Good morning, everyone," she trilled, then paused as if expecting a response none of us were in the mood to give her. She'd revealed a tad too much Magnum-love for our liking. She scowled briefly. "I'm here to guide you through your orientation at the Institute for the Advancement of Immortals." She beamed as if we should be equally excited. Perhaps she even expected applause.

I stuffed another bite of bagel into my mouth and watched her.

She openly huffed, then reached into a satchel she carried across her body and pulled out five new iPhones, the latest model, still in their boxes. She lined them up on the table for us.

"Ummm, what's this?" Layla complained even as she reached for the lavender one and slid it toward her. "I thought we were getting back *our* phones."

Fanny smiled at us, but I wasn't buying her friendly act anymore. "It was decided that these would be better for you."

"You mean, better for Magnum," Brady corrected.

She blinked at us, holding her smile. "Yes. You'll be able to use these phones to communicate with each other, with me, and with personnel on campus. It's been decided it's better to make a clean break with any other friends or connections from Ridgemore at large."

"'It's been decided,'" I parroted bitterly.

"As promised, you'll want for nothing while you're here."

"Except for our freedom," Griffin said, moving to stand behind me. "That's not on the table, now is it?"

Fanny smoothed her fingers along her hair. "That depends on how you view 'freedom.'"

"Oh, you know, the usual way," Griffin bit out.

She merely plastered a tight smile across her face. "Is there anything else I can help you with today?"

As if she were customer freaking service.

"Yeah," Brady said. "I need an RF detector ASAP."

Fanny actually had the gall to look surprised. "Whatever for?"

"Uh, to scan for listening devices to make sure we have some privacy?"

"Oh." Fanny chuckled, waving a hand at us. "There's no need for that."

"Yes, there is," Brady insisted.

"You'll find listening devices in every room of the house, along with each of your cars, even the unfinished ones. You'll also be monitored in every room on campus."

I blinked at her.

"Well, that level of honesty's new," Layla muttered, topping off her coffee.

Fanny nodded. "You'll find Magnum to be very forthcoming if you give him the chance." Her eyes gleamed with hero worship. "The many microphones and cameras—"

"Cameras?" Brady interjected.

"Yes," she said, but one of her eyes twitched for a moment, making me think it had been a slip. "The surveillance is for your protection as well as ours."

"Doubt that," Layla said. "We've never been *less* safe than since we met Magnum."

"True that," I said.

Though it didn't need adjusting, Fanny smoothed her hands down her jacket. "This school is about to be filled with students of all sorts with a vast range of capabilities we have too little idea about. You all may be able to survive death, but these students, some of them are quite skilled at *causing* it. Trust me when I tell you, you want the security Magnum affords you."

A chill ran over my skin and I sat up ramrod straight. "Are these new students going to be used to . . . kill us?"

Her eye twitched in a tell, before she hastily replied, "Magnum has not yet informed me of his plans for you."

"Lie," Layla snapped, voicing my own thought. My girl was definitely in a pointing mood today, as she now aimed her rigid index finger at Fanny. "You just flat-out lied to us."

The assistant didn't deny it. She merely tilted up her chin in defiance.

Layla pressed, "What kind of supes are coming?"

Fanny just stared back blankly.

"Shifters? Vamps?"

"Layla," Brady started. But then Fanny's eye twitched again. Brady leaned back in his seat with a whistle. "No shit . . ."

"Dayum," Layla breathed. "That's gonna be awesome. What else? What other powers?"

"I've neither confirmed nor denied a single thing."

"Yeah, you have," Brady said. "Never play poker with your boss. He'll take you for everything you have and add it to his stuffed vaults."

Fanny huffed, then scowled for good measure. "I personally will not be referring to anyone in the student body of this fine institute as a supernatural or a 'supe,' and I highly recommend you don't either." Her frown deepened. "As far as I know, there is no such thing as a vampire or a shapeshifter. I've not once heard Magnum use those terms. The new students will be blessed with unique *gifts*, with special *abilities*. They are imbued with *skills* from beyond this world. They are not caricature-like paranormal *creatures*. For goodness' sake, this is reality, not fiction!"

"Just like I said," Brady interjected. "I told her this wasn't a book. We're not living in a damn movie."

"Precisely," Fanny said.

Undaunted, Layla's eyes still sparkled. "Hmmmm. We'll see."

Fanny snorted. "This is a waste of my time. We have to get going. You're to meet with the scientists first. They'll perform an examination to get a preliminary baseline reading on each of you. Then we're to meet with your instructors. First, those who'll teach you"—she paused to curl her lips in apparent disapproval—"ninja skills. Next, those who'll nurture your minds." The latter was apparently sufficiently dignified for her; the sneer vanished. "Finally, we'll get all the supplies you need and get you ready to begin your training first thing tomorrow. Now . . ." She cast a sneer at Layla in particular. "Is there anything else I can help you with before we set off for the day?"

"Yes," Hunt answered right away. "We want the titles to our cars, even the incomplete ones, so that when we choose to leave, we'll have no problem taking them with us."

"Of course," Fanny said a little too easily, too graciously.

The lack of titles was the least of our worries in leaving this place, but kudos to Hunt for thinking of it. The more we had lined up in our favor ahead of time, the better.

Without warning or apparent reason, the dishware atop the table began to rattle.

Bobo whined, rushing to my side, where he placed both his snout and paw on my lap. Griffin's hand landed on my shoulder.

"What's going on?" Brady asked, pushing to his feet.

"Nothing," Fanny said, too breezily. "Nothing at all, I'm sure."

Then Brady's spoon began to clink against his bowl. Layla scooped up her mug from where she'd set down her coffee, clutching it close.

The large panes of glass all over the house began to vibrate.

"You sure it's 'nothing'?" Griffin pushed.

Fanny chuckled, but the sound was breathy, unsure, and a bit alarmed.

I stood too, and Bobo pressed against my legs. Hunt, Layla, and Brady huddled around Griffin and me.

The light in the kitchen began to flicker.

"Okay," I snapped at Fanny. "What the hell's going on?"

"I'm sure everything's fine," she answered, her voice an octave higher than before. "But we may want to take cover, just in case."

Before any of us could so much as take a step to do so, a loud and unmistakable *KABOOM* shattered the campus's quiet.

The entire house shook. Dishes and silverware rattled loudly in the cupboards and drawers, and a fine dusting of plaster rained down from above.

The five of us crawled under the massive table, dragging Bobo under with us.

Fanny lay sprawled out on the floor, squawking, "What was that?"

"How the hell should we know?" Brady snapped back. "We were just asking you that!"

"Not you," Fanny snapped back at Brady. "Hush so I can hear."

I placed my hand on the floor. The shaking seemed to be slowing.

"And is he locked up now?" Fanny asked someone.

"Holy shit," Hunt breathed. "She's chipped."

I jerked a stare at him, then Fanny. She didn't have her tablet or phone out, nor had I noticed a comm on her, and I'd looked in her ears specifically.

"Who'd be insane enough to let someone do that to them?" Layla whispered.

As one, all of us, even Bobo, studied Fanny.

Her hands were pressed against the floor as she spoke to the air around her. "Well, then take him out! Get him locked up!"

The shaking settled even more.

"Yes, yes, I'm on my way," she told the invisible person on the other end of the chip in her head. "Yes, I'm with them. But they can make it to the labs on their own. I showed them the way already."

She paused as if listening. "No, they'll be fine." Then she stared angrily at us, as if we were at fault in whatever the hell chaos was going down now. "They'll go straight there. Uh-huh. On my way, but don't wait to get security there. Tranq him if you need to. Keep dosing him till it works."

As if nothing untoward had happened, Fanny rose from the floor, dusted off her flowered skirt, hitched her bag higher, then walked to the window-wall with a view down to the drive where the buggy was parked. I glanced toward it too. Don was standing beside the cart, looking anxiously up at her.

She glanced back toward us. "You're to go directly to the labs, nowhere else. They'll be waiting for you there. When you're finished, someone will be there to escort you to your next appointment."

She powerwalked to the door, and with it already opened, she added, "And hurry. I don't have time today to deal with your bullshit." She stepped out and slid the door shut behind her.

On the other side of the door, she muttered, "I don't have time to deal with *his* bullshit either." She surely wasn't referring to her precious Magnum. "No, I'm not talking to you, Fred. Give me an injury and destruction update."

She walked down the small hill to the buggy, hopped in, and Don took them down the drive.

The five of us looked at each other, and without a single word we dropped everything and raced toward the garage level, Bobo on our heels. Ordinarily, I'd leave him at home. But not when some majorly sus shit was going down like this.

We piled into Bonnie in record time and Brady had us peeling down the driveway after the buggy while it was still in sight.

They didn't want to tell us anything? Fine. That was on them.

But we weren't going to live with anybody's lies any longer. As best we could, we were going to play Magnum's game by our own rules.

15

Appearances Were Worth a Steaming, Stinking Pile of Shit

Though the campus was relatively small compared to many other schools, it was large enough for its roads to snake around and wind up and down hills bordered by the forest. At least Magnum hadn't used his fortune to level the building site, a blessing which afforded us some discretion as Brady tailed Fanny.

With Don at the helm, the cart sped across the freshly paved roads, taking turns without slowing much, so that the buggy's wheels caught air several times. Whatever—*who*ever—Fanny was straining to reach, it was obvious that seconds mattered.

Every time Bonnie popped around a bend and we saw the buggy just about to disappear from sight, I thought Fanny would surely make us.

But she must not have looked back. Too preoccupied with the emergency, too certain we'd follow her barked orders like brainless minions.

"There isn't supposed to be anything out this way," Layla said from my right.

Once again, I was in the middle, squeezed between her and Griffin in the back, with a very restless pittie on my lap. Bobo's claws were digging into my thighs, and I was grateful I'd decided to wear jeans that morning.

We'd already passed the physical training facilities and the staff residential building and were now heading toward what appeared to be undeveloped, densely forested land—with asphalt roads cut through it. Not sus at all.

"Fanny said the buildings she showed us were all there was to the place," Layla added.

I snorted. "And you thought she'd be straight-up with us? That the team that killed and has practically kidnapped us wouldn't keep any secrets from us?" Another snort, then, "Also, remember they're listening to everything we say as we make our way to the *lab*."

"Oh," Layla muttered a bit miserably. "Yeah, right. *The lab*."

"We're so screwed," Brady said with a glance at us in the rearview mirror. "No way can Lay remember we're being monitored before she speaks every time. To do that, she'd have to think before she opens her fat mouth, and we all know that ain't gonna happen anytime soon."

"Hey," Layla protested, but then didn't bother denying it. Even she knew it was the truth: *discretion* wasn't in the girl's vocabulary. We were super screwed, deep-fried and extra crispy.

"It's gonna be hard for any of us to remember constantly," Griffin said, looking out the window. "Basically, we can never let our guard down. Nowhere inside anyway. I foresee us going for a lot of long runs."

"Till they chip our clothes or sneaks or something," Hunt said with a huff from the passenger seat. "You know they fucking will too. They chipped Fanny's *head*."

I slid Bobo's foot a little to one side from where it was majorly digging into the flesh of my thigh. "You really think so?"

"From what we just saw in the house, yeah, I do. The advancements in nanotech recently have been totally sick. I won't even tell you how easy it'd be for them to chip us too and we'd probably never even know it."

The dread that had been pretty much a constant in the pit of my stomach for the last several weeks grew heavier, churning like indigestion. "Great. Just fucking dandy. If you're listening to us right now, Magnum, I will fucking *murder* you if you chip me or my friends without our permission."

"Which you'll never have," Griffin chimed in.

"Never," I confirmed. "So keep that in mind," I continued speaking to the invisible microphone and maybe also camera inside the Mustang. "Having more money than God doesn't actually make you a god. You can still die."

I grimaced as Griff and I exchanged looks. The whole point of this campus and Magnum's power play was essentially to buy immortality like ours.

I plunked my head against the back of the seat. "Shit. We're so fucked."

"That much we can all agree on," Griffin grumbled.

"Yup," Brady commented from up front.

I'd just let my eyes close when I felt the vibration beneath my head. "Please tell me that's the car humming a little extra right now."

"No, def not," Layla said, her pitch strung tight. "I think it's another shake as we make our way to the *lab*."

I rolled my eyes at her and sat up, hugging Bobo close. "What—?"

The car began shaking so intensely that the dashboard rattled and the windows buzzed alarmingly; the seat beneath us vibrated like a massage chair.

Griffin jerked forward to tap Brady on the shoulder. "Pull over, man. We gotta get out of here in case it gets worse and the glass shatters."

The glass and steel of Bonnie only shuddered all the more violently as Brady guided the car onto the shoulder.

"Keep going," Hunt said. "Over there. You can park behind those trees and they might not, uh, you know . . . us so easily."

They might not *spot* us immediately with at least a little bit of cover. Then again, they probably had a tracker on the car too. Fuck, it was all too much. If only we could be transported back in time to before the Fischer House party.

By the time Brady parked Bonnie and we tumbled out of the car, the trees surrounding us on all sides of the road were oscillating in a way trees definitely aren't supposed to.

Bobo whined as he pressed against my legs, and Layla leaned into one side of me.

"I don't like this."

Griffin grabbed my free hand and tugged me toward the road's shoulder. "Come on. We're running if we want a chance at figuring out what's going on."

Without another word, we set off, the rhythmic pounding of our feet a counterpoint to the thrashing unease of nature reacting to whatever *un*natural force was disturbing it.

"I *really* don't like this," Layla amended as we crested a hillock. "Something feels majorly off."

When we reached the top of the incline, we immediately ducked behind the trees, their leaves trembling far above us. Bobo was being an obedient boy; I'd told him to keep "quiet" and "follow" in my command voice, and he was doing exactly that.

The buggy was parked in front of a hill with two thick cement walls lining an entrance leading down into it. Fanny, Don, and half a dozen men in tactical gear swarmed out front, chasing a guy who looked to be about our age as he sprinted back and forth trying to avoid them.

"Damn," Layla whispered, though we were a good fifty feet from the cart, far enough that no one should be able to hear us, especially not with the constant humming and grumbling of the earth and trees. "You weren't fucking kidding. They were keeping mega secrets. That entrance looks like it leads to, like, a secret underground lair or something. It's like a bunker."

"That's exactly what it looks like," Brady muttered, shooting out a hand to steady himself against the trunk of a tree as the ground jerked beneath us. Birds took flight in a sudden flutter of wings. "Fuck them for having something like this."

Whatever it actually was.

"We don't know what's inside it," Hunt said. "Could be pretty much anything. Though no doubt it's not anything good."

"No fucking doubt," Layla seethed as the guy, dressed in jeans and a hoodie, dodged a couple of the guys in tactical gear, then sprinted up and around the hill—only to be pushed back down to the front by another handful of armed men dressed all in black, with what looked like bulletproof vests and panels along their extremities. They all wore helmets, and Don was in the process of passing one to Fanny while affixing his own.

"Shouldn't we help him?" I asked.

"How?" Brady said. "It's not like we have super strength or anything. Plus, if they're dressed like a fucking bomb squad, who's to say he won't destroy us."

"The whole point of us being here is 'cause we're indestructible," Layla pointed out.

Hunt harrumphed. "Maybe, maybe not. We basically don't know shit about ourselves other than we've survived death a bit and we're part of some lifelong experiment. We still know too little."

"Magnum's gonna do his best to kill us anyway," I said. "Shouldn't we at least die trying to help this kid?"

From beside me, Griffin tipped his head, a sign he agreed and was considering.

Bobo whimpered softly as he rubbed against my legs, trying to find comfort.

I crouched and hugged him to my chest, kissing his neck. "Sorry, boy. I didn't mean to drag you into any of this." Whatever the hell *this* even was.

The guy was fast, and he took off at a dead run, evading several of the arms reaching for him as he raced off toward the forest.

Before he could vanish into the camouflage of the tree line, Fanny yelled, "Shoot him!"

"Aw, shit," Hunt growled, standing from where he squatted, observing with squinty eyes. "We can't let this happen."

I was already shaking my head. "No, we can't."

Shots rang out, but the guy didn't fall or cry out; he just kept running.

As one unit, with Bobo shadowing my steps, we crept closer at a crouch, taking cover at the final trees that bordered the open clearing in front of us. Once we stepped out from behind their trunks, we'd be exposed. I mentally prepared for Fanny to order us shot too.

My eyes widened as a thought occurred to me. "Oh no," I breathed. "Oh fuck no."

Griffin leaned toward me so that his lips brushed against my ear as he whispered urgently, "What is it?"

I just shook my head, grabbing Bobo's face in my hands and calling on the no-nonsense command tone I'd used to train him, forever grateful I'd had the foresight to train him for a battle I'd had no idea we'd be heading into.

"Bobo," I whispered sternly. "Danger. Stay. No matter what, you *stay*." Then I pointed to the ground behind the fattest tree trunk around us. "*Hide, quiet,* and *stay*."

There was no way on this green earth I was going to let Bobo get hurt.

More shots sliced the air. The earth shook even more violently beneath our feet. And Bobo looked up at me with dark, desperate, pleading eyes.

"I love you, boy. Now you do as I say. Go." I tapped the spot behind the tree where he was to hide.

His entire body shaking along with the ground, Bobo moped to the spot and sat to look up at me. His eyes begged me to release him from my commands.

Gulping thickly, I forced myself to look away.

The guy was staggering up from the ground—he must have tripped—while Fanny was yelling, "How could not one of you hit him? Give me that!" She snatched a gun from Don, who'd been holding it like he knew how to use it. Fanny sighted as their escapee leapt over a fallen log, then she pulled the trigger. *Bam, bam, bam.*

Boom. Another of the soldiers fired a shot, and this one did hit the kid.

He fell forward with a yelp, arms reaching toward the trees that were just inches away from offering him cover.

Griffin handed Layla and me fallen branches while clutching his own. "It's now or never, guys."

Without further confirmation, we rose and emerged from the trees, leaving a trembling Bobo behind. But before our posse could reach him, the guy lifted his head to look behind him at the soldiers, all with guns pointing at him. He skirted across the line of us with a quick jerk of surprise, and then he slammed both fists against the earth.

Once, twice, thrice—with cracking booms that sounded like thunder.

Like a sheet being fluffed, the ground undulated beneath us, knocking our feet out from under us. We landed back on our asses—hard. The air in my lungs was expelled in a loud, grunted exhale.

Then the kid *roared*, sounding like a trapped and wounded animal many times his size. From far away, the flapping of birds' wings scattered through the air. Wherever they'd deemed it safe to congregate, they decided it wasn't far enough away.

The trees behind the kid swayed as if they were enduring a strong gale.

Fanny, Don, and the soldiers were all getting back to their feet, revolvers aiming at the guy. Blood leaked from his right shoulder area.

Again, he slammed his fists against the ground. Again, cracks of thunder threatened to rip apart both earth and sky.

His enemies fell again. Fanny discharged her gun; based on a grunt, she hit one of the soldiers.

The buggy teetered on two tires. The guy knocked the earth again, and the cart slammed onto its side, wheels spinning.

Sitting, unwilling to stand—duh—we watched him from out in the open.

"Shoot him," Fanny shouted while untangling her flowered skirt to lunge closer to him. "Use the tranqs, dammit."

With his fists already raised, three tranquilizer darts whistled as they flew and stuck into his skin. Two on his neck, close together. Another on one hand.

His arms dropped heavily to the ground, but only caused a shudder. His head wobbled atop his neck.

"He was supposed to be a level two," Fanny yelled. "He's clearly *not* a level two. Use the suit."

A soldier popped up and stalked toward the kid, pressing some buttons along either arm of his uniform; he lit up with an arcing blue electrical field that crackled loudly.

With so much focus on their runaway, we hadn't been spotted yet. A small miracle. Hunt waved us back into the cover of the trees. Without a word, we retreated, stares fixed ahead.

Hunt was right. Our time to intervene had passed. There wasn't much we could do to save the kid now that wouldn't lead to us being captured and possibly killed.

Knowledge was power, and at least remaining free meant we stood a chance of helping him later. We stood a chance of figuring out what the ever-loving hell was going on and what exactly the secret underground whatever was being used for.

From the safety of the trees, we watched as the electrified soldier pressed his hands to the drooping kid, whose body was already nearly flat on the ground he seemed to command. His body stiffened as the guard pumped wattage into his body. His extremities went rigid and rose from the earth as blood spurted from the wound in his shoulder.

Then, finally, he lay limp.

"Is he going to stay down?" Fanny asked loudly enough that we heard her clearly.

"I think so," replied the soldier.

"Then turn off your suit. And where the hell are Fred and Doug?"

Another of the soldiers stood. "On their way. They got held up. A sleepwalker knocked them out."

"For goodness' sake," Fanny muttered. "What, is everyone an amateur now? They should know better! They're the ones who're supposed to be dealing with the rogues, not me. Now I'm late to see Magnum, and I have to pop by the lab first to check on the priority cases."

I swallowed. I'd bet we were said priority cases.

As a few other soldiers joined the one in the suit, now dark and quiet, to drag the kid into the entrance below the earth, and Fanny commanded those who remained to help Don get the buggy upright again, we gathered Bobo and ran.

We were loaded up in Bonnie and rocketing back toward the labs before we heard or saw sign of the cart on our tails.

All too aware we lacked true privacy, we rode in silence till we skidded to a stop outside the science building.

We'd already known we were surrounded by the enemy. But now we also knew we weren't the only ones coerced into attending Magnum's little institute for immortals.

On the outside, it might seem like a classy, upscale academy. Appearances were worth a steaming, stinking pile of shit.

Despite our mansion, cars, and all the fake smiles, we were at war.

As we'd do in war, we'd bide our time—until we struck wherever it would hurt the most.

16

Eyes and Ears Everywhere

Despite our collective silence, I knew my friends were as freaked out as I was. We walked so closely together that we occasionally bumped arms as we made our way down the elegant, ample hallways of the science building with Bobo immediately behind us. Ordinarily, I might have considered leaving Bobo in the car while the rest of us headed into the labs—temperatures were in the low sixties, and in the shade with the windows open he'd be fine for what I hoped would be a brief stint inside—but no way was I letting Bobo out of my sight now.

Though neither I nor my friends had lowered our guard since arriving at the institute, which would have been more aptly named a *prison*, the outward civility of the place and everyone staffing it had lulled me into hoping things wouldn't be so bad. After what we'd just witnessed, that hope fizzled and deflated like a sad, sad party balloon.

The sophisticated architectural details of the campus, which I'd previously admired, now only made me scowl. It was all a façade. A twisted, sick façade. Magnum was as villainous a villain as I'd ever found in any sort of fiction. He was, indeed, the worst kind. Handsome, charismatic, and used to getting his way. He wore his ugly villainy on the inside.

I was sandwiched between Griffin and Brady, and on my right, Brady sighed so heavily that I knew his thoughts were as burdened as mine. He scowled brutally. "Let's just get this shit over with as fast as we possibly can."

Griffin said, "Yep. But only 'cause we don't have a better fucking choice."

I sighed as we pushed through the double doors of the lab, then froze. On a large screen up on the wall was a full-color view of the hallway we'd just exited. The fuckers had been following our progress as if we were ants stuck in a glass farm. What could have possibly been so interesting about our approach?

Tobias (aka the former Orson Conway) pressed a button on a keyboard and the image vanished.

"Smooth, D—" Griffin said, catching himself. This man was no more his dad than mine was. What a total and absolute mindfuck.

But Tobias smiled triumphantly at Griffin's near slip. "Good morning, kids," he announced, a bit too bubbly for the tempered man I'd been around all my life.

The rest of our fake parents hovered nervously around the lab, along with Tracy and a few others I'd never seen before. All of them wore crisp white lab coats but no nametags. Apparently everyone knew each other and their roles. We, the supposed children, were the only ones who didn't.

Unease pushed at my skin some more, making me want to scratch. I wouldn't, not with all of them observing us like we were specimens.

Lynne—formerly Monica Bryson—drew closer with the click-clack of her high heels. "Bobo can't be in here. Dogs aren't allowed in the lab."

"Well, *Lynne*," I said feeling the viciousness of my smile, "I don't care. He's staying."

She tutted me as if I were still her twelve-year-old daughter giving her sass. "The work we do here is very important. We can't have animals messing with the integrity of our data."

"And we can't have liars for parents keeping us trapped on this campus upon threat of death." I shrugged, my smile only growing meaner. "I guess none of us are gonna get what we want today."

She stared at me with a disapproving frown that I actually enjoyed, before snapping at the man I'd known as Reece Bryson, my father.

"Jude, will you talk some sense into her please? I won't have—"

"*Jude?*" I interjected. "Jude?"

Layla was shaking her head, a look of incredulity twisting her features. "He *so* does not look like a Jude. No way. Not a Jude."

Reece aka Jude sighed so that his shoulders slumped. "Judah Corlett, actually. Jude for short."

"Jude for short," I echoed as I tried to get this new reality to pierce through my shock. We'd not just been lied to, but our entire lives were nothing but lies.

I shook my head at myself. How was it that the truth could feel so wrong when it was the lie that should? How could we not have felt any of the hints there must have been along the way that nothing was as it seemed?

Worse, how could we ever trust our instincts again?

"Yeah," *Judah* said softly. "Sorry about that, honey."

Bobo rounded our legs to sit on my feet. Without looking away from the spread of traitors in the spacious lab, I ran my hand along his head. At least Bobo would never betray me. Dogs were so much better than people.

"Were you . . ." I started before having to stop to begin anew. "Were you two ever even together?" I waved my free hand at him and Lynne, unwilling to release the connection to Bobo, whose warm, familiar presence was soothing my jagged edges. "I mean, was there ever anything even romantic between you guys? Or was *Lynne* just boning the sheriff while she played at being your wife?"

Jude spun atop the stool he perched on to look at her, so fast that I knew.

"'Boning the sheriff?'" he repeated in a shrill tone that told me and my friends everything we needed to hear. I didn't even get reprimanded like usual for my choice of language.

"We were supposed to be working on things between us!" he accused. "No wonder things weren't getting better."

Lynne winced but otherwise didn't show what I'd consider an appropriate level of remorse. "What did you expect? Our entire lives were about Joss! About the rest of the kids. I'm a *woman*, and I have needs."

"I could've satisfied those needs! I was showing up and trying. Xander Jones? Really, Lynne? Fucking *really?*"

"What? He gave me what I wanted and didn't ask too many questions. Plus, he's a great lay."

Layla whispered to us, "I'd say this is awesome, but not sure anything's gonna feel truly awesome again."

"I know the feeling," Brady added with a sour frown.

Then, since I owed Lynne the Liar zero allegiance, I added, "Oh, and, Jude? Xander got her pregnant. She had an abortion."

Jude whipped his head around to glare at her all over again. This time, though, he silently seethed.

Finally, Porter-who-wasn't-Porter rose from his stool to pat Jude awkwardly on the shoulder. "Sorry, man. We can talk it through later. But this isn't the place for this right now." So softly that I had to strain to hear, he added, "Eyes and ears everywhere, remember."

Jude only continued to glare venom at Lynne. When *Porter* patted him on the back some more, Jude finally rubbed a hand along his face and nodded. "Okay, yeah, okay."

Slowly, he spun the stool to face us again. His devastation at Lynne's betrayal etched years onto his face.

I almost felt sorry for him—almost.

"What you're feeling right now? Imagine that a thousandfold. Then maybe you'll begin to have an inkling of what we've been going through," I said.

Lynne shot to her feet to glower at me before finally crossing her arms over her chest as if she didn't know what else to do. "Are you pleased with yourself now, Joss? For causing havoc, something you do so well?"

Griffin went rigid beside me. Even Brady huffed in shared offense.

"No, Lynne," I said, "I'm not fucking pleased. You guys, all of you"—I gestured around to encompass all of them, even those we didn't know—"you're fucking *assholes*. You treated us like your stupid pawns in your little lab experiment game when we—" I had to stop to swallow the sudden tears rising up my throat and stinging my eyes. "We loved you," I added, a thready admission I didn't even know why I was fucking making. It only felt like yet another point of vulnerability I had no desire to flaunt in their ugly, stupid faces.

Faux Celia's eyes misted over, as did faux Porter's. "Oh, Joss," she said, "all of you, we promise, we *swear*, we did it all because we thought it was the only way to protect you. We did it for *you*. We did it because we grew to love you, every single one of you, and we wanted to offer you a chance at a real life."

As one, all the pretend-parents nodded. Even Lynne.

A single tear tracked down my cheek before I swiped it away angrily. The very last thing I wanted to do was cry for these people. But my heart obviously hadn't gotten the memo in time.

"Yeah, yeah," Layla muttered with enough snark to make up for my temporary sappiness. I was so fucking glad for it. Not a single one of them deserved to see how much they'd hurt us.

"We've heard the whole sob story before," Layla continued. "Save your breath. It still doesn't excuse your behavior, not even close. What I want to know is what are all your real names? 'Cause I do *not* wanna keep thinking of you as the people you pretended to be. It'll make me puke in my mouth. You so aren't our parents."

Before any of them answered, Tracy edged forward. "Um, I hate to interrupt—"

Layla pegged her with that angry stare. "Then don't."

"Well, we do have a lot of work to get started on, and I know you're supposed to be elsewhere at ten." She glanced at the watch on her slender wrist. Shiny gold with a smattering of diamonds to catch the light. Magnum clearly rewarded them well for their work and fuck-all for scruples.

Layla sneered at Tracy as if she were as culpable as the rest of them. "Then stop delaying us. We're gonna get our answers one way or another."

Porter exhaled so loudly that Bobo jerked his head in his direction. "My real name is Mark Malone."

Layla's jaw ground back and forth a few times. "And yours?" she asked not-Celia.

The woman cleared her throat and fiddled with the lapels of her lab coat. "Jacqueline Pawlyn. I go by Jackie."

"And your real last name?" I asked Lynne.

She didn't avoid my accusatory stare as she answered.

"Hopper."

"Got it," I bit out.

Layla, Brady, Griffin, and I looked at Hunt.

Our friend's serious expression had turned morose. He waggled his lips to one side and then the other before finally nodding to himself and casting a look at *Alexis*.

"What is it?" he asked.

The woman who I might have once described as being adoring of her son smiled sadly, as morose as Hunt. "Marisa Domínguez."

She pronounced the name melodically, with a perfect Spanish accent.

"So you really are originally from Spain?"

"Yes, my son."

Hunt tensed his jaw and neck until tendon outlines strained his skin. "Don't call me that."

"But . . ."

He shook his head, and I looked for his usual turquoise to be swinging from his earring. He wasn't wearing it. "You made me believe my dad died. I mourned him. Every day, I wished he were still alive."

I glanced at Griffin, whose jaw was just as tight as Hunt's as his gaze flicked to Tracy.

"Did you ever even meet the man whose sperm was used to create me?" Hunt pressed.

"Not in person then, no," Marisa replied so softly I realized that never in our shared time together had I heard her be this timid. I'd always thought of her as at least a little bit fierce.

"You know who he is though?"

After a quick look at the others, Marisa nodded. "Yes, but he, along with the other sperm and egg donors, requested his information be kept private. He's not looking to be contacted."

"Of course he's not," Hunt said, working to eradicate any hint of emotion from his voice. Then he looked over at us, a silent request to divert the attention away from him.

Right away, Layla, never one to do anything halfway, clapped her hands, and Bobo barked once; I patted his head to calm him. "Now that all that *fun* is under our belts, and we know what names to use when we cuss you the hell out later, what do you need us to do for dear, *dear* Magnum?"

A few of the adults cringed at Layla's thick sarcasm, but for the most part they seemed relieved to get on track. They beckoned us over, and Jude called out, "Joss, you're with me."

With Bobo at my side, his claws clacking against the tile floor, I sat gingerly on the stool Jude extended for me. This close to the man I'd so long believed to be my loving father, I couldn't wait to get away.

He turned to his workstation to pull up on his computer what was very evidently my file—thanks to the large color photo of me—and then stood to lift my sleeve and attach a blood pressure cuff around my arm. While he waited for it to inflate, he stared at me and petted Bobo's head.

When his attention heated to feel like a brand against my skin, I said, "Do ya mind, Jude?"

He startled, but I couldn't figure out if it was because I'd called him by his given name or just that he'd been lost in thought.

"You're all up in my business," I added.

He jerked his head as if to clear it, studied the readout on the cuff, then made notes into his computer before removing the cuff.

When he waved a thermometer across my forehead, my nose scrunched. "Isn't this a bit . . . basic? I thought you'd be, well, I dunno. But not this."

"Your vitals tell us a lot about how your body's reacting to new situations and stimuli. But yes, we'll quickly advance to other, let's say, *measurements*."

The way he enunciated the word so carefully felt ominous.

When he was flashing a penlight onto my eyeballs, he lowered his voice. "I know you don't want to hear this"—I tensed—"but I truly allowed myself to believe you were my daughter. I-I love you, Joss."

I love you too, Dad sat on my tongue, so very ready to slip out, until I tugged it back. *Stupid.* This man was *not* my father, never had been.

That didn't stop my heart from feeling what it felt.

"I don't want you to ever doubt that," he continued. "I understand you're angry now and feel betrayed. I get that, I really do."

As soon as he clicked the light off, I shut my eyes to put whatever barrier I could between him and my raw emotions.

"But just . . . later, if you ever can, please know that I truly do love you, so very much."

I cleared the thickness gathering in my throat but refused to open my eyes.

Even more softly now, a hint of defeat in his words, he said, "If you ever want to talk or, I don't know, whatever, I'll always be here for you. Even if it's years from now, and even if you don't exactly love the idea right now, in my heart I'll always think of you as my daughter. And . . . and . . ."

When he only trailed off, I eventually peered up at him, my eyes glistening in a way I didn't want him to notice. He never got to see me vulnerable again—never.

"I—we—all want to help you," he whispered as he tucked his mouth toward his chest and reached for my wrist to take my pulse.

It sped up.

He barely breathed: "We're being watched even more closely than you are."

Probably in response to my distress and Jude's, Bobo inserted his head between us and planted it on my lap.

Jude glanced this way and that, then up to the corners of the room, and finally to his computer, which he frowned at. Magnum could definitely be listening in through his computer.

Jude cleared his throat loudly before announcing, "I'm going to draw blood next, and after that we'll see how those bullet wounds are healing. Oh wait. I forgot to check your ears first."

He grabbed an otoscope and flicked on its light, then rolled his stool as far away from the computer as he could get while still being at his workstation. As he pretended to study the inner workings of my ear, he mumbled so faintly I felt myself straining to pick up what he was saying.

"When I take your blood"—he tilted his head this way and that, but it was all for show—"I'm going to roll up your sleeves"—my shirt's sleeves reached to just below my elbows—"and leave them up."

Next, apparently for our hidden audience, he said, "Looking good, Joss. Now turn the other way."

Obediently, I did.

He went on, "I'll tuck a note in the rolled-up sleeve. Wait till you're somewhere outside and in private to read it. Where there'll be no surveillance. That's really important, okay?"

He rolled his stool back to the counter of his workstation, ejected the scope's speculum into the trash can beneath the desk, and began gathering an alcohol swab, a tourniquet, a syringe, and vials.

Even as the needle drove into my vein, all I could think about was the note's content, and whether it would actually offer us any useful information.

Halfway through our collective poking and prodding, Fanny arrived, looking calm, collected, and together. No sign that she'd been in the middle of a takedown of one of their latest kidnap victims. Seeing we were where we were supposed to be, she took off to meet with Magnum, grumbling about how she was going to be so late.

I didn't dare make eye contact with any of my friends. It seemed we'd finally gotten away with something, after Magnum had continually had the upper hand. Though it wasn't much, we had one new piece of information no one knew we had. We knew about the earth shaker.

It wasn't much. It most certainly wasn't enough.

But it was something. A start.

By the time my crew, Bobo, and I finally walked out of the lab, on our way to the training center, the note my dad—*Jude*—had tucked into my sleeve was practically all I could think about.

There wouldn't be any privacy for us for a while still. Not so long as we were in the heart of campus, and certainly not later at the mansion. And Fanny had made it abundantly clear we didn't want to make our new instructors wait at the training center.

But I just had to tell my friends. I needed to share the secret that seemed to have its own pulse as it beat against my arm.

As soon as we were outside, the sun shining brightly above the hills that surrounded us, I told them, "I know we're in a hurry, but let's give Bobo a quick walk. Just back there around those trees for a few. Then we can head to training."

Without protest, they all followed, and the very moment we were hopefully out of earshot—assuming no one had succeeded in chipping our actual persons as Hunt believed was possible—I whispered, just in case, "Jude said he wants to help and he hid a note on me. I can't read it till it's safe."

As I met the eyes of each of my friends, I found them wide and surprised.

"Shit," Layla said. "Me too."

The guys nodded with silent *us toos*.

Brady whistled. "Damn. Maybe we've got a better shot than we thought."

Yeah, maybe.

Just fucking maybe.

17

Don't Walk, Run

We entered the training center at 10:10 a.m., our footfalls sounding uncommonly loud in the mostly empty, cavernous building. The very instant we spotted our instructors on the opposite side of the center, Brady mumbled, "Oh fuck," under his breath, and as one we picked up the pace.

Even with the entire length of the twenty-five-yard pool separating us, I already knew it'd be the last time we'd ever be casual about being late to meet any of them. Even the measly ten minutes was too long when their stares alone seemed capable of committing murder. How, I had no idea. But I still wouldn't put it past them. A tangible sense of danger wafted off them like heatwaves.

The unease that I'd been carrying only expanded, stretching at the boundaries of my skin, causing it to feel irritatingly taut.

The two men and one woman stood in a line, their legs shoulder-width apart, their arms loose at their sides. Their poses were deceptively relaxed. I could practically feel their muscles coiled and ready to pounce.

"Don't walk. Run!" the man in the middle hollered at us, and we didn't hesitate to obey, Bobo keeping pace with us.

When we shored up to stand across from them, the man in the center, who was also the tallest, pursed his lips. "You're late."

"We ran into some complications before coming here," Layla offered, and I was glad that, for once, she stayed her tongue and didn't tack on, "We were busy watching a new student being tranq'd and electrocuted into submission."

"Excuses won't cut it with us. You've agreed to be here. You've made a commitment, and we expect you to honor it and not waste our time."

"Um . . ." Brady said as I shifted uncomfortably on my feet. Already I wanted the three teachers to approve of me, and I didn't like feeling that way one bit. "To be fair, we didn't actually agree or commit to anything, not with any real free will anyhow. We're being coerced into being here by threat of extreme violence, in case you didn't already realize that." Brady laid that all out free of his normal sarcasm.

I expected at least one of them to flinch at that reminder, but none did. Either they were remarkably skilled at controlling their reactions, which they likely were, or they just didn't care enough to endanger whatever incentive Magnum was offering them for being here.

"Free will is relative," the man said.

Is it really though? Shouldn't free will be, you know, free to have and wield? I thought it, but didn't say it out loud.

"The rules are very different once you enter this world."

"And what world is that, exactly?" Hunt asked.

"The world of physical powers. In the societies most people live in, material wealth, social class, and political standing are often the determining factors of power levels, especially when one takes into account the rampant corruption that infects nearly all modern civilizations across the globe."

At this, the man to his right nodded with a stout frown, but didn't otherwise comment.

"But when a person develops their physical prowess so it cannot be ignored, they can overcome the restraints of the limited wealth and social standing they might have been born into. The rules change. And when one also considers powers beyond those commonly found in this world that affect the physical laws here . . ." He shook his head in what seemed akin to awe. "Then it's within the realm of possibility to entirely transform the governing rules."

Griffin crossed his arms and studied our instructors, eventually addressing the man in the middle: "From what we've seen so far, we can return from death. That sounds like exactly the kind of power you were just referring to as an advantage. Yet look at us. We're prisoners here, trapped precisely because of these extraordinary powers."

The man shared a look with the other two teachers before saying, "We'll do whatever we can to teach you how to harness and wield every advantage you have."

"That's right. We agreed to be here because we want to help you learn everything you can do," the woman chimed in with a pretty accent that suggested Spanish was her first language. With her lustrous dark hair, round facial structure, dark eyes, brown skin, and small frame, I guessed her ancestral heritage was connected to the indigenous tribes of Central or perhaps South America. But it wasn't an appropriate time to ask.

Bobo circled my friends to once again sit atop my feet where he could keep an eye on our instructors.

"Dogs aren't allowed in the training arena," said the man in the center while studying Bobo. "It will have to wait for you outside."

"'It' is a boy named Bobo," I said, "and it's important that he remain with me at all times." The man started to shake his head, but I persisted, meeting his dark stare and holding. "These four people"—I angled my stare up and down the line of my friends—"and my dog are the only things that really matter to me in the entire world. They're the only ones I trust, and the only ones I love. My friends and I are supposedly immortal. But Bobo isn't. I have to keep him in sight at all times so he isn't used as leverage to get me to fall into line."

Even though I kept the threat to Bobo vague, it was the first time I'd even admitted it to myself. Once I heard myself say it, I realized how true it was. Bobo was the first one Magnum would threaten to hurt if he wanted me to do something. My sweet boy wouldn't survive death like we would.

Griffin and Hunt, who stood on either side of me, moved up half a step so that they also flanked Bobo.

Our instructors were still examining Bobo when the man to our left announced, "Bobo can stay."

The man in the middle frowned at him before sighing and looking at us again. "If he's to stay, then he must be well behaved."

"He is. Very well behaved," I answered immediately.

"You think so, but will he continue to be 'well behaved' when you appear to be in grave danger? When your body and life are being threatened? When he sees you lying dead on the mat?"

"Laying it all right out there, aren't we?" Layla mumbled under her breath. "So much for pretending we'll actually be safe in our classes."

The man at the center scoffed. "Your abject lack of safety shouldn't be news to you. You're here to be experimented upon, to have the limits of your immortality tested and studied."

Layla huffed. "Still doesn't make it any less hard to hear."

"If you're looking to be handled with kid gloves, then you've come to the wrong people. We're not here to coddle you. We're not even here to take it easy on you. We will push you to your limits and beyond. That's our job."

Brady bristled. "So you're just here to try to murder us? Like everyone else?"

The woman stared at Brady. "No, we're here to teach you how to get stronger. And to see what you're capable of."

"While killing us," Layla deadpanned.

The fact that we were being forced to become more comfortable with this shocking topic of conversation just made my skin crawl all the more. I'd never wanted to run so hard, so fast, and so freaking far away from this damned place.

"We'll be testing your limits," repeated the man in the center. "Whether you die or not is up to you and your ability to defend yourself. I'll warn you now, my colleagues and I are quite skilled at ending lives."

"Great, totally fucking great," Layla muttered before tipping her head to one side in consideration of the man. "How?" she eventually asked him. "How do you sound so, I dunno, intelligent and refined while still looking like you do?"

It was a bit of a weird question, maybe even a stupid one, actually, but I didn't understand why every one of the man's muscles stiffened and bulged—and there were a great many of them now on threatening display. He wore a sleeveless workout tank top and shorts that revealed most of his chiseled thighs.

Through gritted teeth, he asked, "Because I'm Black?"

Layla *tsk*ed. "No, not because you're Black. Do I look like a prejudiced asshole prick to you? Your dark skin's fucking gorgeous. *I mean* how do you sound like a freaking textbook while also looking like you do?" She ran a hand up and down the air in front of his body. "You're jacked."

When he still didn't relax, Layla elucidated some more: "How do you find time to develop your mind along with your body to such an extreme? From how ripped you are, it looks like you'd need to spend hours every day just keeping up your training."

Finally, he visibly relaxed. "Ah. That's one of the first things we'll teach you. Of all the muscles you have, your mind is the most important of all. Though the saying, 'mind over matter' is a bit banal, it's also true."

"There's something I don't understand," Hunt said, and I glanced at him, hoping he wasn't about to follow up on Layla's odd line of questioning. "From everything we've seen, Magnum only wants to test our ability to die and resurrect. Why would he want to train us so we become stronger in any way other than our immortality?"

None of our teachers had a ready answer. When the other two only glanced toward the man between them, he answered, "I've known Magnum the longest. While I won't be sharing many of my impressions with you, I will tell you the man is remarkably perceptive and long-sighted. I think he's training you for what's to come farther down the path we're embarking upon together. Also, he told us you were interested in training to become ninjas."

I waited for at least one of them to laugh or snicker. They didn't.

"Perhaps it's simply an incentive or a reward for you at this time."

An incentive and reward system, like we were actual lab rats. Since Magnum seemed to view us as nothing more than that, I supposed it made a certain morbid kind of sense that's what our training would be about.

The man straightened his shoulders an extra fraction of an inch and clasped his wrists behind his back. "We've wasted enough time talking, and you were already late to begin with. The dog can stay for now. But if he becomes a threat or a problem in any way, he'll have to go, no matter what argument you make."

I scratched behind Bobo's ears and beamed up at the man, who was maybe an inch or two taller than any of my guys, who were all around six feet tall. "Yeah, of course, I understand. He's very well trained though."

The man frowned in obvious disbelief, but I was taking the win for now.

"This is Yolanda," he said with a nod to the woman. "This is

Armando." He tilted his chin to the man on his right. "And I'm Homer. You'll find appropriate clothing and gear waiting for you in the locker rooms. In future, we'll expect you to be changed and ready to go at the start of class time. For today only, you have five minutes."

"We'll be working out today already?" Layla asked. "I thought today was orientation only."

"You assumed wrong. Every day not spent learning, growing, and bettering ourselves is a day wasted. Your five minutes are counting down."

With a "follow" directed at Bobo, my friends and I tore off in the direction Yolanda pointed out to us and piled into a co-ed locker room. As I grabbed the pile of clothes under a label with my name on it and scooted into one of the many changing rooms, I had mere moments to decide what to do about the note still tucked into the folds of my sleeve. I could leave it with my clothes in the locker room and hope no one snuck in here to snoop, or I could take it with me, hoping there were no cameras here to spot me transferring it from one hiding place to another. Beyond the noise we were making, the training center was completely quiet. But in the same way I didn't trust enough to let Bobo out of my sight, I didn't trust leaving behind the potential help of our faux parents either. We were one hundred percent being spied on. Did that include rifling through our possessions when we weren't looking? Short of someone sniffing our undies, I didn't think anything was off limits around here.

Without a better idea, I pretended to wipe down my chest with my discarded shirt in case there were hidden cameras. I had no good reason to rub my shirt over my chest, but people did peculiar things all the time. The action could be dismissed as such an oddity. While I was "wiping," I pushed the sleeve into my sports bra and managed to wedge the note under my cleavage, where it tucked securely beneath my boobs with the tight elastic band underneath keeping it in place. For now, it was the best I could do. My exercise clothing had no pockets, and I didn't think the note would fare any better stuffed into one of my socks.

After possibly the fastest pee break of my life, the five of us and Bobo ran back out into the gym, only to find Homer studying a digital clock on the wall, one with a readout similar to that of a stopwatch.

"You're fifteen seconds late," he announced. "That'll cost you fifteen laps around the gym, one per second."

When we just gaped at him, he added, "Make that twenty and counting."

I told Bobo to "follow," and we broke into a steady jog. A narrow, open path skirted the entire length of the spacious building's walls—and now I understood why.

Okay, so Homer was obviously a hardass. But maybe we'd learn a lot from him and the others. At least that part was genuinely exciting.

The killing part, not so much. In fact, not at all.

I pushed away the thought and the immediate panic it delivered. Still, my breath squeezed in my chest, and my heart gave an irregular thump that made me wince.

All the comforts we'd enjoy would come at the expense of our lives, our freedoms. Shackles might as well have clanked with every step we took.

How long till one of us was forced to die again? Till the rest of us were forced to watch?

Bile crept up my throat; I had to swallow it forcefully down.

Welcome to the Institute for the Advancement of Immortals, where dying is part of your coursework.

Welcome to hell on earth.

18

The Correct Response Is to Be Freaked Out

"If this was just their assessment of us . . ." Brady said, eyeing Hunt in the passenger seat then the rest of us in Bonnie's rearview mirror before shaking his head. "Then, *shit*, I can't decide whether to be freaked out or excited, 'cause there isn't a single doubt they're going to hand us our asses."

Again in the middle seat in the back, since Griffin had taken to leaving shotgun to Hunt so he could sit beside me, I let my head plunk heavily onto the seat, trying to carve out some space between my chest and Bobo's body, which was a freaking furnace. I'd shucked my drenched workout clothes and once again wore my jeans and snug quarter-sleeve shirt, but the fabric was sticking to my sheen of sweat.

The note I'd tucked under my boobs was soggy and damp. I'd been well on my way to kicking my own ass for deciding it was safer with me than in the locker room until I realized the clothing I left behind had definitely been rifled through. I'd paid close attention to how I'd left my pile of belongings, and my jeans and the sleeves of my shirt were at slightly different angles than I'd left them. Whoever had gone through our stuff was good, but not perfect. Had I not anticipated how very complete our lack of privacy was, I might not have even noticed.

I could only hope I'd still be able to read whatever Jude had written on the paper. I hadn't yet had the chance to properly examine it, sneaking it from one place to the other without unfolding it because of the surveillance of hidden cameras. Even with the risk that the text might now be a challenge to decipher, at least Magnum wouldn't be privy to Jude's secrets. With the odds stacked against us as they were, it barely seemed like a win. But we'd had so few, I was going to count it as one anyway.

When the others hadn't yet answered Brady, I told him, "The correct response is to be *freaked out*, def to be freaked out. Now that they know we're all in shape and that we know what we're doing at least a little, they're not going to hold back. And when they hand us our asses, I'm afraid it's gonna be in the *dead* way."

Homer, Yolanda, and Armando had made us sprint till our leg muscles burned, climb up and down ropes tied to the very top of the maybe fifty-foot ceiling, spar and grapple with each other, kick and punch and strike every which way. They'd even made us break slabs of wood with both our hands and bare feet. They'd shoved us to see how well we'd catch ourselves or if we'd fall, and they'd swept our feet out from under us any time we weren't paying attention.

My mind was as exhausted as my body—and there was no way we could let down our guard. Not as long as we were stuck on this campus.

"At least we know we'll learn cool stuff though, right?" Brady said. "I can't wait to see what they can do. The three of them look like total badasses."

"Again, not necessarily the best thing when their job descriptions literally include killing their pupils."

Brady slowed as the admin building loomed up ahead.

"Whatcha doin'?" Layla asked.

"Looking," he said.

"For what?"

"Something sus."

Griffin huffed. "Well, I don't think you have to look far to find that. It'd be harder to find something *not* sus around here."

"No kidding," I said on a heavy sigh, leaning my head against Griffin's shoulder as Bobo tried to circle around my lap to get comfy. I patted his rump and guided him to sit before his foot could press against my full bladder.

When Homer had finally dismissed us, he informed us we had exactly an hour and a half before our academic teachers expected us over in the academic building. It wasn't all that much time for the showers we all desperately needed, plus a quick lunch for us and Bobo, but we'd decided the relative privacy of our own house was better than exposing ourselves to the locker room showers and figuring out the dining hall.

Brady slowed nearly to a crawl as we passed the office building, leaning forward to peer at it through the windshield.

Griffin rubbed Bobo's ears. "It's time to get Clyde back up and purring. I'm thinking tonight would be a good time to grab some cold ones and start working on him. You guys down? It'd be good not to have to all pile into Bonnie every time."

We were in the midst of agreeing to the plan for the evening when Brady brought Bonnie to a complete stop.

"OhmyfuckingGod, Brade!" said Layla, throwing her hands up into the air. "Get us home already before we get any riper in here. We stink like a pile of sweaty jockstraps. I can literally smell your ass crack."

I was prepared for Brady to give her shit in return when he muttered, "I've got a bad feeling."

Three seconds later, Hunt snapped, "Guys, *look*!"

With Bonnie in the middle of the road—granted, there was no other traffic—Hunt cracked open the passenger door but didn't push it open.

Bobo was still standing on my lap and his head lifted as he stiffened with sudden alertness—blocking the front window. I wrestled him out of my view while glancing through the side windows across my friends' laps. I didn't manage to make sense of whatever was going on before Hunt pushed his door the rest of the way open and jumped out of it, immediately breaking into a run.

"What's going on?" I asked urgently, but Brady was already pushing open his door to follow, and Griffin and Layla were getting out, too. When Griffin reached his hand back in to me, Bobo stared up at me, waiting for my permission to go.

"Good boy," I said in a hurry. "Go. Follow."

From my lap in the middle, he leapt out onto the ground, waiting for me.

The second I was out, I whirled in Griffin's arms, trying to look everywhere at once and asking, "What the hell's happening?"

For the second time today, a man was running with such desperation and scrambled speed it could only mean he believed he was running for his life.

The administration slash office building was at his back as he scrambled down a steep hill.

"Do you see who's chasing him?" I asked Griffin and Layla, who remained beside the car with me, trying to make sense of the scene before we ran out into possible danger. Hunt was already running toward the man, Brady jogging more slowly after him.

"No," Griffin said. "I see no one. Let's go."

As we all ran toward him, the man noticed us and switched direction to aim for us and our car.

But when his attention crawled across Hunt, he stumbled and fell to his knees, his mouth agape for a few seconds before he pushed up to his feet to continue running.

"Holy fuck," I mumbled under my breath as the man and Hunt intersected, both stuttering to a halt to gape at each other.

Even with a good twenty feet still separating us from them, their resemblance was obvious.

The man and Hunt shared the same sharp nose and high cheekbones, although Hunt was a little leaner than the older man, who appeared to be in his mid-forties. Their hair was the same shiny black, their skin a similar brown, their eyes dark. They were both tall, although Hunt had a couple of inches on the other man.

"Holy motherfucking shitballs," Layla breathed. "Is that . . . ?"

"His father?" Griffin whispered so reverently I didn't want to correct him to say "sperm donor."

Two men simply could not look this much alike and not be related.

The stranger was studying Hunt like he was seeing a ghost. Gingerly, he reached for Hunt with both hands. His long hair had come partially free of the long braid that draped down his back, framing the wildness in his eyes; they burned with the urge to flee while being apparently unable to look away from Hunt.

Brady, Griffin, Layla, Bobo, and I all drew up around Hunt as his father cleared his throat and rasped, "Son?"

Hunt's throat bobbed while his forehead bunched into lines. "I . . . think so?"

The man's eyes, a darker tone than Hunt's chocolate brown, glistened. His voice was an awed croak. "How truly mighty the Great Spirit is. I believed you were lost to me forever, my son."

"I was told you were dead."

The man's lips pursed, making the fact that they were thinner than Hunt's more apparent. "*Lies.*"

"Is someone after you?" I interjected. In his shock, the man seemed to have forgotten whatever he was fleeing. "Do we need to help you get out of here?"

When his eyes landed on me, they widened. "You."

I flinched until he added, "You walk my dreams. I thought you were a witch come to steal them."

"Nope, no witch here."

He studied me for several seconds we probably didn't have to waste before nodding. "Not a witch. You look like the white man, but my ancestors stand with you."

"Your ancestors of the Eastern Band Cherokee?" Hunt asked.

His father glanced at him. "No. My tribe, the Aquoian people."

Hunt harrumphed. "I thought you were Eastern Band Cherokee. That's what they told me."

More lies. The explanation went unspoken.

"My ancestry—*your ancestry*—lies to the west. The blood that runs through my veins is all Aquoian. It's their secrets and power that the rich white man wants, that he kills for."

"Then we need to get you out of here, right now," Griffin said, and I nodded as a sense of urgency undulated beneath my skin, urging me to move.

The man stared at Griffin, then me again, next Layla and Brady, before his gaze returned to his son. His brow furrowed, causing his eyes to narrow. "I don't understand how or why, but my ancestors have chosen all of you."

His attention focused solely on me until the force of it made me shudder. But I refused to look away. Something about this man made me want to draw closer, to learn every possible thing there was to know about him.

"Especially you," he told me. Then to all of us, "You'll defend the knowledge entrusted to us."

He stopped as if to listen to something—perhaps the ancestors—that I couldn't hear. Frantically now, I glanced behind him at the admin building; still no one appeared to be in pursuit.

He smiled sadly. "For many generations, my tribe's given everything to keep what we know safe. I speak with the ancestors. You'll protect our secrets now too."

"We, uh, can come back from death," Hunt admitted.

The man's eyes widened again, this time tinged with panic. "A gift of the sky people," he whispered in a thready pitch I could scarcely hear. "Shit. It might already be too late. We have to hurry."

"Yes, *hurry*," I repeated, all too happy for us to get moving.

I turned and started jogging back toward the car with Bobo at my side, prepared to pile up into each other's laps to make room for this man, when a hoarse scream rang out before quickly stuttering to a strangled end. Whirling, my mouth dropped open.

Blue light crackled and sizzled as it wrapped the body of Hunt's father, now rigid as a board. A web of blue trapped every hair and every limb. His features were twisted with pain, his skin cast in the eerie hue of lightning—

And a dude I'd never seen before, with Magnum right behind him, stood at the crest of the hill the man had run down, with strings of a haphazard blue light wrapping his bare forearms to shoot from his fingers—straight into Hunt's father.

The father gurgled helplessly and shook all over. His eyeballs vibrated and even seemed to swell—not fucking good—before they rolled into the back of his head.

I sprinted back toward him. The loose strands of his hair stood on end as he staggered and pitched forward, unable to do anything to catch himself, and fell straight into my open arms.

The electricity jumped from him to me, racing into my own body, and then into Bobo's as he pressed his snout to my bare arm in a worried whine.

No, Bobo, no! Don't touch me! But I couldn't get out my warning. Either way, it was too late.

My teeth clamped together; I couldn't get them unstuck. Even my eyeballs felt like they rattled in their sockets. My head trembled uncontrollably atop my neck. Everything was too tense, too tight, too overwhelming.

My friends screamed—maybe I did too—while I struggled to keep my eyes open long enough to save Hunt's father.

But his eyes took on a glassy and empty sheen as the tattoos that wove down my forearms leapt from my skin to his. Somehow, some inexplicable way, they climbed across his fingers and hands to latch on to his arms. My tattoos hooked in, hung on, trying to keep him with us.

Crackling blue coated our bodies and Bobo's as I gawked at the inked lines distorting from their usual geometric patterns of Layla's design to snake around the man's arms like vines. Was I hallucinating? Was the current making me see things that couldn't possibly be?

Arms wrapped around me. I heard more whining and cries and realized with a start that I was no longer staring at my tattoos as they *moved*, but was now blankly studying the sky. At some point, Hunt's father had slipped from my grip and I'd slumped to the ground. Around flashes of my friends' faces that I couldn't get myself to focus on, the air vibrated, differentiating itself into an infinity of sparks and fractals. The air, which I'd always believed was just empty air, as it appeared to the naked eye, was actually composed of millions—bajillions!—of geometric designs. The air was a puzzle made up of more pieces than I could ever possibly count, each fitting into the next with perfect precision. I was staring at translucent designs more wondrous than any mandala, a beautiful reflection of the many symmetric and harmonious patterns all throughout nature, both in plants and animals.

In a way I'd never imagined, *the air was alive.* Writhing, interlocking, inhaling, exhaling, moving, dancing, pulsing, *being.*

As I gaped and gawped and stared at the designs filling my vision, desiring to memorize each and every one of them, I tried to decide: *Am I dying again?* Or was I becoming more alive than I'd ever been before?

19

Somebody Wake Me the Fuck up Already

Groggily, I blinked awake to discover I was lying in my bed at the mansion. The room was bright despite the drawn blinds, suggesting it was the middle of the day. But was it the same day?

Vague recollections flooded my mind: heated arguing while I lay on the ground, overcome by visual evidence of a reality I'd never realized coexisted with our own. Screaming, moaning, and then I was in Griffin's arms, being carried. Then here, slurring like a drunkard as I insisted on taking a "suuuuuppah fassssht" shower to wash off the sweat before I collapsed into bed. Then beneath the rainfall showerhead, crying out as the water somehow reactivated Magnum's lightning energy. Every one of my friends swarming into the shower, desperate to help me escape the pain that had me shrieking and whimpering.

I groaned at the memory. Besides seeing me being all wimpy, they'd also seen me all naked, including Griffin. Including Brady, the self-declared boob connoisseur. He'd probably never let me hear the end of it.

Fuck, the note! I hadn't gotten into the shower with it, had I?

I lifted the duvet in case it might be tucked into my fresh clothes, but nope—I wasn't wearing any. Not even underwear. *What the hell?*

Yanking the covers back down, I blinked up at the ceiling for several moments while trying to remember what else happened.

I couldn't.

Eventually, I tried to get up. But my entire body ached like I'd gone ten rounds with Homer, Yolanda, *and* Armando all at once, and lost to every single one of them, badly.

So instead, I croaked out, "Uh, guys? Bobo?"

Instantly, several sets of sneakers squeaked and ran across the floor, growing louder until they reached me.

Griffin was first to rush into the room, his eyes wide as they jumped across what was visible of my body—from the shoulders up. The concern tightening his brow softened, and he walked into the room as Hunt, Brady, and Layla piled in behind him.

Automatically, he reached for me, but then he pulled back. "I should wash up first. I was working on Clyde. I didn't want to leave your side—"

"But then I made him," Layla interjected, plonking down at the foot of my bed with a bounce. Even if the guys had all been working on the Mustangs, knowing Layla, she'd probably just sat beside them to sketch, as she preferred to do more often than not. Whereas grease smeared a line across Griffin's cheek, Layla looked freshly clean.

"He was fussing over you the whole time," Layla continued, "but you were just sleeping and sleeping and, shit, *sleeping*. Girl, you've been out for, like, three days again."

My own eyes widened as I moved to sit up, but then I remembered my state of undress and slunk deeper under the covers. "Three days? How's that possible?" I did have to pee something fierce though.

"You tell us," Hunt said, standing to hover beside Layla at the foot of the bed. "It's not just been Griff. We've all been pretty messed up about it."

"What happened—where's your dad?"

Hunt's face fell. "They took him."

I moved to sit up in bed again only to recall I'd be flashing titties if I did.

I shook my head. "You know what? I need to hear it all. But first ya gotta let me pee and get dressed. I didn't exactly expect to wake up full-on naked here."

Griffin grimaced, but Brady only grinned. "Joss, dude, your body's slammin'."

Layla reached across Brady to smack him on the arm. "Bro, not helping! You don't want her to think you were all perving on her when she was passed out, now do you?"

Brady's smile dropped, his eyes widening in alarm. "No, Joss, you know I didn't mean it that way. We'd never—I'd never. I was just messing with you."

I waved away his concern. "I know, Brade. I'm just not in the mood to give you guys another show while we talk."

Brady relaxed, laughing easily. "And what a show you gave us, girl—"

Layla smacked him again before standing and shooing him out. She and Hunt followed. When Griffin lingered, I glanced up at him.

His gaze trailed across my face. "You really had me so majorly worried. Don't ever fucking do that again."

I chuckled darkly. "Well, I'd say 'sure,' but I don't really know what I did."

"Yeah, I know. Get dressed and we'll catch you up. You want me to get your clothes out for you?"

He seemed to recognize how exhausted I felt. I smiled up at him. "Yes please."

He rummaged through the chest of drawers, pulling out sleep shorts to start, obviously expecting me to keep resting. "Layla couldn't sit still while you were out. She put away all your clothes."

"Hmm, that was nice of her."

"Yeah." He spun. "You want a bra or not?"

I blinked at the unexpected question. Was this a best friend or a boyfriend thing to do? We were both, I thought, and there'd been too much dying and upheaval recently to figure out our new relationship.

I smiled gently, refusing to let myself feel awkward with the boy I'd known forever. "How about a camisole with a shelf-bra? Do I have anything like that?"

He was already pulling one out like there wasn't a single strange thing about him selecting my undergarments. "We would've dressed you before helping you into bed, but you were hurting so much and it was hard enough to get you out of the shower and into the room. We didn't even get you fully dried off before you fell into bed. It seemed worse to leave you exposed while we dressed you, so I just covered you up." His eyes grew heavier. "We had no idea you'd be out this long."

"I understand," I murmured, though I didn't. Not even a little bit. My friends seeing me naked was the least of my worries when I'd apparently lost control of my body and mind.

Not good. So not good. I was going to motherfucking kill Magnum for this.

Griffin placed my clothes on the bed and leaned over to press a lingering kiss to my head. Then he walked out, pulling the door shut behind him.

Despite my sluggishness, I dressed, peed, and brushed my teeth in record time. When I got a good look at my bare skin—and the totally batshit cray-cray going on there—the need for explanations snaked beneath my skin like desperation. My tattoos—the ones that weren't supposed to be able to just up and move, because, you know, they were *tattoos*—had freaking *up and moved*.

The many designs Layla had painstakingly etched across my skin were now different in size or location—or gone entirely.

Maybe I was still sleeping? Shit, I half hoped I was.

I was barely climbing back into bed when I called for my friends to join me again. "And bring me water too, please! And Bobo!"

Hunt delivered a pitcher of water and was filling a glass for me when I pressed, "Where's Bobo? Is he okay? I remember him touching me when I was being, well, whatever the fuck that all was. Please tell me he's okay. And tell me more about what happened to your dad."

Hunt stared at me for so long that I started to get back out of bed, ready to rush off to save them somehow, though I had absolutely no idea what I could do to help.

But Hunt shook his head till I sat back down, swallowing thickly. "I really wish I could tell you that both my dad and Bobo are okay, Joss, really, I super fucking do. But I don't know if either of them are, and as far as I can tell, there isn't a single thing any of us can do to change that for the time being."

"What do you mean?" I asked, draining half my glass. God, I was so thirsty!

I stared up at him with imploring eyes. "Your dad's not . . . *dead*, is he? Tell me he's not. He can't be."

"No. At least, I don't think he is. He was unconscious when Magnum had him dragged off."

I sat up straighter. "Wait, you guys let Magnum take him?"

Griffin climbed up on the side of the bed to lean against the wall, while Brady and Layla lowered to the foot of the bed, settling in.

Brady said, "We didn't *let* Magnum do a damn thing." His eyes blazed. "He threatened us. It's the fucker's M.O. Threaten us till he gets us to do whatever crazy crap he wants."

Hunt raised one of the blinds and, gazing out the window, added, "Actually, he threatened my dad. Said if we didn't let him go, he'd kill him."

I gasped, though surely I couldn't have actually been all that surprised. Death and threats of death had quickly become our new way of life.

I didn't like it one stinking bit.

"When we still hesitated," Griffin said, "he upped the ante. Threatened to run enough voltage through you to power the entire campus."

"You knew I'd come back," I whispered.

Griffin and Brady were shaking their heads. Griffin said, "There's no guarantee, not that it'll happen every time. There's too much we still don't know about all that."

"Besides," Brady said, "you took longest to come back last time."

"Yeah," I said. "But I still came back."

When my friends just stared at me, their expressions terribly heavy, I chuckled awkwardly. "The whole deal with us being here is accepting that we're going to die over and over again." I swallowed the lump building in my throat.

"We talked to Magnum about that," Griffin said. "We made a deal."

I whipped my head in his direction. "What kind of deal?" When he didn't answer immediately, I pushed, "*Griff*, what kind of fucking deal?"

"The kind where the rest of us die but you don't."

"What?" I looked to the rest of my friends as I laughed like this was all some big fucking joke. If it was, it was the worst joke in the entire universe.

My friends all wore somber expressions that made them seem years older than they were.

"You can't be serious! You actually expect me to just sit back and twiddle my thumbs while you all suffer the consequences of, well, shit, all this? Whatever the fuck *this* is? 'Cause I'm gonna be real here, guys, I truly don't know anymore, and that's assuming I ever had a clue, which I really don't think I did."

"Yes," Griffin said. "You heard Hunt's dad. He said you're different."

"But he didn't say I was different in that I could actually die. Or did he? I actually don't remember all that much after the guy shot him up with the lightning . . . juice . . . stuff. And so I don't keep sounding like a total moron talking about this, what've you all been calling it?"

"We haven't been calling it anything much," Layla said, deadly serious for once. "Just lightning. Haven't been in the mood to talk much given that we have an uninvited audience to everything we say."

As one, the five of us shot accusatory glares at the electronic panel inside my bedroom.

I started: "None of this would be stuff Magnum doesn't know."

"Nope," Hunt said. "The issue is that the asshole isn't telling us shit. He expects us to plaster smiles on our faces while we keep playing along with his stupid little games when he lies to us and doesn't tell us diddly squat. He's obviously messing with our lives just so he can become some glorified superhero or some other insanity. The fucker's ruining lives left and right so he can play dress-up!"

I glanced up at Hunt, who remained standing by the window. "Do you know why your dad was here?"

He stuffed his hands into the pockets of his jeans and sighed. "No. I don't know anything beyond what you saw. Once they started shocking him, he didn't say anything else you didn't hear."

"Will you be allowed to see him again?"

He shrugged. "Magnum said *maybe* I'd be able to, if we do what he asks."

"Generous as always," I muttered, drinking the rest of my water. I took a deep breath to steel myself, already knowing I wouldn't like their answer. "And where's Bobo?"

Griffin crossed his legs into a lotus position and leaned his head back against the wall my bed was pressed up alongside. "Last we saw, he was on your thigh."

I laughed. "No, seriously, where is he?"

Griffin just stared pointedly at the outline of my body beneath the blanket.

I looked at Layla.

"He ain't shittin' ya, girlfriend. Seems like he should be, I know, but nope. It's like we're on a 'shroom trip and it's turned bad and now we can't do anything but wait it out and hope we come out the other side in one piece."

"'Shroom trip does track with the shit I saw," I muttered as I flung off the duvet to reveal my legs—

My attention whisked across the tattooed skin of my thigh.

I felt my eyes widen and my mouth drop open before my mind properly registered what I was looking at. A tattoo, yes. But . . .

I blinked, I stared, and then I blinked and stared some more.

But the scene didn't change.

From my right thigh, where a year ago Layla had inked a pair of frogs guarding a crystalline pyramid just their size, bordered in psychedelic mushrooms, now a tattoo Bobo smiled up at me instead. His tongue lolled out of his mouth as his lips spread into his goofy wide grin as his tail wagged behind him—across my knee.

"What. The. Fuck?" I breathed.

"Pretty much sums up what we thought of it too," Layla said. "Sure as shit didn't see that coming, I'll tell ya that much."

"What the fuck?" My voice was squeaky. "Guys, are you also seeing Bobo moving around and hanging out on my frigging *leg*?"

"Can't help but," Layla said. "I actually watched him gobble down the frogs, pyramid, and shrooms. I'm thinking maybe he morphed into them, or something? They seriously don't write manuals for this shit."

My eyes strained to stretch wider. "Please tell me Bobo's not about to start tripping balls on my leg." I shook my head across the pillow. "You know what, guys? I've just figured it out. I'm dreaming, that's it. Somebody wake me the fuck up already."

"You know," Hunt said in that way of his when he was about to spout some scholarly shit, "communal dreaming is believed to be a possible thing."

"Then let's all wake up," Brady said. "Go back to before the Fischer House party."

Hunt finally turned to face us, taking a seat in the corner armchair. "Even if communal dreams are possible, this isn't one of them."

"How can you be so sure?"

"Because I've already tried everything I've ever read about that's supposed to wake you up from dreams. Besides, if you die in a dream, you wake up in real life. Either that, or you die in real life if your mind believes that the body is actually dead."

He slumped farther into the chair, crossing his hands over his waist. "This is all too real."

I studied Bobo some more. His mouth was moving as if he were barking, but he made no sound. He wagged his tail some more. At least he seemed happy enough.

I sensed a butterfly a moment before it fluttered over to Bobo, landing on his nose. When I thought it would fly away, it did, and Bobo chased after it, growing smaller as he appeared to put distance between me and him.

While he was still an ink figure on the skin of my thigh.

And Layla had tattooed no butterflies on me anywhere.

"This has gotta be a bad trip," I muttered to myself, still desperate to make sense of the situation that made no damn sense no matter which way I examined it. "Do you think I need to . . . feed him in there? In here?"

I shook my head at the absurdity crossing my lips but didn't bother commenting on it again. My friends were definitely not missing how crazy life had gotten for all of us.

"Seriously, dude, who the hell knows?" Layla said. "Just keep an eye on him. He seems fine for now."

"At least now you don't have to worry about Magnum using him against you," Brady said. "Silver linings, you know?"

I leaned my head onto my pillow and allowed my eyes to close for a few breaths. Bobo was prancing across my skin, just the outline and some simple shading, and I didn't feel a thing.

"Do we know exactly how he got in there?" I asked.

"I watched it happen," Griffin said, and I opened my eyes to look at him. "When you touched Hunt's dad, and that guy's zappy lightning jumped over to you, Bobo touched you, and when he did, he just kind of got sucked onto your skin. One second he was standing outside of you like usual, the next . . ." Griffin gestured to my leg. "Talk about freaking the rest of us the hell out."

"And where did the clothes I was wearing then end up?"

Brady huffed. "What do you want those for? They reeked. You were right to want a shower, even if you did just about give us a heart attack trying to get you out of it before it fried you alive."

"So that memory was real. *Sweet*. How did the current reactivate or whatever? I majorly need more accurate ways to describe all this stuff that's happening to us."

"No kidding." Hunt's eyes were grave. "*We don't know*. Apparently, that's the theme of our lives lately." He frowned severely. Nothing bothered Hunt, the one with a beach-ball-sized sponge for a brain, more than not knowing. "But when we meet with our academic instructors, I'm going to ask to learn about everything that has even the slightest chance of affecting us. Magnum agreed meeting them could wait till you recovered."

"So, my clothes?" I asked.

Layla waggled her brows obnoxiously at me in a blatant message. "I grabbed them." For good measure, she also winked.

"Got it," I said, in a hurry to stop her gestures which were so exaggerated she could have starred in an early silent film. "You know, I thought I wanted to wait to grab some fresh air, but now I think it'll do me a lot of good."

Griffin leaned forward. "Are you sure you're up for it? It looked like you took some major voltage—twice."

Layla said, "I'm surprised our girl can string two words together."

Fuck my life. I smiled tightly. "I'll be fine if I just go slowly. I really just want the fresh air and to think things over."

One by one, I looked at my friends, trying to silently broadcast to them, *Bring your notes.*

We still knew pretty much jack squat. I was beyond over it.

With Griffin's arm wrapped around my waist to steady me, we trudged beyond the pretty flower garden and its perfect clusters of outdoor seating until nothing surrounded us but wild forest.

"If they're watching us all the way out here," Brady said, "then there's really no escaping them, and we should just accept that we're as fucked as fucked gets and move on with our lives as best we can, being Magnum's fucking puppet bitches."

After a squinty-eyed scan of the forest, Brady added, "Now, guys, whip 'em out so we can compare 'em."

When the four of us jerked our heads in his direction, he cackled. "Not our dicks, you dirty fuckers. The notes, obviously."

"Obviously," Layla muttered, but her eyes danced in delight. She and Brady were definitely twins when it came to a crass sense of humor and ill-timed jokes. It was part of their highly dubious charm.

As Layla handed my note to me, still folded, still unpleasantly damp, I asked, "Have you guys looked at yours yet?"

"No," Griffin said. "We decided to wait for you."

"Even though it might've helped with something?" I asked him.

"Yes. We've been a united team forever. Not about to change that up now."

Hunt nodded. "We waited. But I'm super curious, so let's not wait any longer."

The five of us set to unrolling our tightly folded scraps of paper. I moved slowly with mine, relieved to find Jude's familiar cramped handwriting scrawled in pencil instead of ink. It was faded and difficult to read, the letters tiny to maximize space, but at least the words hadn't smeared. With some patient deciphering, it was all still there.

My dearest Joss,

I hope that someday you'll learn to forgive me for the many lies I told you. I promise, I only ever did all I did because I genuinely, with all my heart, believed it was the only way to help you. We had to get you out of the lab. Things were really bad already, and they were only getting worse. Remember when we admitted to cutting off the stalks of plants to see how quickly they'd regrow? I'll just say this: It wasn't plants. I'm too ashamed to say more. We decided we had to do something. When our boss told us the lab was going to close and we were to euthanize you all, we took you and ran.

Magnum Chase wants to become an immortal. He's convinced many of his staff that he intends to cure disease the world over with his findings. He says he intends to eradicate poverty and suffering around the globe.

But he will stop at nothing and will use anyone he thinks will help him to achieve his ultimate goal. It's not just to become a man capable of living forever, but also to be the most powerful man alive. He doesn't want just immortality, as if that weren't enough: he wants it all. Like in the superhero movies you used to love watching when you were younger. Picture that. He wants actual superpowers.

When the Aquoians refused to give him the information and biological material he wanted, he took them by force. And he started looking elsewhere for other legends of what I've come to consider "magical powers." He searched especially in the ancient tribes that still preserve some of their previous ways of life. We believe he didn't stop there, that he's searched the world for more hints of abilities that science cannot explain.

Even though science can't properly explain a condition as remarkable as immortality, it can confirm it. Joss, my sweetheart, I fear what might come of his continued insistence on forcing a natural, though mysterious, condition into a box of science. As much as it pains me to admit, there are some abilities beyond the scope of my beloved science.

There is so much we need to discuss. If you'll learn to trust me again, we can help each other. I fear that Magnum will want to experiment on you. A man like him will never take the risk of absorbing the totality of the powers he wants before testing them. You already have immortality. He'll next want to test if we can add more powers to your arsenal. He wants it all, but not at the risk of unexpected side effects to his person.

Don't worry, my Jossy girl. We'll figure it out together. Just be careful. We're all being watched. We'll have to be discreet.

I love you with all my heart. Please don't ever doubt that.

Even if it's just in my heart,

Your Dad

20

I'm Harmless and I'm Here to Help

I'd barely had time to register that Jude was a total sap, and that my friends seemed to have received notes with similar apologies and warnings, when footfalls crunched through the forest.

Bobo launched himself front and center across my thigh to bark out a warning none of us could hear. Hurriedly, I urged him to hide beneath my clothing so whoever was approaching wouldn't see him. I couldn't tell if he responded to my spoken commands or to my frantic gestures, but either way, he obeyed. Bless my sweet boy and his constant obedience, no matter how unlikely the situation.

As my friends hid their notes, I stuffed mine down into my cleavage before Fanny, along with several armed guards, came tromping toward us.

"What are you doing out here?" Fanny shouted ahead. "We were worried."

"Yeah, right," Layla snorted so only we could hear. "Worried when you lost sight of your precious, obedient pets, more like." Her lips twisted. "Wait, erase that. Forget I ever called us the dipshit's pets. *Yuck*. I'd rather die than be his pet."

"Well," Brady said with a scowl directed at Fanny and the others as they continued advancing, "let's hope that choice isn't about to be on the table."

Fanny plodded awkwardly across the uneven forest floor. "Joss, you should still be in bed."

"Sure, and whose fault is that?" I asked.

Fanny pretended I hadn't said anything against her perfectly twisted boss or about the person he'd wielded as a weapon.

"You need to be checked out before you have the all-clear to move about."

"I'm fine," I told her. She was now fifteen feet from us and closing in. "Just needed some fresh air."

"It's non-negotiable. Part of the agreement of you getting to live and study at this beautiful campus and in this beautiful house completely free is that you're to show up for your check-ups when they're required."

"Uh, we didn't make such an agreement," Brady said. "Not quite like that, anyhow," he mumbled.

Up close now, with half a dozen armed security guards surrounding her—none of whom I recognized—Fanny's face was flushed, her eyes jumpy. "Joss, I need you to come with me right now. It's urgent that I get you to the lab."

Griffin, Hunt, and Brady silently shored up to stand in front of me. Layla rolled her eyes at our guys and leaned her head to whisper to me, "When will they ever learn we don't need their protection? Jeez."

"Maybe when I haven't recently had the crap zapped out of me?" I muttered back as Brady told Fanny, "She's not going anywhere right now."

"She is." With two fingers, Fanny waved a pair of soldiers forward. They drew their sidearms and pointed them at us. "Your only choice is: we do this the easy way, or we do this the hard way.

Personally, I don't care which you choose. I've had quite the day already, and I think I might just appreciate the opportunity to vent some of my frustration."

"By killing a bunch of teenagers?" I hissed before I realized I was going to. "This pointing guns at us is getting *real* old, lady. You should be fucking ashamed of yourself. You told us you were some cool, fun aunt who just wanted to help us. Fuck you for thinking you have the right to treat us this way. Where's your sense of human decency?"

Fanny stared back at me, her rising anger coloring her neck until it matched the pink of her cheeks. "I'm doing this *for humanity*, you entitled, selfish, narrow-minded brat! You could be offering yourself up for study to rid humanity of all its suffering and torment. But *nooooo*, we need to threaten you to do the right thing, because if not, you can't be bothered." Her voice pitched to a mocking taunt, and I half wanted to punch her straight in the face. The other half understood that, if she actually believed that crap, Magnum had brainwashed the fuck out of her.

"You're coming with me right now," she snarled with a curl of her lip that made her appear feral, so unlike the façade of the professional, composed woman we'd first met.

Griffin wove his arm through mine. "She's not going anywhere without us."

Fanny glared at him until her eyes shone, revealing the crazed maniac I was starting to see she was. Then she jerked her hand in the air between us. "Fine. But you'll all be getting checked too, then. We need all the data we can get to speed things up."

"Speed what things up, exactly?" Hunt asked.

She whipped her head in his direction—just to better sneer at him, apparently. "And I was told you were the smart one."

Hunt's brows arched. "You weren't well informed then. We're all highly intelligent."

She *tsked*. "Not smart enough to see that the five of you have the power to fix every wrong in the world." Without so much as glancing my way, she pointed at me. "Her especially."

"Wait," I said. "Why me especially?"

Fanny smiled and batted her lashes, taking her taunting—for whatever reason—to the next level. Now I *really* wanted to punch her.

"You're somewhat different from the others," she eventually answered. "Which is why you need to get to the lab immediately so we can figure out all the ways you are. Now, final warning. Move out or we'll move you out."

Layla grabbed my free hand and started leading me back toward the house, Griffin walking with us, his hold on my arm tighter than before.

"Damn, lady," Layla called over her shoulder at Fanny, "you're a real psycho bitch. You know that, right?"

Fanny didn't bother to answer as Hunt and Brady fell into line behind us, the armed soldiers still pointing guns at our backs.

Apparently, just another Tuesday around here.

Though I still didn't understand pretty much any of the nuttiness that was going on with Bobo, he seemed to comprehend my verbal commands. I'd stared at him across my thigh—yep, that wasn't getting any less weird—told him there was "danger" and that he was to "hide." Instantly, he'd run up my leg—still ever so strange, especially since I didn't feel a thing—leapt over another of my tattoos, and then scrambled to hide under my shirt.

Even so, I'd dressed in jeans and a long-sleeve t-shirt to make sure no one saw him. I had no idea what Magnum and the zealot Fanny would make of him wandering my epidermis, and I had no intention of finding out.

Though my friends and I were firmly inside the lab, Fanny stood watch with several of her sentinels, as if we'd shimmy out the shoebox-sized windows and make a run for it. Even if we did manage some miraculous escape from the heavily monitored lab, Magnum and his staff of loony goons were making it all too clear there was nowhere we could go that they wouldn't retrieve us from.

Once again, I sat atop a stool at Jude's workstation, only this time Lynne stood beside him as he dutifully checked my vitals. Lynne leaned against the counter, very much in the way of Jude's keyboard, which he needed to input my results. When she crossed her arms and ankles, settling in, I realized she was deliberately blocking the nearest camera along the ceiling line.

Jude didn't even glance at her, proceeding with my examination as if nothing were amiss, showing me once again how very good at acting the two of them were. No wonder none of us had suspected a single thing over the years. They were so smooth; they were like superspies.

When Jude leaned in to examine my face, actually measuring the breadth and height of my features—merely for show, I hoped—he spoke softly and without moving his lips, making him sound like a ventriloquist. Still, it was far from the weirdest thing that had happened to me so far today.

"Don't react to me speaking," he said in that very bizarre, stilted way. "They can't know I'm talking to you when they can't hear."

"Mmmm-hmmmm," I hummed without moving my lips.

He shone a light across my eyeballs next. "Things are about to get worse. Magnum's worried about something big. He's moving the timeline up."

"Timeline of what?" I asked. Unlike him, I hadn't practiced ventriloquism. I sounded like a toddler with a lisp and no good handle on consonants. But he got the message.

"Not sure. Think someone maybe found out what he's doing."

"This is taking too long," Lynne complained, picking up the blood pressure cuff and telling Jude, "Trade places."

Jude huffed at her in annoyance but did as she asked, likewise positioning himself to block the view from the nearest camera. He pretended to reach for a pen, using the movement to ensure Fanny and the soldiers remained by the door.

Smooth operators indeed. My faux parents would have me fooled if I were Fanny.

Lynne bent over the blood pressure cuff, allowing the sheet of her loose hair to obscure much of her face. Even staring at her mouth, I didn't see it so much as twitch when she said, "No time. Need to help."

What the fuck? Had they taken ventriloquism classes while I was at school? Dudes were freaking pros.

"Restore your memories while you still can. Okay with you?" she asked.

What, *now* they were asking for consent? That was fresh—and also appreciated.

I nibbled at my bottom lip. I had a metric shit-ton of questions about that, and I couldn't ask a single one without possibly giving away what they were doing. But I couldn't just say *yes* without knowing more either. Were these potentially missing memories what Brady's nightmares had been all about?

Think, Joss, think.

"Can I ask some questions about some of the upcoming experiments I'm guessing you'll be doing on me?" I asked in a normal voice.

Lynne met my stare, her eyes sharp. She understood what I was asking. "Sure, honey," she said, also normal, for our surveillance. "Anything I'm allowed to tell you, I'll be happy to."

"Well," I fumbled. "I actually have no idea what you guys are planning on doing to us. What are the possible risks and side effects of some of these procedures?"

"Oh," Lynne said with a smile that conveyed: *I'm harmless and I'm here to help.* I had to swallow a snort. "All of what we do here is cutting-edge and exploratory. No one else in the entire world's doing what we're doing. But this team's truly the very best and the most capable of doing any of this, including Jackie, who is absolutely a top expert on the brain." She paused so that last point would linger and settle in.

Brady and Layla's pretend mom was indeed supposed to be the foremost expert not just on the brain, but on its memory functions in particular. Whatever process Lynne and Jude were offering up to restore the memories they'd stolen from me originated with Jackie. Did that mean the same offer was being made to my friends?

I glanced at them, spread out across the lab, and noticed nothing beyond the expected examination from their faux parents.

Lynne pressed a stethoscope to my chest beneath my shirt. With her face so close to mine, she continued for our audience.

"Everything has an intrinsic risk because this is an entirely new, unexplored part of science, which is what makes it so incredibly exciting. But I promise you, we've done absolutely everything within our power to minimize any possible risk or side effect of every single procedure we'll ever perform. Plus, thanks to Magnum's funding, we have every possible piece of state-of-the-art equipment we could need."

Jude piped up: "We promise, honey, we'd never recommend a procedure or test for you if we didn't truly, with all our hearts, believe it was the best path for you and the others."

He sure was throwing around this "all our hearts" shit a lot lately.

Softly, reverting to ventriloquist-speak, Lynne added, "It's gonna be rough. A lot of info coming in for you all at once." She moved the stethoscope around my chest, her hand beneath my shirt. "But this may be our only chance. And you need to know, if you're going to fight back."

Fight back? Surprised, I jerked my stare to hers. Immediately, she rolled the stool away, taking the stethoscope with her. She sat next to where Jude now stood, neither of them showing any sign they'd be moving closer again. Their message was clear. If they pushed it more, someone would suspect—and if someone would suspect when they'd been this careful, this pristine in their performance, then we were being monitored even more carefully than I'd imagined.

It was a big decision to make, and surely it would have been wise to measure the pros and cons carefully, to really study the risks.

But everything about our stay at the new *Institute for the Advancement of Immortals* was a risk. Magnum was open about his intentions to kill me and my friends. I'd bet everything I had to my name, including the bones of Cleo, my soon-to-be-beautiful-and-purring 1999 Ford Mustang SVT Cobra Coupe, that this place was designed entirely for the purpose of advancing Magnum's desires to achieve superhero status. All risks to us were acceptable to him on his way to gaining what amounted to paranormal abilities.

Normal risk assessment went out the window. These weren't normal times. We weren't dealing with a normal man or his normal goals.

I saw only one reasonable path forward, and it actually felt quite unreasonable.

As Jude removed the cuff from my arm, I asked them, "Okay, so what's next? I felt pretty crappy after being zapped by that lightning light stuff."

Jude put on a smile that said, *I'm compassionate and I'm paying attention to you.* Ventriloquist style, he whispered, "He's gonna steal powers. More students arriving. He'll take. You must be ready."

"Do you have something that could help me feel better?" I asked. "I understand the risks of new procedures."

Jude and Lynne looked at each other. Lynne actually brought a hand to her chin as she feigned considering what procedure they could do to help and study me next.

Jude scratched his neck, as if distractedly, before suggesting to Lynne, "Hmmm, maybe something along the lines of hypnotherapy? To diminish the trauma of the incident?"

Lynne tipped her head this way and that before shrugging. "Yeah, that might help. Plus, then we'll get more insights into how her brain reacts to interaction with the powers of others." I was guessing Lynne was dangling that tidbit to win over Magnum.

"It could give us data on how different powers can assimilate in a subject's brain," she added.

Jude's eyes widened. "Wow, Lynne. That's a great idea." He stood. "Let's get it set up with Jackie right away. It'll help Joss, and we're bound to learn something new."

When Jude and Lynne continued the charade by leading me into an adjacent room, I followed. But when they guided me to lie down as Jackie entered, nerves pulsed under my skin.

Ultimately, I didn't trust them. I might trust them a smidge more than Magnum, Fanny, and their trigger-happy security force, but only because at least I didn't believe our faux parents actually wanted to watch any of us die.

As a standard, it wasn't all that impressive.

"I want at least one of my friends in here with me," I said. "Someone to look out for me."

"We'll look out for you," Jude said, his eyes as earnest as I'd ever seen them. But dude had also just proven he was an amazing actor, worthy of a freaking Oscar.

I met the earnestness in his gaze. "Griffin, Hunt, Layla, or Brady, any of them will do. But I'm not doing a single thing more unless one of them's in here with me."

"Well?" Lynne snapped at Jude. "Go get one of them. Seconds matter right now."

And with that, Jude rushed from the room even as Lynne dimmed the lights to prepare me for a process I guessed I wasn't near ready for.

Apparently, when it came to our lives recently, we learned like baby chicks did. I was about to be pushed from the nest to see if I could fly.

Within minutes, Jude returned with all four of my friends—along with the rest of the pretend-parents. They all squeezed into the windowless room that had felt spacious enough moments before, but now was crammed full of people.

"We have to hurry," Jackie said, gesturing them to shut the door behind them and then fiddling with some dials on an odd-looking sound system and plugging headphones into a port.

She was already extending the headphones to me where I lay atop a padded medical bed. I sat up to stare at my friends even as Jude tucked a thin blanket around me. "Watch my back."

Layla huffed. "Dude, obviously. But what the fuck's going down here?"

The *parents* looked at each other, cracks showing in their usual cool façades. Finally, they all looked at Jackie.

Her eyes widened as an idea plainly dawned. "Joss is going to undergo a proprietary sort of hypnosis I developed that will help her accept any new adjustments to her powers. I've prerecorded a quick explanation of what's going to happen to put her at ease with the procedure. Here, sweetheart, why don't you have a quick listen while I finish getting Joss ready? We don't have much time before you have to head to your classes."

As far as I knew, we weren't going to classes today. But I lay back down as the already low lights dimmed further, probably to make it more difficult for the cameras to make out our expressions. First, Layla listened. Then, eyes wide as saucers, she passed the headset to Hunt, who passed it to Griffin, who in turn handed it off to Brady.

When all of my friends had listened to whatever Jackie had recorded, they looked to each other and to me, then Hunt announced for them, "We're doing it too."

Immediately, Jackie shook her head. "There's not enough time today. We—"

Brady stepped forward. "*Mom*, make it happen. This hypnotherapy to feel better about the process will help us too."

When Jackie hesitated, he added, "I know you can make it happen."

Jackie winced but then jerked her head at the other adults. "I need a headset for each of them that can be jacked in, and audio jack splitters. Mark, there are some in my bottom drawer."

As the adults hurried out the door to fetch the required items, Jackie told my friends. "There isn't time to get you properly set up—we don't want you to be late for your classes. So if you still want to do this, lie down on the floor and position your heads close to the sound system so you can be plugged in."

Griffin stalked over to lie right beneath my bed so he could reach me if he needed to, and the others plopped down beside him.

"Who's gonna have our backs though?" I asked them.

Jackie was the one who answered. "*Us*. We're going to have your backs. No one's going to hurt you while you're under." She was so ferocious about it that I actually believed her.

Besides, our choices were, yet again: A: shit. B: shittier. C: royal shitstorm. And D: all of the above.

As the adults rushed back in with the supplies, so did Tracy.

"What the hell's going on here?" she demanded.

As one, the adults visibly calmed for her benefit—fucking masters of illusion they were.

Jackie smiled beatifically at Tracy. "I'm doing a group hypnotherapy session to help ease the trauma of Magnum having the subject apprehended in front of them. I'm not sure if you're aware, Tracy, but Joss was also hit by that beam. She slept for three days after, and they're all a bit shaken from the experience. I'm going to smooth things over for them and, while I'm at it, also smooth the path for future experiences that have the potential to be traumatic for them. Give them more coping abilities for what's to come, so to speak."

Jackie sounded like an infomercial. Calm, collected, and convincing.

Tracy peered at the scene with suspicion. "I'm going to call Magnum."

Jackie's beatific smile barely faltered as it spread across her face. "Of course. I'm sure he'll be happy to learn what we're doing here."

The very instant Tracy prowled off to tattle, Marisa closed the door and locked it.

Jackie lined her face up directly over mine on the bed, as if she might be about to kiss me on the cheek. She breathed, "I have to delete the explanation the second you hear it. You're going in right now. Keep your eyes shut at all times."

Then, before I could so much as squeak in reply, her voice, pitched to be soothing, rang out through the headphones.

"*When I altered your early memories, I didn't delete them. I simply built a pathway that bypassed them and then constructed other memories along that bridge to replace the ones you no longer accessed. What I'm going to do now is delete the bypass. What will remain are your original true memories of your early childhood, before we got you out of the lab and went into hiding with you. Since time is of the essence and we want this process to stick, I'll be injecting you with a drug I developed that makes you susceptible to suggestion and will rapidly lull you into a theta state. Don't resist the process. It will be painless, though it will likely still be shocking as you adjust to the reality that we've kept hidden from you all these years. Be gentle with yourselves afterward. It's a big adjustment. Now, let's begin.*"

I felt the cool wipe of what I guessed was an alcohol swab, then the prick of a needle.

Within moments, I felt my breath deepen, my muscles relax, and then I knew nothing at all.

21

More Hyde than Jekyll

Awareness swooped in, and it took several groggy, disoriented moments to recall where I was and what I was supposed to be doing.

Right. Hypnosis.

Kind of, anyway. Whatever it was, the process would be Jackie's modified version of it.

Was it over already? I didn't feel any different, but I guessed that was the point. The adjustments happened in the unconscious mind.

When I attempted to open my eyes, my lashes rubbed against soft, slick fabric. One of the pretend-parents must have found an eye mask for me after the process started. My arms rested beside me on the med bed beneath a warm blanket. I was so cozy I didn't want to move.

"You think that disrupted the process?" my dad whispered softly yet insistently.

"No, no, I'm sure the quake wasn't enough to interrupt the signal," answered Brady and Layla's mom. "The reprogramming is proceeding as normal. The recording still has nearly half an hour to go."

And yet, no sound was coming through the headphones still pressing against my ears. I prepared to open my mouth to let them know—but *wait*. *Not* my dad. *Not* my friends' mom.

We were trusting the proven liars to get a leg up on the "devil we know." Good God, when had life turned to such shit?

"You're a hundred percent sure?" Jude pressed.

Jackie *tsked*. "Of course I am, Jude. How many times have we done this to them already? You'd think you'd trust me by now."

"I do trust you," he whispered. "It's just that it really needs to take."

She tutted. "Of course it's going to take. It *always* takes. They always believe everything from the procedure without a single problem. And you can talk normally, you know. They won't absorb a thing we're saying."

Suddenly I was twitchy all over and eager to rip off my headphones, flip them all the finger—double-fister, for good measure—and get myself and my friends the hell out of there like rabid hounds were chomping at our heels.

Instead, I made very sure that my breathing remained deep and steady, and that I did nothing that might reveal I could indeed hear every single traitorous thing the rat-turd bastards were saying.

"You and Lynne must've put on quite the show to get Joss to agree so readily," Jackie said conversationally, sounding like she was preparing to chat it up to pass the time till the recording ended. "She's usually much more resistant."

"Yeah, well," Jude said, "I really hope this is the last time we ever have to do this. It's getting harder and harder to pretend with them."

"Really? I find that every time it gets easier. I've gotten to the point that it's almost easier to believe the lie than the truth. Though it doesn't help that Magnum keeps making us mix things up. It does get tricky to remember some of the details. Like this time, he wants to try Joss and Griff remaining just friends, and for Zoe to get closer to Hunt. They're supposed to be dating this time. And the kids are supposed to think his nephew Rich is a nice guy." She snorted softly but didn't follow up, suggesting that even though she was unaware I was hanging on to her every crappy word, she didn't believe she had the same immunity from Magnum's pervasive observation.

"And Magnum's going to be a long-time family friend, right? He was a TA grad student when we were all undergrads. That's the story?"

"You did read the memo, right?"

"Of course I did," Jude said huffily. "How else would I know the details? Come on, Jackie. Don't treat me like I'm a novice at this. Just making sure I have it all straight. It really is a lot to keep track of when the stories keep switching."

Holy fuckballs, how many times had they altered our understanding of our lives and our pasts? Nausea roiled deep in my gut, and I had to force myself not to grimace. Only my eyes and ears were covered.

"That's all that's new this time though, right?" Jude pressed.

"I'll have to read through the memo again."

Jackie hummed as if distracted—perhaps checking her equipment. "Ah, yeah. Oh wait, no. They won't have any memory of Kitty Blanche."

"The reporter?"

"Yeah, she's gone."

Gone. Meaning six feet under, not on vacation, I was guessing.

"Good," Jude said. "She was a pain in the ass."

"For sure she was. I'm surprised Magnum let that go on for as long as he did before dealing with her."

"He had his reasons, I'm sure. He always does."

"Doesn't he just?" Jackie said. "As usual, they won't remember they died, and since none of their other powers revealed this time, we don't have to deal with any of that."

Other powers? OhmyfuckingGod, what other powers?

"So I guess that's it. Oh, nope, never mind. Just thought of something else. Griffin's getting a new car that'll look like one they worked on. They couldn't get his other one done in time. Too much damage from the crash."

"Makes sense."

Makes sense? *Makes sense?* I was ready to shank a bitch. Any one of the lying, two-faced assholes I'd believed to be our parents would do at this point. I wasn't going to be picky.

How could they? How *fucking* could they? This was so much deeper and worse than I'd ever imagined. This was next level shit, that's what this was.

Minutes of silence passed during which my rage grew to such levels that I had to focus on calming myself so my body's reactions wouldn't give me away.

Jude, sounding pensive, asked, "You really aren't bothered by all the lying?"

Jackie sighed loudly enough that I thought there might be a chance she was actually burdened by their awful behavior. "I used to be, at first. Now, it's just normal. At least we have plenty of good reasons for it."

"We do."

"That's what I think of any time Layla or Brady do something cute or loving. I just focus on the *why* of what we're doing, then I remind myself it's probably the only way to get them to do what we need them to do, so . . ."

So? That was it?

And *why*, for fuck's sake, WHY were they doing this? *Don't leave me hanging now, Jack-fucking-ie.*

Eventually, Jackie added, "But yeah, I hope this is the last time I have to do this too. It's going to happen at some point. Everything's going to eventually line up, so why not this time?"

"It'll be so incredible to finally get to move on to the next stage, after all this time," Jude said.

"We've devoted the last twenty-plus years of our lives to this. We deserve it."

They *deserve* it? I couldn't remember the last time I'd had to work so hard to resist the desire to kick someone's ass.

"We really do," Jude said, and I could feel the smile in his voice.

The fucking fuckers!

It was a good thing they weren't monitoring my vitals now, because they were certainly spiking.

The bed beneath me shook enough to make my limbs, purposely loose, wobble.

Jackie huffed. "What is going *on*? How long can it possibly take to immobilize one kid on his own? It's not like it's rocket science. I mean, come on already. You juice him or tranq him till he's out cold. It's not that complicated."

I was struggling to reconcile this woman and what she was saying with the Celia Rafferty I'd known growing up. Were the whole lot of them more Hyde than Jekyll?

"Maybe it's a different one," Jude suggested. "Magnum's been bringing new ones in fast."

"Hmm, maybe. Go find out what's happening."

"Why? I'm sure they're on it. They're not going to let any of them out on the loose."

"Because I don't want to have to re-drug the kids and start over. I've already dosed them pretty heavily to make them properly susceptible. If I do it again, they'll sleep forever."

Nothing, then Jackie insisted, "Go."

"The others are right there," Jude complained. But then I heard the door open and close anyhow.

My bed shook again, this time much harder. My blanket slid across my body as I restrained the natural urge to reach out and catch it before it could slip to the floor.

"What the shit?" Jackie muttered, again making it difficult to reconcile this cussing woman with innocent-looking Celia

Rafferty who enjoyed homemaking when she wasn't in the lab. Was any of it real? At this rate, probably not. For all we knew, in her spare time, Jackie might rock shiny black pleather and ball gags.

Yet another quake rattled my bed, and when it did, Jackie's voice, pitched to be soothing, suddenly sounded through the headphones in a lulling monotone.

"—preschool with Ms. Gail. Then I attended Ridgemore Elementary, then Ridgemore Middle School, and then Ridgemore High School, where my friends and I are currently seniors. I love the town of Ridgemore and have no desire to ever leave it. It feels happy and comfortable here. I love my home with my parents, Monica and Reece Bryson—"

Ah, so we each had our own individualized brainwashing recording. *Peachy*.

"—in the Periwinkle Hill neighborhood. It's the only home I remember. I love my parents and trust them implicitly. With them, I am safe. I trust their guidance."

How much of this hogwash drivel had my poor, abused gray matter been subjected to over the years?

On and on the recording droned, listing out basic facts of my life I'd long taken for granted—but never would again. The asswipes apparently didn't leave anything to chance. There were even comments about how much I enjoyed keeping up my physical fitness and eating my freaking vegetables. Was my love of brussels sprouts and lima beans all just another lie? I mean, seriously? What the actual fuck was wrong with these people?

Few facts differed from what I remembered—and I had no way to tell whether or not those were true memories. Jackie didn't mention our time at the lab at all. I had no way of knowing what scintillating tidbits of programming I'd missed out on while she and Jude discussed deceiving us as if it were any ol' ordinary part of their job.

I was coming to realize it was.

They were indeed superspies, ones with a fully outfitted laboratory primed for all sorts of evils, plus unlimited funding. A winning combination.

From what I was gathering from the partial hypnosis, we weren't to remember any of our time here at the facility, but would experience a new enthusiasm for attending the Institute for the Advancement of the Gifted, a new school soon opening in Ridgemore. *How lucky we were!* They were already planning how to get us back right where we were, just with a different backstory.

Before today, I hadn't believed I could grow any more shocked by our circumstances. How very, *very* wrong I'd been.

With minor—yet crucial—deviations, we were to proceed with life as normal. Unless our *parents* and Magnum had even more devastating secrets stuffed up their sleeves, we'd likely simply be biding our time until they killed us again. Only we were supposed to believe we were dying for the first time, and to experience that terrifying panic at the possibility of losing one of our dear friends forever.

These weren't scientists. They were monsters.

In the headphones, Jackie rambled on with a final litany of thoughts:

"I only practice safe sex and am very careful to avoid pregnancy." (If my mom's previous theatrics were to be believed, that was probably her addition.)

"I accept my parents' regular checkups as a normal part of my care."

"I never enter my parents' office when they aren't present."

"Ridgemore High School is lucky to have a newly built gymnasium for us to use. Magnum Chase is a generous donor and we appreciate all he does for our community. We're very fortunate he moved here years ago to share time with our families."

"When I wake, I will feel well rested. I will believe I went to sleep in my bed last night in my bedroom at home, as always. I will get up and go to school for the day. I will greet my friends as if no time has passed and everything is as it always has been."

I was in the middle of wondering how the *fuck* they were going to pull off this kind of production when no one in town was likely to forget the resurrection of the "Miracle Kids" anytime soon when, without warning, the blanket was pushed back to expose my arm and immediately something wet and cold swiped my arm. Another alcohol swab, I guessed too late, after I'd already flinched at the touch before instantly relaxing again. A stool swiveled with a soft whir of metal against metal as I focused on not holding my breath, on not doing anything else to indicate I was alert when I shouldn't be.

The whir came again, and then a pinch that told me I was getting another injection.

No one said anything, allowing me to hope that Jackie had already been mid-turn away from me to reach for the syringe when I jerked. If she was the only one in here with us, and it seemed like she was, and no one was reviewing the footage of us to catch my tell, I might've just gotten away with the first real advantage any of my crew had ever had.

Jackie's footsteps scuffed along the floor as she presumably injected my friends as well. My need to pretend ended as the second shot she gave me pulled me completely under, at the mercy of the devils we apparently didn't know at all.

22

No Drugged Bait-and-Switch Going on Here

I awoke to someone gently shaking me. In a groggy haze I wasn't feigning, I blinked open my heavy eyelids to find Jude's face close to mine.

He smiled at me like he had a million times before when I'd believed him to be my plain ol' loving dad. His hair was damp, his cheeks ruddy, like he'd recently returned from his morning run. Just an ordinary day at the Bryson household. No drugged bait-and-switching going on here . . .

Fuck. I had no idea how I was going to pull this off. At the best of times, I wasn't one to bite my tongue. And this was most definitely *not* the best of times.

"Hey, sweetheart," he said, as smooth as honey. "You overslept. It's time to get ready for school."

I realized I was gaping at him and hurried to rub my eyes and groan. "I don't wanna go." That, at least, was an easy truth.

He chuckled, so naturally that I questioned whether all of it had been a dream. Had I made up Brady's death at the Fischer House party and everything since? It was possible, wasn't it?

He rose from where he'd been sitting on my bed. "You say that practically every day. But Griffin'll be here to pick you up for school soon. You don't want to make him wait, especially not today." He gave me a meaningful look I had no idea how to interpret.

Especially not today, meaning the day after our "parents" fucked us in the ass and then tried to pass it off as familial bonding?

"What's up with you today?" he asked, putting me on alert that I needed to get my shit together and fast. "You never forget the anniversary of the day Mitzi skipped out on them."

Ohhhhh. The fake anniversary of the fake abandonment of Griffin's fake mother. *Gotcha.*

I sat up in bed, doing my best not to react to the fact that I was wearing familiar PJs which I had *not* had on when I was last awake. Who the hell changed my clothes while I was unconscious? What a violation. But then, it was all such a terrible violation, wasn't it?

Bobo was sleeping on top of the covers, along the length of my legs, and he let out a soft, comforting snore. So he was back to being my real dog? I stroked his exposed belly, and he cut off mid-snore. At least he was all real doggy love.

I had no clue how he'd gone from this flesh-and-blood companion to being a tattoo moving across my skin, and I had even less of an idea how he'd gone back to being his regular self.

I looked up at Jude. "Thanks for reminding me, Dad." I smiled more at the fact that I'd been able to get the endearment out without choking on it than anything else. "I must've been sleeping really hard when you came in. It's taking me a sec to catch up."

That should be believable to him. He alone was supposed to be aware that I was waking up from being motherfucking drugged and not just from some restful Zs.

I rose to walk into my ensuite bathroom, then returned with my toothbrush in hand—the same purple glittery one as before. "How's Orson doing?"

God, was I glad I hadn't adjusted to our faux parents' real names yet.

My dad paused at the threshold to my room, leaning on it as he gazed back at me. "Oh, you know." He shrugged, a movement I'd seen him make so many times I couldn't help but get swept up a little in the familiarity of the scene. "He's moping but trying to pretend he isn't. I don't think he'll ever get fully over Mitzi. She really took his heart with her when she left." He exhaled slowly. "Porter and I are gonna take him out for lunch and some beers. Take his mind off things. It's a good day to break our rules. Hey, it's always five o'clock somewhere, right?" He winked, like he was some cool dad joking around with his kid about how he overlooked our underage drinking.

A true laugh slipped free as I stuffed the toothbrush in my mouth to keep from having to say anything else. This was too weird. Too bizarre. Too quaintly comfortable.

Maybe it was all some giant . . . dream?

Psychosis?

Hallucination?

The very instant I hopped into Griffin's idling Mustang out front of my house, I knew without a doubt I hadn't dreamt a single thing.

"Hey, Joss," he said in that usual deep, grumbly voice that whisked across my skin like a full-body *hello*. But his eyes burned a fierce hazel as they held mine. They told me what his words wouldn't, courtesy of the hidden mics in our cars.

Our entire lives were a lie. And he knew it too.

Plus, Clyde was still a 1976 Ford Mustang Cobra II Coupe. Only instead of the silver I remembered, the car was a shiny black.

"Hey, Griff," I eventually answered. "Thanks for picking me up, especially today. Sorry your mom was such a shithole to leave you and your dad like she did."

He cruised down our long driveway, his eyes widening as they flicked to me. It looked like Orson hadn't delivered the day's scheduled prompt.

"I know it was years ago," I added, "but still. I'm sorry."

His throat bobbed. "Thanks. It's intense."

"Fuck yeah, it is." I was assuming he was referring to the many things we weren't openly discussing. "Have you talked to the others yet?"

Do they know too? Did the hypnosis recording cut out for all of us? And did we all successfully pretend it hadn't?

Since the recording had apparently cut off but then turned back on, it seemed likely that the hiccup had been with the audio system and not any of the individual headphones. I was *really* hoping we were all on the same page now. It would royally suck to have different memories and realities from the only people I truly trusted.

"Nope, no word yet," Griffin said. "No texts either."

Our phones had been confiscated. I'd found mine on my desk, fully charged.

I lowered the window and leaned my head back against the headrest, enjoying the rush of fresh air. That, at least, wasn't fake. "The day hasn't even really gotten started yet and I'm already wanting it to be over."

"Yeah, me too. Me too."

He shifted gears, then his hand stretched toward my thigh. At the last moment, when it already hovered over my body so that I could feel the heat of his skin, he reined it back.

We weren't supposed to be anything more than friends—by parental super-spy fucking decree.

I groaned obnoxiously and let my eyelids sink closed.

Fuck. My. Life.

After all these years of secretly pining for him, after we finally found the courage to come out about our feelings for each other, and we discovered our friends to be miraculously fine with it, now we had to hold back?

"Tell me about it," he grumbled in shared frustration, slamming his now free hand against the steering wheel.

When we pulled into the parking lot of Ridgemore High we found Brady, Layla, and Hunt already there, waiting for us beside Bonnie. Their eyes were wide as they took in the new color of Clyde, who we knew wasn't really Clyde at all. Gone was the Mustang we'd all worked on so lovingly for so many months.

Their reaction to the difference was all it took to release some of the tension I was carrying in my neck and shoulders. Whatever the next act of this shitshow would reveal itself to be, at least we were all in on it together.

"Thank fuck," I muttered under my breath as I got out of the car to find Griffin already at my door, ready to close it for me. I arched my brows at him, but he simply shrugged.

"Hey, chivalry's not dead."

I supposed he had always treated me a bit differently from the others, even Layla. His gaze had lingered, his touch had drifted in my direction as if of its own volition, his smile had lit his eyes. At least, from the last cycle of memories I had, this was how he'd behaved. It wouldn't arouse suspicion, and even if it did, fuck it, I wasn't ready to give up more of Griffin than this crazy situation was already obligating me to.

I smiled up at him, remembering how he'd told me he loved me. "Thanks." Now at least he knew I loved him back.

The wins weren't many, but they were there if I searched for them.

After the door shut behind me, his fingers traveled to my lower back, trailing softly along the one-inch stretch of exposed skin between my low-slung jeans and my cropped shirt.

My eyelids wanted to drift closed as I leaned into his touch. Just knowing I wouldn't be able to have it openly and with ease made me want to throw Griffin to the ground and have at him right then and there in the rapidly filling parking lot.

As if he could read my thoughts, his grip tightened with what felt like searing possession, and softly, so softly that no secret mic would pick it up, he moaned. All on its own, my body leaned back into him.

Layla cleared her throat. Through what felt like a haze, I dragged my attention over to her.

Her light eyes danced with awareness as she grinned at us. "Good morning, guys. We've been waiting for you."

Griffin gave them a guy-nod *hello* while I just stared at them all, fully back here with them now. I wanted to bellow out, "What the fuck are we supposed to do now?"

But none of us could openly share the panic that was undoubtedly scrolling through our minds.

It was so royally messed up.

Our invisible audience was possibly already on the edge of their seats, wondering if we were acting strange because something had gone wrong or if that's just how we were. We couldn't risk them trying to reboot us again. The next time, their hypnosis very well might stick and we'd be completely at their mercy again. Or maybe next time they'd do something worse, more difficult to overcome.

No, we had this one chance to figure this all out and come out on top. This one opportunity where we were in the know. We had to play our parts as convincingly as the *parents* did, even if the deception felt wrong.

"Whazzup, guys?" I said. "Looking forward to another day of boring classes?"

Were our classes the same as the last time we'd been in school, before we were gunned down? I'd have to keep things vague until

I could check my school schedule, which I typically kept in my planner in my locker. If my locker combo was different, we were screwed.

Brady chuckled darkly. "When am I ever looking forward to classes? I am looking forward to lunch though. And maybe a group run after school today? My legs could use a good stretch."

"Mine too," Hunt said.

"Yeah, I'm down," Layla added, even though she was the one most likely to complain about our group runs. When Hunt found his stride, he pushed to keep going. One time, he'd convinced us to do fifteen miles. Layla had never forgiven him for that.

But running outside was the one place where we could actually talk.

Unless we were chipped, like Hunt thought we might be, in which case we'd lost the game already. We *had* to be able to communicate without resorting to passing notes like we were in the third grade.

"It's a plan," I agreed, knowing Griffin would definitely be on board. "I'm also down for a good workout session with the dummy. I'm in the mood to hit something."

"Girl," Layla said, "I want to beat the fuck out of something. Or someone."

Brady somehow managed to get out a good-natured laugh that sounded so authentic I peered at him. "Aw, my little sister, always so fucking sweet."

"I'm not your little sister," Layla protested right away, as she'd done possibly a thousand times over the years. At least this was familiar territory that would put our eavesdropping *parents* at ease.

"You were born after me. That makes me the big brother. Or did you need me to help you figure out that math? Not simple enough for you?"

"Fuck you, Brade. You're only like five minutes older than me."

"Still older."

"Def not more mature though. Just means I'll get to call you an old fart."

"At your own peril," Brady threatened. His tone was convincing, as was Layla's, but their body language wasn't behind it. They were putting on a show to buy us time—but time for what? We *had* to have a way to communicate or we were never going to make real progress.

I was foreseeing *a lot* of running in our futures.

Hunt pulled his iPhone from his back pocket, tapped and swiped at the screen. "I've already shown Brade and Lay, but I wanna get your opinions too. I'm not sure what to answer. I don't want to mess up my chances here, but I also don't wanna just say yes."

"Dude," Brady said, "like I told you, she's already putty in your hands. Just keep playing it smooth and you're all good." But again, Brady's eyes weren't into it.

Hunt passed the phone to Griffin, and I huddled next to him.

Zoe Wills was in Hunt's contacts as "Zozo," a nickname I doubted he'd give her himself in a hundred years. Layla, sure—probably even. I might even go there if the girl and I became super close friends. But Hunt? Nope.

Now that we knew to look for signs of artifice, I suspected we'd find them everywhere.

Zozo: Hey babe, wanna hang tonight? 🐱
Me: Sounds great, babe. Pick you up at 7?
Zozo: Can't wait! 😉💋

I glanced up at Hunt, whose lips were pursed. Those text messages were supposed to have been from a couple of days ago. Griffin scrolled to reveal a whole long line of them going back an entire month before he stopped, brows raised in Hunt's direction.

"Not sure what to respond to her latest one," Hunt steered. "I'm obviously super into her." Which had to suck so badly for

Hunt, because I didn't think he really was. He'd liked her well enough, but if she was part of their master ruse, then how could he? And she had to be at this point, right? Or were our psycho pretend-parents hypnotizing other people too?

What a fucking quagmire.

Griffin scrolled back down to the bottom of the message thread. One came in from Zoe this morning.

Zozo: I think I'm finally ready to go all the way, babe. I want you to be my first more than I want to keep waiting. Date night tonight????? 🌶️👄👅🐝🦴🌿💥🌺🐲

Griffin and I glanced up at Hunt.

Layla scowled. "She's really laying it on thick there, right? No doubt about what she's gettin' after." Then, as if she all at once realized this wouldn't be her usual response, she added, "But hey, gotta give kudos to a bitch. She knows what she wants, and she's going after it. Lucky for Hunt, it's his sweet ass. What's even your hesitation, man? She's cute."

"She is cute, and I really like her, obviously." Since the phony-ass text messages on his phone were apparently proof of that. "But I kinda wanted to wait a bit more. You know, have it be *really* special."

What else was the poor bastard supposed to do but play the born-again virgin card? The faux parents were going to have him fucking a girl he didn't even love. That might've worked for someone like Brady, who was fond of chasing tail, but Hunt was different. He didn't want to just have sex, he wanted to make love. Which was why he'd only had sex a few times.

I'd purposefully not been vocal about how few times I'd actually done the deed myself. It was challenging to really get into some other guy when all I wanted was the one standing next to me. The one who, for so many years, had been off limits.

If Magnum or the *parents* had manipulated Griffin and me apart more than this one time, I was going to deliver an ass-kicking on a platter for that reason alone. I would have much preferred to share my first time with him than the dufus I had, *shit*.

Griffin was *the one* for me.

Griffin handed the phone to Hunt. "Then that's what you should do, dude. The right time with the right person really matters."

My skin buzzed as I couldn't help but feel he was also talking about us.

"Tell Zoe how you really feel, man," Griff went on. "Tell her you really like her, and you maybe will eventually want to share something so special with her. But you're not ready yet, and you don't know how long it'll take for you to be ready. If she's really into you, she'll wait however long you want and need. If she's not"—Griffin shrugged—"then she's not the right girl for you anyway, and fuck her."

"Just don't actually fuck her," Layla said with a bit of her signature mischief tipping up her lips. "'Cause that would really defeat the purpose of the whole 'I wanna wait' deal."

"Always such a help, Lay," Brady commented.

She twirled, framing her face with both hands and batting her lashes at him. "I know, right?"

Brady snorted, and this time I thought it was for real.

Even so, this charade was going to drive us all bonkers—me first. I knew it, they all knew it. I did not do well with holding back my true thoughts.

Layla perhaps even less so.

What we really needed was telepathy or some shit, one of these nebulous "other powers" Jackie had teased us with and then not revealed. Of all the times for her not to elaborate on a damn thought.

But hey, if we were all, you know, *immortals*—and that was totally, wholly, and absolutely in-fucking-sane—then maybe we could do other things, like speak to each other through our minds. Crazier things had already happened.

<Maybe all I've gotta do if I wanna tell Griff how fucking sexy he is and how much I wanna kiss him all over and then jump his sizzling bones is push the thought into his mind.>

Directing the thought outward while chuckling to myself at the absurdity of it, I glanced up—

Only to discover not just Griffin but all four of my best friends in the entire world gaping at me.

Hunt dropped his phone. It crashed to the asphalt of the parking lot. He didn't even look at it.

Their astonished stares were locked on me.

"What?" I asked.

23

It's Groundhog Day!

Layla shook her head in what appeared to be astonishment. "'What,' she says."

"Yeah, *what*? Why are you all looking at me like that?" I asked.

<*Because we all heard you being a total sap about Griff, my bestie bitch. You want to kiss him 'all over'?*> Her face puckered.

Despite my total awareness that we were almost certainly being monitored right now in some way or another, I couldn't keep my eyes from widening to the proportions of cartoon flying saucers.

My mouth dropped open until Griffin subtly elbowed me. I jerked my jaw shut before glancing up at him. His grin was devilish, drawing me closer.

<*You heard me too?*> Layla's shocked voice filtered into my mind as if it were my own inner dialog, but not quite. It sounded like her.

I whipped my head around to study her. <*Yeah, I can hear you,*> I attempted experimentally.

Layla's forehead scrunched into accordion lines with her mounting shock.

<*Can we . . . can we all hear each other?*> I asked.

<*I think so?*> Brady "said" in an uncharacteristically uncertain tone. <*Assuming you guys can hear me now?*>

<*I can,*> I said.

<*Me too,*> said Layla.

<*And me,*> added Griffin.

As one, we glanced at Hunt. <*Holy crap, you guys. This is actual fantasy-level shit. We're like Galadriel from* Lord of the Rings.>

I snorted. <*Not bloody likely.*>

<*How come you guys didn't seem to hear me earlier, then?*> Brady asked. <*I was trying to push thoughts into your heads before Joss did.*>

<*Dunno, bro,*> Layla said. <*Maybe you're just a weakling and you needed a girl to give you a boost.*> She shrugged as if she'd spoken aloud, snickering. <*That tracks, for me.*>

<*Guys!*> Griff said urgently, even as Brady's body stiffened at his sister's goading. <*We gotta be really careful here. If someone's watching us right now—and my money's on them being up our asses—then they'll know something's up if we keep being so obvious about having silent conversations.*>

So true. Shit. Now I was going to have to play a part for Magnum and our faux parents and *also* pretend not to be hearing my friends' voices in my head? I didn't have the self-restraint, discretion, or finesse for that. Layla had even less. And I didn't think Brady could pull it off either; he led with his reactions. Only Hunt and Griff had that quiet introspection down already.

<*They'll catch on fast,*> Griffin added, <*especially if this was one of the 'other powers' we displayed before. Even if it's new to us, they'll be on the lookout for signs of it, and whatever else.*>

<*Dammit, so true,*> I said.

"Fuck, I hope your phone screen didn't just crack, man," Brady told Hunt aloud to fill the suspicious silence we'd allowed to stretch.

"Yeah, me too," Hunt said, but made no move to retrieve his phone from where it had fallen.

"Hunt!" a girl's voice yelled, and as one we turned. It was Zoe.

"Hey," she called ahead with a smile as she bounded across the parking lot toward us, her backpack bouncing. When she reached us, she didn't bother with individual greetings, just wrapped both arms around Hunt's neck and pulled his face down for a kiss.

<*You're stiff as a board,*> Layla told him urgently through our apparent mental bond. <*Too obvious. Loosen up, dude.*>

Hunt's arms had been clamped to his sides, but now he wove them around Zoe's waist. His touch was still light, but it was definitely an improvement.

When it became evident Zoe was slipping Hunt tongue, and my friend's fingers were clenching and unclenching behind her back, Layla whistled obnoxiously before patting Zoe on the back.

"Whoa, Zo. Lay off a bit there, will ya? We need you to leave some of Hunt there so he can make it to class." She snorted a laugh that to my ears was fake, but I doubted Zoe would notice.

Zoe pulled back with a lick of her lips but left her arms looped around Hunt, gazing up at him dreamily. "Good morning, handsome. You're looking especially hot this morning."

Hunt blinked away the deer-in-the-headlights look that wanted to creep up on him and forced a smile to his glistening lips. "Thanks. You look . . . great too."

<*Oh, nice one,*> Layla said. <*How'd you come up with that smooth line?*>

I realized at once we were all in even more trouble than we'd thought. Now we'd have Layla heckling us inside our minds too? Talk about a mega distraction when we definitely needed to keep our shit together and all our stories aligned. But I already knew she wouldn't be able to help herself. Layla would be Layla, even when playing the part of herself.

Zoe, appearing unbothered by Hunt's modest enthusiasm, continued to gaze up at him with evident adoration.

"You're such a sweetie," she told him. Her hands traveled from his neck to his shoulders, then his arms, where she squeezed. "Did you, um, did you get my text?"

Right. The one where she wanted to bone our friend to carry out some orchestrated ruse. Talk about a violation for Hunt. This took our situation to a whole new level of fucked-upness.

I shuddered, drawing a questioning look from Griffin. <*Just wondering what else our pricks for parents have done to us that we don't know about.*>

I'd intended the thought to travel solely to Griffin, but Brady answered, meaning I'd once more failed to deliver my words as precisely as I'd intended.

<*I'm going to kill them all for this, every single one of them.*>

Then, because every time we spoke to each other, silences inevitably drew out for anyone observing us, I told Zoe the first thing that came to mind.

"Hunt dropped his phone."

Zoe looked down to find the phone abandoned at Hunt's feet and arched a brow at him. "And you didn't even pick it up?"

Layla popped into my thoughts. <*Fast, Hunt, repeat after me. 'I felt you coming.'*>

Hunt, appearing somewhat frazzled, for once did as Layla directed without prior deliberation. He parroted for Zoe.

"Your beauty easily outshone my stupid phone," Hunt told her. "I completely forgot about it once I saw you heading my way."

Despite Layla's lines being more cheese-licking than I thought she had in her, and despite the fact Brady looked like he was about to burst from trying to hold back an eyeroll, Zoe beamed up at Hunt, who was several inches taller than her.

"So, what was the message about?" he asked, echoing Layla's instruction.

Zoe blushed—actually blushed—and trailed a finger along the tattoo across his collarbone. She wore mascara, which I didn't remember her usually doing, and batted her thickened lashes at him. "Well . . ." Her finger ran back and forth across the neckline of his t-shirt. He looked like he was trying hard not to pull away. "Maybe we can talk about that tonight, on a *private* date?"

"Man," Layla interjected, "I'm sure he'd really love to, but we've got dibs on him tonight. Gotta work on Joss's car if we're ever gonna be able to move on to Hunt's, and he's next in line. You want him to have his own car up and running for your dates, don't you?"

For the first time, Zoe appeared unsure what to do. "Uh, yeah, of course."

Brady made a performance of checking his cellphone for the time while Layla swooped down to pick up Hunt's.

"It's almost time for the first bell," Brady said. "Catch up with you later, Zoe."

It was as clear of a dismissal as it could get, and yet Zoe clung to Hunt a bit longer.

<*Fuck my fucking life,*> Hunt mumbled miserably into our shared connection, when he was the least likely to ever say something like that. Then he leaned down to give her a goodbye kiss. "Catch you later?" he asked her, pulling off what passed for a hopeful expression.

Zoe's lips spread into a grin before she licked them in a way I suspected she intended to be enticing. "Of course, babe. I'll always be here for you, no matter when."

Hunt gave her a chaste peck on the lips, leaving her wanting more, then pulled out of her arms. "Perfect."

Layla handed him his phone and he pocketed it without looking, even though Zoe's stare followed his movements as if urging him to read her message already.

"Bye," Layla told her, then looped an arm through Hunt's and led him away toward the lockers, not waiting to give Zoe the chance to come with us.

"See ya later, Zoe," I said with a smile of my own that felt as brittle as the rest of the show we were putting on. I stuffed my arms through both Griffin's and Brady's and hustled them after the other two.

<*What the* fuck?> Brady snarled through our super-duper cool and now extremely helpful telepathic connection. <*That was all shades of wrong, guys. All shades. Fuck them for this, fuck them wrong. Hunt, you will* not *follow through with this sick plan of theirs. If it were me they were trying to pull this with, it'd be one thing. I'd just bang her and get it over with, and hope they'd order her to move on. But you? Nah. So messed up. You don't do it like this, dude, and we all know it, which means they know it too.*>

We pulled up to our lockers and held our collective breaths as we entered the only combinations we remembered. When the doors all popped open, we exhaled loudly.

<*Seriously,*> Layla said. <*Fuck them for putting us under this much stress. I don't handle stress well, you all know that.*>

I retrieved my calendar first, relieved to find my class schedule waiting for me at the front. <*Everyone have AP World History first today?*>

<*Yep,*> Griffin said.

I blew out another relieved exhale. <*Good.*> As I loaded the books I'd need into my backpack, I shared, <*What I want to know right now, I mean, 'cause there are like a billion things I'm still trying to figure out, so one at a time . . .*>

<*Like two billion over here,*> Layla interjected from a few lockers down.

<*Is Zoe in on it? Was that all an act?*>

<*If so, she's damn convincing,*> Brady said.

<*No shit,*> Hunt said. <*I can still feel her tongue trying to push its way into my freaking throat.*>

<*You sound like she tasted like ass,*> Layla said.

<No, I sound like I showed up to school after one of the very worst experiences in my entire life to have a girl I thought of as a friend, maybe a bit more, but not even crush levels, kiss me like she wanted to taste my tonsils.>

Layla's head popped out of her locker just to waggle her eyebrows in his direction. <And that's before the date she's trying to wrangle you into.>

<Not cool, Lay,> Griffin said. <How would you like it if Rich came over, shoved you against your locker, and started making out with you?>

Her expression soured. She slammed the door of her locker shut hard enough to rattle the whole row of them on this side of the hallway.

<That's what I thought,> Griff said.

<If Rich puts his hands, tongue, or any other body part near her,> Brady growled, <I'll throw him off a balcony onto rebar, see how he likes it.>

<Guys,> I reminded them. <We're doing too much talking in our heads. Someone's gonna notice if we aren't careful. We aren't known for being quiet.>

Layla frowned. <No, we aren't.> She sighed, then, "Joss, have you decided what color you're gonna paint Cleo once she's finished?"

Right. The normal details of our previously normal lives that had never been normal at all.

Closing my locker and swinging my backpack to hang from one shoulder, I pretended to think about it. "I'm leaning toward the cherry black. I mean, let's be real here, I'm a cherry black kinda girl. Though I do love the electric green too, so still not a hundred percent decided."

Car talk, at least, was safe territory. We could go on and on about our Mustangs without much thought, and it shouldn't arouse suspicion.

<*Good idea, Lay,*> I told her—and everyone else too, apparently. That was a tad inconvenient. A private channel, to Griffin especially, would have been helpful. Maybe we'd figure it out as we honed our skills.

<*We should make sure we have car talk running in the background whenever we do the telepathy thing,*> I added. <*I'm still not over the fact that we can do this in the first place. It's almost as cool as the dying and coming back thing.*>

I made myself sound relaxed about the immortality issue, but just the thought of having to again face my death or that of my friends made a rush of panic squeeze my lungs.

<*Or ninja talk,*> Brady said as we joined the throng of students heading toward their first classes. As usual, they tended to part for us, as if they knew there was something special about us. <*You guys know I'm always down for the ninja talk.*>

<*Yeah, Brady, we know,*> Layla snarked. <*Still haven't gotten over seeing you in your Ninjas "R" Us costume. It'll probably haunt me for the rest of my days, till you're an old fart and I'm still a spring chicken.*>

<*Hey, just 'cause you wanted to look as cool as I did—*>

<*No, Brade, I didn't. Your junk was all on display just behind a bit of black spandex. Maybe the skanks in this school are all up for that, but not me. Keep your kink to yourself.*>

Brady scowled at her. <*You make me sound like a fucking perv, you asshole. I'm apparently the only one who understands the line that divides appropriate from inappropriate in sibling relationships.*>

"So, cherry black, huh?" Griffin asked from where he walked on one side of me. Hunt, now on the other, appeared lost in his thoughts, but that wasn't all that uncommon.

I smiled, though even I could feel how tight it was. "Yeah. I'm picturing a really shiny finish. She's gonna look so hot."

<*You look so hot,*> Griffin said, and from behind us, I could hear Layla gagging.

Griffin glanced at me. <*She's gonna be the one to give us away, isn't she?*>

Brady sighed loudly enough to reach us from behind. <*Yep, no doubt. We're all gonna have to work to keep her in line.*>

"Hey," she protested aloud, all but proving our point. <*You can't all blame me. What we're doing, how they're forcing us to live, this is what normal people call* nuts. *This is too fucking much.*>

<*It's too fucking much, all right,*> Hunt said before adding aloud, "If it were me, I'd go with the electric green. That color is so bright you'll be able to spot Cleo from a mile away. She'll make an impression, that's for sure."

"She will," I conceded, "but then she'll just pop that much more for the cops."

<*Who might just be in on this façade too,*> Brady grumbled.

<*Who knows who's in on what anymore?*> Griffin asked.

"Maybe I should consider some other colors too," I said for no one but our hidden audience. How fucking inane. "Open it back up. There are so many to choose from."

"This day feels eternal already," Layla grumbled. "Please tell me it's 2:59 and that final bell's about to ring."

"Nope, little sis," Brady said. "Wish I could."

"This day is gonna go on forever," Layla complained.

The rest of us grumbled our agreement. How were we going to keep up the ruse so well that none of the expert liars studying our every move would notice, while also figuring out our immortality and now telepathy, while *also* discovering a surprise way out of this situation?

"It's fucking *Groundhog Day*," I muttered as Griffin pulled open the door to the classroom for me and held it for our friends.

<*In every which way,*> he said. <*We gotta find a way out of the loop before they start thinking they need to hypnotize us again and start over.*>

Because then they'd probably just kill us and hypnotize us while we were coming to. No need to convince us to fall in line. And if that wasn't an option, they'd just do something else I doubted we'd like. Maybe it would be worse.

<*It's a good thing we can all pass this class with our eyes closed,*> Brady said. <*We're going to need 'silent' class time to talk things through and figure our shit out.*>

<*Yeah, we are,*> Hunt agreed.

It wasn't a plan yet, that was for damn sure, but it was the start of one. Or the start of how to find one anyway. Beggars can't be choosers, and all that.

For once, I settled into my seat two-thirds of the way through the classroom with some pep in my step. We had fifty minutes of time during which no one would expect us to be talking—that was fifty minutes to work everything out, and by every standard, we were geniuses.

For the first time in a long while, things were looking up—*Groundhog Day* or not.

24

A Vengeful Bitch, Out to Get Us

So much for our genius statuses . . .

We talked telepathically during the entirety of our five classes that day, discussing every aspect of what we'd learned through the failed hypnosis, our impressions of the two other students with abilities we'd seen at the institute, everything we knew about our supposed parents, Magnum, and his staff, about our burgeoning powers, and everything else we could think of—and *still* we didn't come up with a single winning plan. We hadn't even come up with a *came in fourth place* kind of plan. All we'd get was a participation trophy.

The five of us were waist-deep in a pit of quicksand, with no rope nearby to save us. The more we examined the conundrum, the more the pit sucked us farther down toward an inevitable conclusion: as long as Magnum possessed unlimited influence and wealth, there was nowhere we could go that was far enough. No place we could hide. No way to avoid the long arm of his constant threats of death.

It didn't matter that the blinders were off or that we could at last speak to each other privately again. Whatever advantages we had this time around were nothing when compared to our many disadvantages and limited knowledge. We didn't even know how many times we'd been rebooted, how many times they'd adjusted this and that about our life stories and sent us back out into Ridgemore to be studied.

And Magnum had already proven he'd kill us as many times as he wanted, no matter where we were, even surrounded by other people.

In the age-old scenario of *fight or flight*, if we couldn't run, our only other option was to defend ourselves.

But how exactly did one fight someone with such a massive upper hand?

It was during our run after school that day, which we'd gone on solely to work off some of our mounting frustration, that we'd eventually agreed: we had to face off with the monster and lop off its smugly handsome head.

If we killed Magnum, there'd be no more funding, no more labs, no more sneaky *parents* or gun-toting soldiers to carry out his orders.

We ran an extra three miles just to cruise on the high of finally reaching a decision. None of us wanted to kill anyone. Unlike Magnum, murdering wasn't part of our life plans.

But we'd do what had to be done.

To protect my crew, I'd break through his chest and rip out his still-beating heart with my bare hands. I absolutely would.

I refused to let any one of my crew die again.

Now, grinning in anticipated relief, we crowded onto the porch to our treehouse slash ninja training space, chests heaving, before spreading out to cool down. We'd run nine miles, and Layla hadn't complained once.

Bobo was panting from the run and lapping up water beside me. My sweet boy was thankfully healed enough for the exertion since as far as we were supposed to know, he and I had never jumped from a moving Clyde. According to Jackie's hypnosis, the thin scar on his leg was from a bad scratch.

I was stretching out my hamstrings when steady footfalls warned of someone approaching. Many someones, actually. Bobo stiffened as he came to full alertness.

From the winding path my crew and I had carved through the forest that surrounded our homes, our traitorous *parents*, all together, emerged into the clearing in front of the treehouse; they led Homer, Yolanda, and Armando toward us.

"Hey, kids," Celia called ahead with a friendly smile splitting her face. Had I not known better, I would have believed it was genuine. "We have an awesome surprise for you!"

<*I feel like ripping that fake-ass smile right off her stupid face,*> Layla commented into what I was beginning to think of as our "group chat."

"You're going to be so excited," Porter claimed, rubbing his hands together in what I now couldn't help but notice was high theatrical fashion.

<*And I feel like slapping the shit out of Dad's wrists after that little move,*> Brady said. <*What a bunch of sus motherfuckers!*>

As our faux parents and almost surely future-ninja-instructors-slash-extra-superspies crowded around the porch, I couldn't help but notice that *Lynne* wore a pair of dangling pearl earrings that I recognized.

Weeks ago, when I'd searched my bedroom for wiretaps, I hadn't found any. But I had found a pearl earring I'd never seen before.

Of course it belonged to my snooping, lying faux mother, who must have dropped it when she'd been searching my room for who-knew-what. I hadn't remembered her wearing them before because my previous memories had been overridden.

Now that we recognized the signs for what they were, they were everywhere, impossible not to notice.

<Guys,> I told my friends. <Check out Lynne's earrings. Remember how weird it was when I found that one rando pearl earring in my bedroom?>

<Damn,> Griffin said, drawing closer. <And there it fucking is.>

<There it fucking is,> I echoed.

<How the fuck are we supposed to keep ourselves from strangling them when they look at us like they're just a bunch of innocent schmoes?> Layla asked. <Asking for a friend, ya know.>

Before any of us could answer, Alexis beamed at the five of us. She even smiled down at Bobo for a second. And she never smiled that big. She was the least smiley of the whole lying bunch.

"You've been asking us for what feels like forever to find you an instructor to help you advance your fitness skills to the next level." With excitement dancing across her face, her eyes bright and shiny, she glanced back at the other adults before looking at us again. "Well." She bit down on her lips as if she couldn't contain her excitement, her brows arching. "We finally did it! We finally found someone perfect."

She looked to Hunt first, then the rest of us, no doubt waiting for us to lose our shit over the wondrous news.

<I can't believe I ever trusted her,> Hunt said.

<How could you not?> I protested. <Her act is so fucking believable.>

<I'm half believing it right now even though I know it's all a lie,> Layla said.

Alexis, who was without a doubt the least bubbly of them all, *bubbled*. "We found not just one, not even two, but *three* perfect teachers for you!"

"Wow. Seriously?" Brady said. He probably didn't sound quite as delighted as I'm sure they all hoped, but at least he was able to play their game. I still needed a moment to tighten my mask and make sure my true face wasn't showing.

"That's amazing!" Brady added, sounding peppier now. "Like, sooooo super amazeballs. We've been wanting to up our game for so crazy long. I can't believe it's finally happening."

<*Okay, bud,*> Layla warned. <*You might be laying it on a bit thick there.*>

But the *parents* were lapping it up. Celia actually bounced on the balls of her feet and clapped before Porter wrapped an arm around her shoulders, making me wonder if the two of them actually cared about one another. Or were they putting on a show of loving each other just as my *parents* had while my mom was out banging the sheriff on the side?

Said lying mom and dad gestured for Homer, Yolanda, and Armando to step forward, and after they did, my dad introduced them. At least the teachers kept the same names, which I was grateful for. No one needed the jumble of alternate names I currently had burdening my mental Rolodex. The more lies we had to keep straight, the more likely it was for one of us to trip up in a mistake that would clue them all in.

"It's a pleasure to meet you all," Homer said, taking the lead just as he had at the institute. "We're looking forward to working with all of you. We love having capable students who are ready and eager to learn what we have to offer, and between the three of us, it's quite a lot."

Just as back at the training center, Homer, Yolanda, and Armando were dressed in form-fitting clothing designed for movement that revealed honed bodies, sharp as weapons.

"Yeah, it's nice to meet you all too," Brady said.

"For sure," Griffin added, glancing at our *parents*. "How'd you guys find them?"

Orson pushed his glasses up the bridge of his nose and stepped forward. "You know that new post-secondary institute over by the abandoned outdoor amphitheater? The one that's almost finished?"

<Were we supposed to know about that?> I asked my crew while Layla offered a noncommittal "Yeah" aloud.

<Must've been in the part of the hypnosis we missed out on,> Hunt answered.

"Well, it looks like it's going to be a really amazing place," Orson continued. "The best not just in academics but also in extracurriculars."

<Uh-oh,> Layla said. <Tell me they're not lining it up for us to go there next year after graduation.>

Damn, she was right. That's exactly what they were doing. I glanced at her and found her smile looking too tight.

<Chill, dude,> I told her. <You're gonna give us away.>

<Joss is right,> Brady added. <You look like you're trying to hold in a wheezy fart. Relax your face, dude.>

To make up for her slip, I pushed my own smile to grow brighter, pinning a purposefully attentive stare on Orson.

He went on to say, "They're only hiring the best of the best teachers over there. Everything's really top notch." Again, he pushed up his glasses. "Really impressive."

My dad clasped my mom's hand and twirled her so her back leaned against his chest. "Actually, guys, we were going to save this for later, but why not just tell them now, right?" He made a show of searching the gazes of the other *parents* for permission. When they gave it, my dad grinned, "Well, guys, another reason we were able to find these wonderful instructors for you is because . . ."

<Is he waiting for a fucking drumroll?> Griffin asked.

"Drumroll please," my dad joked, and I almost snorted aloud. "They've offered us amazing positions there, working in their state-of-the-art lab."

"That's cool," I said. "So would you guys be teaching? Or just doing research?"

"Probably just research, especially at the start," my mom said, running a hand along my dad's arm as if they were happy lovers.

Celia squealed. "Oooooooh, let's just tell them the whole shebang. It's too exciting to keep under wraps."

Once more, the *parents* shared looks I would have previously bet my entire savings were genuine.

Alexis gave her a generous smile. "Go on, then. Tell them."

Celia clapped and squealed some more. "Well, guess what? Okay, never mind. You'll never guess."

<*Wanna bet?*> I snarked, and Layla tittered. Lucky for us, Celia's act was so spot-on everyone assumed Layla was already reacting to this incredible news.

"If we decide to take the positions—" Celia said.

"And we probably will," Porter interjected.

Celia's smile revealed her perfect teeth. "Of course we will, because . . . *pum-para-pum* . . . when we work there, all five of you will get full scholarships to study there!"

"Including room and board," Orson added.

"Everything's included," Celia told us. "And because you happen to already know and love the super-top-secret founder of the place, who's only just now letting us tell you. . ."

She waited until Hunt offered, "Magnum?"

She pointed at him as if he were some lucky winner. "*Ding-ding-ding.* It's your Uncle Magnum."

<*I will call that man 'uncle' over my dead body,*> Layla said. <*Maybe I'll call him that over* his *dead body though.*>

"Your Uncle Magnum is so generous, he's actually built the place keeping you lot and your special gifted levels in mind. In fact, he's even built you five a special house just for you, where only you'll get to live as a special welcome bonus. Isn't that just beyond words incredible?"

"Wow, Mom," Brady said, "that's really amazing. I can't believe it."

"We hardly could either," Porter said, tucking a strand of his wife's hair behind her ear. "Now you don't have to even worry about applying to other universities. Your Uncle Magnum's making it super easy for you, and your parents couldn't be more grateful."

He removed his glasses to rub at his eyes as if emotion were getting to him. "You don't know what it's like to be parents. We worry so much. Now that we know your futures are supported and looking bright . . ." He shook his head, sliding his glasses back on. "It's such a relief. The costs of a university education nowadays are no joke. And you can't beat the education your Uncle Magnum's going to make sure you get. He's even chosen these guys"—he gestured to Homer, Yolanda, and Armando, who continued to stand still like props in the performance—"to teach there 'cause he knows how serious you are about learning self-defense and that kind of thing."

<*I'm never believing a single other word that comes out of my dad's mouth,*> Brady told the four of us. <*Not even a simple 'hi.'*>

<*No shit,*> Layla answered. <*Dude gets an A+ in acting.*>

"Have you put together the best part yet?" my dad asked.

"I . . . don't think so," I said. "It's all kinda shocking. Unexpected. We asked for so long we kinda thought you'd forgotten or maybe just given up."

"We'll never give up on you, honey." I was afraid of that. "But now that Homer, Yolanda, and what was it? I'm sorry, what's your name again?" he asked Armando as if they were truly newly introduced.

Armando smiled generously and tipped his buzzed head to one side. "It's Armando." He, like Yolanda, had a pretty, melodic accent.

"Oh, that's right. My apologies," my dad said. "Now that Homer, Yolanda, and *Armando*"—he smiled at the lithe man who, though about my height and slim, was majorly ripped—"have agreed to be your teachers, the even better news is that they'll be able to continue as you transition over to the institute after you finish at Ridgemore High."

"Assuming we want to go to the institute," Griffin said. "That will be our decision."

"Of course it will, my son," Orson said, and I glanced up at Griffin to see his cheek twitch. He scratched at it, playing it off as an itch. "Whatever you guys decide in the end, we'll support you."

"That's right," Alexis said. "You can count on us."

I didn't mean to, but I found myself looking toward Hunt. He did a better job of pretending and ignored my questioning look.

"We know we can count on you," Hunt said. <*To betray us,*> he added privately. "Thanks."

Homer clasped both hands behind his back and cleared his throat. "Perhaps that's enough chatting for now? We'd like to perform an assessment today to get a better idea of what we're working with here."

"Oh, of course," Celia said with a delighted chirp at the end. "I'm sure they can't wait to get started."

"But," my dad said, his astute gaze skirting across the five of us, "before we do, we should ask you: do you want to proceed?"

<*Oh, like they're all about getting our consent to everything,*> Layla said. <*What total dickbags.*>

"Yeah, of course we want to, Dad," I said, trying to make up for the few stealthy looks I'd shot my friends without meaning to. "This is gonna be so awesome. We're stoked, aren't we, guys?"

"Totally stoked," Griffin said.

"Ready to start," Brady added.

"All right, then," my dad said. "We'll leave you all to it, then."

Our *parents* hovered for a bit, but when Homer, Yolanda, and Armando moved up to stand directly across from us, they turned and started down the path that led to the houses.

Bobo sat at my side, his eyes trained on the strangers.

"We just got back from a long run," Layla told the instructors as she gestured to her sweaty running shorts and tank. "Not sure it's the best time for an assessment."

"It's the perfect time," Homer said. "You'll be warmed up."

"More than warmed up," Layla said. "We ran, like, ten miles or something."

Homer arched his brows. "Oh, is that all? Well, it gives us something to build on."

Layla gaped at him. "Something to build on?"

Homer nodded his chin at the treehouse. "Show us what kind of equipment you're working with here."

My body went rigid. The treehouse was supposed to be sacrosanct. Yes, our *parents* had violated the crap out of that sacredness, but still, I didn't want anyone else to violate our special space.

Brady was the first to nod with acquiescence. "Come on. We'll show you."

"Excellent," Homer said. "We'd like to see you work the equipment you have, gauge our starting points."

Why were they so intent on these assessments? Were they going to compare them with the ones they gave us mere days ago? Did they expect our bodies to perform differently when we were aware of our immortality and when we weren't?

Who fucking knew?

After sharing a reluctant look with Layla and then Griffin, we followed Brady, the three teachers, and Hunt, along with Bobo, into the space we'd built as children. When we'd still believed in the easy joys of our companionship.

Before the world had revealed itself to be a vengeful bitch, out to get us.

25

Mess with Me and You'll Die

Our teachers' assessment that day was just as brutal as it had been at the institute's training center. With keen stares, they'd studied the five of us as we'd cycled through striking and kicking every dummy, bag, and board we owned. They'd had us do pushups, burpees, sit-ups, and every other exercise I'd ever heard of that used our bodies as resistance. They'd noted how much weight we each could lift, what weapons we thought we were proficient at—while making it plain their opinions of our skills weren't nearly as high as our own.

I *of course* understood we weren't actual ninjas. I wasn't an idiot. Compared to the levels of mastery of, say, a Shaolin monk we were probably more like baby ninjas just learning to walk.

At that point, we hadn't yet seen our instructors in action. It was easy enough to guess they were royal badasses. Not only did their sculpted physiques suggest it, but there was something about their postures, ready for anything at any time, a vibe they put off that said, *Mess with me and you'll die.* Goals, right there.

I only truly began to comprehend a bit of why they seemed so utterly unimpressed with us when, after they lamented that the treehouse didn't boast climbing ropes like the institute's training center, they asked us to climb trees instead. As children who'd spent more time in the forest than indoors, we'd spent our fair share of time climbing trees. Hunt was a freaking monkey, and Griffin was nearly as agile, swinging from branch to branch.

But after we'd all taken turns going up and down a few trees, first untimed, then competing against our previous records, Armando had shucked off his shirt and shown us how it was motherfucking *done*.

I'd never again think of Hunt as a monkey, not after Armando's performance. The man was Tarzan, so fluid and swift I had no trouble accepting that he'd grown up in Brazil's Amazonian jungles and later become a master teacher of capoeira, among other martial arts.

That night, the five of us collapsed into our beds. I was grateful I was so exhausted that my mind quieted, putting the gazillion worries on hold until the next day.

When they'd attack with renewed vigor.

Several days eked by like this, and we settled into a pattern. In the mornings, we exited our houses as quickly as possible to diminish our time with our traitorous not-parents. During school, we largely kept to ourselves, which was pretty much our norm anyway, and occupied our time during classes searching for a way out that didn't involve us murdering Magnum. The more we discussed, the more convinced we became that it truly was the only way to secure our freedom.

After school, we trained with the badass trio until we sweated our guts out and every muscle felt like it was dying a torturous death. Then we did a little homework while we hung out together before finally stumbling to our beds.

Every day like this contributed to lulling me into a growing sense of complacency—like maybe this time no one would try to kill us, maybe they'd let us live our merry lives and forget about us and whatever powers we had.

But then I would observe the five scars on my chest and be reminded how very close to death my friends and I were in all moments. The hypnosis had explained away the continually shrinking scars as hornet stings, but I couldn't see them without remembering in too vivid detail what it had been like to watch Layla and Hunt gunned down in front of me. To witness Griffin's anguish when he'd thought he might be about to lose me forever. To hear Brady's heart shattering as he screamed and attacked the soldiers.

I'd never forget what it felt like to stare down the barrel of Jaggar's gun, knowing it might be the last sight I ever saw.

No, the feeling of growing complacency only made me all the twitchier. Like really bad shit was just on the horizon.

<*You're rubbing at your chest again,*> Griffin said into my thoughts one afternoon in Ms. Tott's British Lit class, in that gentle tone I'd only ever known him to use with me, though our other friends would hear it too.

Despite how much we'd practiced our telepathic communication since we'd returned home, the channel continued to broadcast to all of us no matter our intentions. We'd also discovered we could only speak like this so long as we remained somewhere in the range of a couple hundred feet of each other. Across the length of a football field, yes. From the newly constructed gym to the cafeteria, also yes. But from the gym to the classrooms on the other end of the school campus, no. And we couldn't reach each other when we were in our separate houses either. Whenever Layla and Brady were in their house together, they could speak to each other without us hearing since the rest of us were out of range.

After a final rub of my chest, I leaned back and dropped my hand to my desk, absently looking at Ms. Tott. Our British Lit teacher seemed trapped in the wrong decade, more at home as a flower child of the '60s. Today she wore one of her usual long, airy, ruffled skirts and a fitted shirt that revealed much of her ample bosom. She spun expertly on velvet-lined platform heels, her long hair swinging behind her as she lectured about . . . Jane Austen, I realized. I hadn't heard a thing she'd said in quite a while.

<You okay, Joss?> Hunt asked from my left. Griffin sat on my right.

I blinked a few times, bringing myself back to the present. <Yeah, fine. Just kind of got lost to how crazy the last few days have been.>

I glanced at the clock at the front of the classroom. <Ugh, we still have twenty minutes left? Did I miss anything good while I zoned out?>

<From Ms. Tott, no way,> Brady said. <If she mentions Mr. Darcy in that swoony voice one more time, I'm gonna puke in my mouth.>

<That's rich, coming from you,> Layla said. The twins sat beside Hunt. <You've been talking in that same swoony voice about the triple-threats of badassery. I swear, if you talk about how fucking tight our ninja teachers' techniques are one more time, I'm gonna puke in my mouth.>

<And if I talk about how tight Yolanda's ass is?>

<That would be marginally better. Though I don't believe you for a second that you're focused on her body and not how fucking sick her moves are.>

Brady sighed so dreamily that a couple of students around us glanced his way, but he didn't care. <You can't blame me, Lay. They're insane. Everything they do is so fucking lit.>

<Keep it in your pants, bro, jeesh. How am I supposed to make it through my day like this? Even when we're not with them, I have to listen to this crap. Don't worry, Brade, in no time they'll be barking orders at us while they try to kill us with sheer exhaustion alone.>

<Don't even pretend you're not loving it too.>

<I don't have to pretend. I'm not a sadist. Every single muscle in my body hurts. Even my fingers hurt, and I don't even know how that's possible.>

<*I'm definitely not complaining,*> Hunt started.

<*That's 'cause you're a maniac,*> Layla said. <*You actually enjoy running till your legs and lungs give out. It's not normal to want to run marathons every day, Hunt. Not normal.*>

I felt a wry chuckle from Hunt travel down the line of our internal dialog. <*That's not what I was talking about. I meant Zoe.*>

Since we'd come back and Zoe had pushed her tongue into his mouth by way of hello, he'd been using our training as an excuse to delay the date she kept pestering him about.

As one, we looked to where she sat immediately in front of us. When we'd arrived for class, she'd lingered around us, no doubt trying to snag a seat next to her "babe." So we'd guided Hunt toward the middle of the rest of us and occupied the entire row of seats. She'd already snuck a hundred glances at him so far this class.

<*You're not going to be able to put her off forever,*> I said. <*And that's a problem.*>

<*Yeah, a major one,*> Brady said. <*If she tries to make out with you one more time, I might just punch her, and you know I don't punch girls.*>

<*You've punched me before,*> Layla pointed out.

<*Of course I have. You're the most annoying sister a brother could ever have. I'm practically a saint for putting up with you.*>

I glanced down the row at Layla. She didn't usually get offended. In fact, I was often shocked at just how much didn't seem to bother her. But Brady could get to her sometimes, and when he did, she did nothing to hide her hurt.

She merely smirked and rubbed at the tattoo that wound around her wrist. <*You. A saint. As if, dude. You might just spontaneously combust if you ever try to walk into a church.*>

<*I haven't punched you since we were twelve,*> Brady responded. <*Now I'm thinking it's been too long.*>

While they squabbled, my thoughts drifted again, back around to the questions I'd asked myself dozens of times already.

What if one of these times one of us doesn't come back to life? No power can be completely foolproof, can it? Can we even risk a single other time?

And if the only real way to avoid anyone coming for us is to kill Magnum, how will we feel after we do the deed?

When I'd seen Brady broken across that pillar, the rebar puncturing his heart . . . when I'd heard Griffin go over the cliff to his death in a groan of crunching metal . . . when I'd had to watch Magnum's soldiers kill Layla and Hunt and threaten the others . . .

In those moments of terror and loss and anguish and righteous rage, I would have killed Magnum, had I known he was responsible. Gutted him from neck to balls or cut off his fucking head, without hesitation.

But contemplating the act now felt more like premeditated murder than self-defense. And unlike us, we'd be ending him forever. I still couldn't shake the sense of wrongness every time I anticipated what we'd have to do.

Why couldn't there be a super-max prison that could actually keep filthy rich assholes like him for a lifelong sentence instead?

Something bumped my leg and I glanced down to find Griffin nudging my foot. Ms. Tott was busy listing the many noteworthy qualities of Mr. Darcy on the whiteboard up front, so I turned in my seat to really look at him.

He didn't speak. But his eyes said what he didn't. Their hazel was bright, his brow furrowed in evident concern for me.

I smiled my reassurance. But it didn't look like I managed to convince him, probably because I wasn't actually okay, and the man knew me as well as I knew myself.

My fingers twitched with the need to reach for him. My skin longed for his touch. I'd only gotten to really kiss him that one time in my bed at the institute, and now it felt like every single minute I suffered from the urge to kiss him.

I didn't realize I was biting my lip until I felt his gaze on my mouth.

I grinned. He grinned back.

Fuck our *parents*. I was going to have to have at him today after school, hidden away in the forest where the many sets of prying eyes wouldn't follow.

"Ms. Bryson," Ms. Tott's voice suddenly interrupted. "Is there something more interesting going on than what I'm teaching that you'd like to share with the class?"

<*Practically anything's more interesting than what she's been saying,*> Brady groaned into my mind.

Along with several other students, Zoe swiveled in her seat to look at me, her stare immediately traveling to Hunt.

Every single thing about Griffin was more interesting than this class. My blood simmered just looking at him, feeling him this close. He was so fucking beautiful, everything about him. I wanted the fuck out of him.

But I'd be damned if I'd share any of him with the rest of the students or Ms. Tott.

He was all fucking mine.

His eyes danced with mischief. His mouth tipped up on one side. And he winked at me.

"Ms. Bryson?" Ms. Tott pushed, her tone stern.

Still staring at the man I loved, I answered, "My apologies, Ms. Tott." I turned to face her. "I got distracted."

She frowned. "I can plainly see that."

<*She can't blame you for that,*> Layla said. <*You and Griff've got no choice but to eye-fuck each other since our 'parents' are cunts.*>

I very nearly snort-laughed out loud. With effort, I composed my expression into a respectful smile and told the teacher, "I'll be paying attention now."

<*Yeah, right,*> Brady said into my mind with a chuckle.

As Ms. Tott finally turned back to the whiteboard, I couldn't help but wonder if the Rafferty twins and their constant snark would be our undoing. They, at least, never changed.

What remained of class rolled by slowly enough that I checked my cellphone against the classroom clock twice to make sure the school clock hadn't fallen behind. Ms. Tott mentioned the swoony Mr. Darcy sufficient additional times that Brady was the first to barrel out of the room, desperate to flee.

When the four of us filed out with the rest of the class, we found Brady in the hallway, facing off with Rich. Brady's arms were coiled at his sides, and he was leaning ever so slightly toward Rich, as if the momentum of his internal ire were pulling them together.

<Brade,> I told him right away. <Remember, we're supposed to be friendly with the prick this time around.>

<I don't care. Look at the twerp. He's already checking my sister out.>

Only, I wasn't so sure that he was . . .

I looked from Rich to Layla, then across Hunt, who had Zoe clinging to him like she had four arms and intended to never let go.

Rich craned his neck to see around the mass that was Brady and all his muscles and stared straight at me.

"Hey, foxy Joss-y."

Students walked by, avoiding our group while also rubbernecking to make sure they didn't miss any action.

Rich sidestepped Brady and stalked toward me. Suddenly, Griffin was pressed against my side, staring him down.

Rich ignored him, doing nothing to conceal his appreciation as he dragged his gaze up and down my body. "Mmmhmmm." He wagged his head, running a careful hand across the surface of his gelled hair. "Lookin' fine as always."

After a strong reminder that in this timeline he was supposed to be the nice nephew of our dear family friend, Uncle Magnum,

I forced my distaste into a smile. "Thanks." The guy had pestered Layla for years. My fingers kept wanting to curl into fists as I fantasized about punching in that sleazy smile.

In truth, who knew if he'd been a creep to her solely in the latest timeline we remembered? He had denied sending her notes and gifts when I'd confronted him about it, though now that small bit of stalking had somehow become the least of our problems.

Rich openly leered at me as Brady shouldered his way to my other side.

<Will the dudes ever stop thinking they need to protect us from the assholes?> Layla asked, almost wistfully.

I was too concerned that one of us—maybe even me—was about to knock the guy out and blow our cover.

<Steady, guys,> Hunt said. <Let's just walk away.>

When none of us budged, Hunt added, <We can kill him after we kill his uncle.>

Sandwiched between Griffin and Brady, the anger rolling off them both was a tangible heat against my limbs.

"Can we help you with something?" Griffin snarled at Rich when his stare began to drag down my body another time.

Rich snapped his eyes up to meet Griffin's for a quick instant before grinning down at me. Mr. Charm himself waggled his brows.

<Dude does not know how to read a room, does he?> Layla commented.

"Don't want anything from the rest of you," Rich answered Griffin, "but I wouldn't mind a little help from Joss here."

"Oh yeah?" I asked, injecting danger into my voice. "And what's that, Rich?" I practically spat out his name.

"Why don't you come closer and I'll tell you?"

Griffin growled and stepped between us. His jaw was clenched hard, and from the corner of my eye I saw Hunt disentangling himself from a reluctant Zoe, preparing for the fight that seemed inevitable at this point.

"What?" Rich asked Griffin. "You've got no claim on her."

"Claim on me?" I repeated just to be sure I'd heard him right, treating me like I was some fucking object to be owned.

Rich ignored me to tell Griffin, "You and Joss are just friends." He paused as if he might know exactly what he was doing, might know we had feelings for each other. "Right?"

"What we are or aren't is none of your fucking business," Griffin barked back in a tone that seethed with suppressed violence. If I were Rich, I would have taken a giant step back.

Rich had no such street smarts.

His hungry gaze landed back on me, and I had to wonder if this was part of his role this time around, or if he just enjoyed perving on chicks and any of us would do.

"Whaddya say, Bryson?" he asked. "Wanna help me out with something?"

Then he adjusted himself.

I waited for one of my friends to cry out a warning through our shared bond. To remind us we had to play it cool. We couldn't beat the asshole to a pulp. We had to keep up the act if we were ever going to break free of Magnum's hold on us.

But the group chat was silent.

"Do that one more time," Griffin seethed at Rich, "and I'll break off your dick and feed it to you."

Rich barked a laugh that was purposefully loud, drawing even more attention our way. I spotted a similar crew from the Fischer House party heading our way from both sides of the wide hallway. Slater Moore and Duncan Mills headed in from one direction, Pike Pills and John B. from another. And Wade Jones and Reed Carter eyed us warily. Their dads were the sheriff and deputy sheriff.

Noticing his buddies inching closer, Rich laughed again. "You wouldn't be able to wrap both hands around *my* dick to get a good grip on it." Rich eyed me again. "It's made just to be slick."

Beside Brady now, Layla crossed her arms over her chest. "Yeah, sure, Rich. Your dick's so big it's round as a fucking hoagie." She huffed incredulously as she held up both hands, pretending to barely be able to hold said hoagie in the circumference of her fingers. Seen like that, the girth he was implying was laughably absurd. "No wonder you scare all the girls away. You're just too much man for them." Sarcasm dripped from her words.

"Watch your mouth, Rafferty," Rich said.

Instantly, Brady lunged, meaning to wedge himself between Rich and her.

But Layla pushed a hand to her brother's chest, keeping him at her side. Layla stalked into Rich's space. "Go find somewhere else to be."

"I pretty much fucking own this school."

"Not you, your uncle."

"Same thing."

"No, Rich, it's not the same thing."

<*We really will have to kill both of them,*> Brady said. <*I just decided. I call dibs on this asshole.*>

After another glance to either side of the hallway, where he spotted his jock friends among the crowd, near enough to rumble on his behalf, Rich pinned his stare on me as if my friends weren't even there.

"I'm not talking to any of you. This only concerns Joss."

"Whatever concerns Joss concerns me," Griffin said, his voice still deep, like building thunder moments away from booming into existence.

"I'm pretty sure Joss can take care of herself," Rich insisted.

"Of course I can," I snapped. "But I'm not interested. Not now, not ever."

"Aw, come on." Rich put a "how can you resist this?" look on his face, causing our audience to laugh on cue. "We'd have so much fun."

"And we'd *have fun* beating your ugly face in," Griffin said. "You heard her. Now fuck off."

I wouldn't have thought violence did it for me until I heard it from Griffin's beautiful lips.

Rich got up in Griffin's face, his buddies moving in. "You don't tell me to fuck off. I'm gonna tell you to fuck off."

"That doesn't even make sense, Rich," Layla grumbled with annoyance. "Just—"

"What's going on here?" a teacher called out, and the crowd began to scatter.

While Mr. Lauderbeck walked toward us, the football coach's eyes narrowed at the members of his team. Rich leaned in so that his cologne felt like an assault.

Eyes narrowed to slits, distorting his objectively handsome face into something truly ugly, he hissed at Griffin, "Tonight. At the crossroads. You and me. We'll settle this then."

The "crossroads" referenced an old farming route at the edge of town that was never used at nighttime, where locals met up to drag race.

Without hesitation, Griffin responded, "You're on."

Rich leaned back a few inches and smiled good-naturedly. "Great. I can wait till then to beat your ass."

Then, without missing a beat, he spun to offer a blinding smile to the approaching teacher. "What's up, Mr. Lauderbeck? What do you think of the upcoming game against Mountain Laurel? What are our odds?"

As Rich steered him away, and everyone else dispersed, I exchanged looks with my friends.

"Well, that didn't go to plan," Layla said.

"It sounds great to me," Zoe piped up. I'd forgotten she was there. "I love watching you guys race. Hunt especially." She paused, seemingly only to moon up at him.

Hunt swallowed a long-suffering sigh, but I didn't think anyone other than the four of us would notice. Of all of us, he was actually managing to keep it together the best, even with Zoe draping herself all over him every chance she got.

"I'll be there tonight for sure," Zoe added.

I smiled tightly. "Great. Can't fucking wait. Guys, ready to go train?"

"So fucking ready," Brady snarled.

"Fuck yeah," Griffin echoed.

Griffin and Brady looked ready to pulverize something Rich-Connely-shaped. And I *knew* I was ready. After blowing off steam with our new instructors, we were going to need to order new dummies.

26

Rinse and Repeat

My admiration of our instructors' demanding, unwavering discipline had evaporated about forty-five minutes ago. In the open clearing next to the treehouse, sweat dripped down my face in annoying, tickling rivulets, and I couldn't stop myself from glaring at Yolanda. I really, really wanted to stop. My anger seemed only to delight her.

"*Vamos, vamos!*" she barked at me. My appreciation for her pleasantly exotic accent had also vanished somewhere around the hour mark. "I don't train quitters."

I snarled and hit the targets she held out—*one-two-three*, then again, and again, and fucking *again*. My shoulder muscles burned like they might actually be about to catch fire.

"Who said anything about quitting?" I bit out at her as I followed through with another jab-jab-uppercut. Her long ponytail swung as she received the brunt of my blows with an ease that suggested she could do it all day long.

<*Me,*> Layla said, but only to us, never to our teachers. <*I'm so ready to quit, it's possible I might not've ever wanted something so much in my entire fucking life.*>

Only, there was a reason Layla was whining to us and not them. No matter what she said, she wasn't a quitter. None of us were. And right then, that was feeling like a massive problem for my arms, legs, back, abs. Hell, my ass muscles ached.

<*It's been, like, three-and-a-half hours of this,*> Layla continued. <*Do our workouts really need to be four hours long every single day?*>

<*Yes,*> Brady said into my mind while he grunted aloud. He, Griffin, and Hunt were cycling through complicated kicking and striking combinations, hitting Homer's moving targets first, then Armando's, then running to the back of their short line to do it again—and all over again.

<*Tell me you don't love the burn,*> Brady said.

<*I don't love the burn,*> Layla answered drily with a wince, hanging upside down from a pullup bar, doing sit-ups. Yolanda had ordered her to do five hundred repetitions.

<*I don't believe you,*> Brady said over the rapid smacks of Griffin's flesh connecting with the targets. <*You love this shit almost as much as I do.*>

<*No. What I love is being able to walk without looking like I have a stick shoved up where the sun don't shine 'cause my ass hurts too much to relax it. I love being able to laugh without my stomach feeling like it's about to crack in half. I think they might actually be trying to kill us.*>

"You know," Yolanda said in a loud voice in Layla's general direction, "if you want to be the best at something, you have to give it everything. You can't hold back any single thing. You give, give, and give."

I would have worried Yolanda could somehow hear us talking, but it didn't take a mind reader to interpret the blatant discontent scrunching up Layla's face. My friend hissed as she crunched up for another rep.

When she was upside down again, Layla asked, "Who says I'm not giving it my all?"

Yolanda just arched a brow as she held up the targets for me to keep going. "It takes complete dedication to become a master at anything. And we were told you all want to become masters of your bodies and minds, *sí*?"

"*Sí*," I answered even though she wasn't specifically addressing me.

"We're loving this," Brady said with a grin. When he executed a flying kick then spun smoothly to deliver a roundhouse kick, Armando grinned back with an encouraging, "*Bom, bom.*"

Since he wasn't currently torturing me, I enjoyed his musical Portuguese. He tacked on a translation for Brady, saying "Good, good," in case Brady hadn't already gotten the message, which he had, judging by the pleased smile that continued to tug at his lips.

"Twenty-five more," Yolanda told me. "Then we'll take a short break."

Obediently, I cycled through twenty-five more complete exercises, then sagged.

"Twenty more."

My stare snapped to her. "What? You said that was it."

She smiled for a second, then dropped it like the act it had plainly been. "I changed my mind."

<*If she tells me to do more after I'm finished with the five hundred,*> Layla said as she hissed though another crunch, <*I will rearrange her face.*>

I scowled at Yolanda but didn't bother complaining. What was twenty more in an endless succession of them? But I did pull out some extra *oomph* to put into my next strikes, and I didn't bother hiding my real smile when she stumbled backward with one of them.

When we all stood around taking our five-minute break and guzzling water, Layla asked our teachers, "Why do you guys care so much?"

As one, Homer, Armando, and Yolanda turned toward her.

"What do you mean?" Homer asked, using a crisp towel to dab at the sweat on his brow. He even sweated elegantly. "Why wouldn't we care?"

<*Because you work for a man who only wants to kill us?*> Layla told us before answering him. "Well, it's not like we're planning to start competing or fighting or anything. We just love martial arts, honing ourselves, that kind of thing. But it's nothing official."

Homer studied Layla long enough that anyone even remotely self-conscious—which she wasn't—would have squirmed. She just stared back at him, anticipating.

Eventually, Homer said, "The five of you don't strike us as people who do things halfway."

"We aren't," Brady chimed in. "Not at all."

Homer gave him a nod of recognition that Brady lapped up like he'd earned some kind of prize.

"Well," Homer said, "neither are we. If we're going to train you, we're going to train you to the best of our capabilities, no matter what your intentions are for the future, or what said future holds."

The way he said it made me think he understood as well as we did that our futures might indeed be brief—if Magnum got his way anyhow.

"If you show up for us," Homer continued, "and you're all in, then we'll show up for you the same way."

"We're all in," Griffin said, and I peered at him.

The moment he felt my gaze on him, he tilted his entire body in my direction. I didn't think either of us would last much longer without touching each other.

"Yes, we are," I said, for everyone else—though I was privately referencing the magnetism between Griffin and me.

Armando started rolling his shoulders, stretching out his arms and bouncing on his feet.

"Uh-oh," Layla muttered under her breath before she thunked her head on my shoulder. "Dude looks like he's prepping to kill us."

Armando laughed, a bright, uncommon sound, and his eyes crinkled at the sides. "No, just some sparring."

He turned to remove his zero-drop shoes, his back muscles flexing with each of his minor movements.

<*You know what?*> Layla said, mostly to me I thought. <*I don't think I mind tussling with that man. Is he fine or what?*>

<*He looks like he could take any opponent down in one-point-five seconds flat,*> Brady said with equal levels of admiration.

"You are very close to each other, *sí*?" Yolanda asked, startling me from my thoughts and those of my friends.

I looked over at her as Hunt nodded and said, "Yes. We've been friends all our lives."

She studied us with open curiosity. "I can see that. I hope it will serve you well."

<*What the fuck does that mean?*> Layla asked.

<*Dunno,*> I said, but it did sound a bit like she might be sympathetic to our plight.

"Come," Armando called out. "Break is over. We fight."

<*I think I'm in love,*> Brady said, before adding, "I'll go first."

I was already chuckling at Brady's eagerness to have his ass whupped when I heard a single bark. Whipping my head toward the treehouse's porch, where Bobo stood just as I'd asked him, I saw him looking down the path that led to the houses.

"Someone's coming," I announced, though by then everyone was already looking that way.

"Stretch," Armando told us while we waited. "No waste time."

I leaned into a soothing stretch for my shoulder until none other than Magnum fucking Chase waltzed into the clearing with an ease that suggested he owned it. Knowing him, it was possible he did. It seemed like he pretty much owned our faux parents and everything they did.

He wore jeans that looked ironed, a light sweater that draped as if it were made of silk, an important-looking watch that gleamed on his wrist, and a charismatic smile I wished I could peel from his face with acid.

"Hi, everyone," he said cheerily.

I had to suppress a shudder that threatened to tear through me. Turned out I disliked a pleasant Magnum even more than a menacing one. At least when he was threatening us it was obvious what we were dealing with.

"Hello, Mr. Chase," Homer answered. "We didn't expect to see you here."

"I happened to be in the area and thought I'd drop in to see how the training was going."

As if a man as conniving as him did anything by chance.

"Well then, it's good timing," Homer offered. "We were about to end the day with some sparring."

An already annoyingly perky Magnum seemed to perk up more at that. "Excellent. That's the most fun part." He then looked at the five of us expectantly.

It was only then that I realized my friends and I were standing around openly staring at him, our postures tight and angry—and he was supposed to be a longtime family friend we adored.

Not the man who'd orchestrated everything in our lives only to study and murder us, study and murder us, rinse and repeat.

Fuck. Him. *Hard*.

Any qualms I'd had about wiping him from the face of the Earth: gone.

My previous exhaustion: gone.

I was jittery with the desire to pounce and attack until his bloody corpse lay on the ground.

But we couldn't fuck up. Not now, and especially not with him.

Before I could overcome the disgust of being near him, I forced myself to paste a smile on my face that said I was happy to see him, not that I was in that very moment fantasizing about clubbing him to a bloody death with a fallen branch.

"Hey, Uncle Magnum," I heard myself say like the words didn't make me want to gag. "How've you been?"

I had no idea how we were expected to interact with him and hoped that was a safe bet. "No hugs today unless you wanna smell like you've gone ten rounds with these beasts of instructors you sent us."

Magnum studied me for a beat too long, long enough for me to worry we weren't huggers. But then he smiled again.

"Aw, then you'll owe me double hugs next time."

<If I'm forced to hug him,> Layla warned, <I'll be stabbing him in his cold, black heart. Just so you all know.>

<Only if I don't beat you to it,> Griffin said.

Magnum drew closer to me, and I felt Griffin move to my back.

<Cool it, Griff,> Hunt cautioned.

Griffin remained where he was.

Magnum's gaze traveled from me to him and back. "How's the training been going?" He glanced at our teachers for a moment. "How've they been treating you?"

I chuckled, surprised I was able to. "Like they don't think we'll need to be able to walk tomorrow."

Brady stepped forward. "Like they're trying to kill us."

From behind Magnum, I caught Armando's reaction—he jerked, then tried to pretend he hadn't.

Brady laughed and palmed Magnum on the back. "You know us well, Uncle Magnum. We're eating this shit up. Guess we're gluttons for punishment."

"Not me," Layla said. "I'm not."

Laughter circled our group, and I felt my body relax, even if it was all fake.

"What, Lay, can't keep up with the others?" Magnum teased.

<You've gotta pull this off, Lay,> I immediately told her. If I was wrestling with the urge to twist his head till his neck went *pop*, then so must she be.

Lay was *our* nickname for her.

Eventually, she smiled and chuffed a laugh, even running a hand through her bangs, currently tinged a pale powder blue. "Better be careful there, Uncle Magnum, or I might feel the need to prove myself and challenge you to a round."

While Magnum threw his head back to laugh, Layla glared at him like she had laser vision and was trying to burn him up.

Our instructors were observing her. There was no way any of them missed how her look only turned friendly again when the billionaire looked back at her.

Shit. Our instructors were too sharp for us not to be busted. The question was: would they give us up?

When theirs and Magnum's backs were turned, my friends and I shared a loaded, anxious look. But then everything proceeded more or less as expected.

Yolanda played a berimbau, a stringed percussion instrument commonly used to accompany capoeira, while Armando kicked our ever-loving asses in his personalized melding of its constant dancing with crazy effective sweeps, strikes, and kicks, some of which I recognized from karate and kung fu, making me wish I were as proficient as he was. Hell, I wished I were as skilled at any martial art as he was. The man, small and light as he was, was an obvious *beast* in the ring, on a mat, on the grassy floor of a forest clearing—anywhere. He leapt and twisted and turned so quickly and with such agility that none of us stood a chance against him.

An hour or so later, when training was finally over for the day, my friends and I plopped onto the ground and looked up at our instructors and Magnum, who were speaking together off to the side.

<*Why does he even care if we get good at fighting?*> Griffin asked via the group chat. <*I'm really convinced after this that he does. But why? I don't get it. Why would Magnum give a shit?*>

<*I don't get it either,*> Brady said.

<*I've been wondering about that too,*> Hunt added. <*Maybe he thinks this'll somehow draw out some of our other powers? We're at a disadvantage since we're the only ones who don't know what they are.*>

<*I'm really fucking over all the disadvantages,*> I said.

<*Ditto, girl,*> Layla said. <*Dit-fucking-oh.*>

Magnum approached, our teachers a few steps behind him, and I had to coach my body not to react when, boy oh boy, I wanted to launch at him, claws first.

"All right, guys, I have to go. Rich texted saying he wants to borrow the Aston Martin tonight, so I have to get home to talk him out of whatever trouble he's planning on getting into."

Griffin chuffed a rasp of a laugh. "Good luck with that."

Magnum smirked as if we truly were all friends, and we all knew no one was going to be talking Rich out of anything. In a time when I wasn't certain of much, I'd bet Rich wouldn't admit to the drag racing. He'd lie through his teeth.

Unless.

Unless of course the drag race was all part of the plan.

And why wouldn't it be?

Everything about our lives seemed to be planned down to their minutiae—it's just that we weren't in on any of it.

After more promises of owed hugs I hoped to fuck we'd never have to deliver, Magnum left the way he came, and our instructors stood around us.

"We'll see you again here, tomorrow at four," Homer said. "And soon we'll start meeting at the institute. Better equipment."

Tersely, I smiled up at him. The last place I wanted to go was the institute. We'd only just escaped the cursed place.

We said our goodbyes, and when the three of them walked off down the path toward the houses and their cars, Armando was a pace behind them. He flicked a lingering look at us before swallowing markedly enough that I couldn't miss the action despite the growing distance.

Then the path curved, and the forest swallowed them whole.

"Well, that wasn't encouraging," Griffin said.

"Nope," I replied. "Don't race tonight." The plea spilled out of me before I realized it would.

When Griffin looked over at me, his eyes were troubled. "I have to."

"No. You don't. Not really."

"And let Rich win?"

"That's not the game we're playing right now."

"No. We're playing a game we can't win."

As that sentiment sank into my bones, Hunt promised, "We'll go over the car with a fine-tooth comb. We'll check everything before Griff drives."

"Everything'll be fine, Joss," Brady said, and I nodded numbly in response.

I'd never been so sure of anything in my life: everything would *not* be fine.

It already wasn't.

27

Not a Play-It-Safe Kinda Crew

"Bobo really didn't look happy to be left behind," Layla commented from the back seat.

We were all piled into the new Clyde, and with Griffin at the wheel I rode shotgun.

"When he gave me those eyes of his," she went on, "all sad and shit? I swear, I was crazy close to smuggling him in the trunk."

It wasn't like I never left Bobo at the house when I went out. With school alone, he was used to it. But my sweet boy and I were connected. Undoubtedly, he could feel the tension vibrating through me. He'd protested my leaving more than usual, his insistence pushing the limits of all the training I'd done with him.

"The crossroads is no place for him," Brady told his sister.

"Well, obviously. I wasn't actually suggesting we turn around and go pick him up. He just . . . it made me sad, that's all."

"It made me sad too," I said softly, gazing out the window, taking in the trees the headlights illuminated as we zoomed past them.

Griffin zipped around a curve, shifted gears, and brought his hand to my thigh, squeezing my leg through my tight jeans.

In the car's near darkness, I couldn't make out the intensity of his eyes, just the contours of his beautiful face, the gentle curves of his lips.

"We could still go back though," I ventured. "Order pizza and get cozy with some beers, maybe some herb. Binge watch some more *Warrior*. Get inspired with some of its sick fight scenes before Homer and them kick our asses tomorrow. Remind ourselves why we're training."

Griffin glanced at me before fixing his eyes back on the winding road up ahead, pulling his hand from my leg to shift again.

Instantly, I missed his touch. I'd gotten too little of it lately, while we all played the parts Magnum had assigned us in this farce.

"That show is so totally lit," Brady said. "Makes me want to be able to fight like they do right the fuck now. Get sticky as much as they do too."

"That show makes even me want to get sticky," Layla chimed in, as if either of them wanting to get laid more often was unusual.

"Shall we do it, then?" I asked, my question hopeful.

"You know we can't," Griffin said.

I'd already tried to talk him out of racing several times in the last hour. Even though I expected that answer, I sighed. "Can't we though? Who cares what Rich and all his stupid friends think?"

"It's not about that. I don't care one shit what any of them think." Griffin switched to speaking to us alone. <*Rich needs to learn he can't push us all around. I'm fucking done with him. I'll never forget what he did to Brade.*>

<*Nor will I,*> Hunt said.

<*I'm not gonna stand by and watch him push himself on you now. It was bad enough watching him perv on Lay. I won't do nothing while he plays his sick little game with you too.*>

I swiveled in my seat to fully face Griff's silhouette. <*What happened with Brade was an accident. Maybe. Regardless, it's not like* he's ever gonna stop being an asshole. I'm pretty sure that shit's built into his DNA.>

<He must get it from his uncle,> Layla said with a chortle.

I insisted, <Our only focus right now should be on staying alive. Everything else can wait.>

<It's not like I'm taking any unusual risks,> Griff argued. <We've raced at the crossroads dozens of times before, and that was before we knew we could come back from the dead.>

I faced forward, unwilling to search the shadows of his face while I asked the question that weighed on me more than any of the other unknowns. <And what if one of these times one of us doesn't come back? What if they kill us for good?>

No one said anything to that, leaving me to assume they'd been wondering the same thing.

Finally, Hunt said, <Then it'll be the same as with anyone else.>

<Only everyone else doesn't have an entire team of professionals out to kill them,> I pressed.

<That much is fucking true,> Layla admitted. <But, Joss, that's a constant of our lives now. Until we find the way out, we've gotta accept it and keep going best we can.>

<I refuse to accept that.> I turned in my seat to shoot her a look even though she wouldn't be able to make out much of it. <I won't accept that any of you guys could be taken away from me at any time. No fucking way.>

Again, a deep silence spread through the car as I faced forward. We were probably less than five minutes away from the crossroads now.

After a minute, Layla said, <You're extra freaked right now 'cause it's Griff, and he's, like, your secret boyfriend.>

<Of course I'm extra freaked 'cause it's Griff. But that doesn't mean I'd be any less freaked if it were any of you. This all just . . . I'm not handling it well.>

Brady huffed. <*None of us are handling it well, Joss. Some of us are just better at shoving down our feelings and pretending. I can barely sleep at night anymore. I keep feeling like one of you'll be gone when I wake up.*>

The weight of our reality only grew heavier.

<*We have to find a way out of this,*> Hunt said. <*A real way.*>

<*Well, we're all fucking trying, aren't we?*> Brady asked. <*No luck yet. I don't understand how we can be the freaking immortals and still be the weak ones.*>

<*Because we aren't willing to kill indiscriminately,*> Griffin said.

<*At first I didn't know if I'd be able to kill Magnum,*> I admitted. <*But now I know I can. Now I can't fucking wait to get my hands on him. I can't keep living this way, just waiting for the other shoe to drop. For death. It's fucking insanity, man. Insanity.*>

<*So we set up to kill him ASAP,*> Layla said. <*Like, tomorrow.*>

<*Why tomorrow specifically?*> Brady asked.

Some rustling told me Layla shifted in her seat directly behind me to stare at Brady. <*'Cause why wait? I'm feeling this shit just as bad as Joss is.*>

<*Me too,*> Hunt said. <*I'm in. Let's figure out where he's going to be and take him out.*>

<*Okay,*> Griffin said. <*I don't think they'll be expecting us to come in hot, guns blazing. I think they've bought it, that we don't know shit right now.*>

<*Even with us knowing more than usual,*> I said, <*I still feel like we don't know shit.*>

<*Me too,*> said Hunt. <*And I don't like not knowing something.*>

Hunt exhaled sharply, and I turned to see Layla grinning after jabbing him in the side. <*Must be a new feeling for you,*> she teased. <*Not knowing something, you fucking brainiac.*>

"We're getting close," Brady announced aloud.

I pleaded, "Please don't do it, Griff. I have a bad feeling about it."

To be fair, I hadn't had a good feeling about our life expectancies since we'd discovered we were "extraordinary."

Griffin glanced at me, slowing to take a sharp right. Closer to the old farming route, the trees had been cut centuries ago to make room for cultivation. The streets were straighter here than they were around our stomping grounds, where the roads wove through the forests.

His strong, warm hand rubbed my leg some more. "It'll be okay, Joss. We've checked Clyde over. He's running great."

Indeed, we'd practically dissected the car in our need to verify that no part of the Mustang had been tampered with, that every component was where and how it was supposed to be. The brakes were in perfect working condition, as was the steering, the souped-up V8 engine, all of it. We'd even stolen defibrillator paddles from the school and stashed them in the trunk, just in case. None of us were fans of stealing, but if we tried to buy them, we worried someone would rat us out to Magnum and the jig would be up before we'd had the chance to make substantial progress.

"It's a short, straight run," Griffin persisted. "It'll be smooth sailing. I've driven it tons of times. As have you."

"That was before . . ." I hadn't meant to say that aloud. Hurriedly, I adjusted. "Before Rich asked Uncle Magnum for the Aston Martin. How are you gonna beat the Aston Martin Valkyrie?"

Griffin chuckled smoothly. "You know as well as I do. The car's part of it, sure, and the Aston Martin's a fucking beauty, no doubt. But more than the car, it's the driver. And I can outdrive the fuck out of Rich Connely. Besides, Clyde's a sweet ride too."

"Fuck yeah he is," Brady agreed.

<It's not the same car we worked on,> I said, growing desperate. We were on the final stretch of road that would intersect the crossroads. We were almost there.

<I know,> Griffin said. <I don't like it either. But all the upgrades we made are still there. And for all we know, they've switched Clyde out on us several times. Maybe Bonnie too.>

From the seat behind Griff's, Brady sucked in an affronted gasp. <*Blasphemy!*> Then he pretended he'd choked, coughing for our likely eavesdroppers.

<*Maybe she used to be bubblegum pink,*> Layla said.

<*Take that back!*> Brady snapped.

Layla laughed, and it came off as if she were laughing at her brother as he choked on his spittle. Knowing the two of them, it was believable.

Once more, Griffin's hand found its way to my thigh. If anyone had planted night-vision cameras in here, we were fucked; the darkness wouldn't conceal that we desperately wanted to be more than friends.

Griffin's deep voice filtered softly through my mind. <*It's not enough for me to stay alive, always looking over our shoulders, just waiting for them to make a move. If I'm going to fight so hard to stay alive, I need to really* live, *Joss. I want to be* me. *To do the things that feel good to do. If we don't do that, what are we even fighting so hard to live for?*>

<*To be together? To all make it into our twenties and beyond?*>

<*And we will. However we do it, I know we'll find the way. Together, we can do fucking anything.*>

<*Hell yeah we can,*> Brady said.

<*All we've really got right now is this moment, and then the next and the next. But Joss, that's it. We don't know what the future holds. None of us do. That goes for everyone. We've gotta live the shit out of right now 'cause it's what we've got. It's the only for-sure we've got, and I don't want to waste a second of it.*>

<*But you could enjoy the fuck out of the moment without taking any additional risks.*>

<*Then I wouldn't be me. We've never played it safe. Never lived safe.*>

<*He's got a point there, girl,*> Layla said. <*We're not a play-it-safe kinda crew. Not even you. Fuck, especially not you.*>

<*Exactly,*> Griffin said. <*Don't go changing who we are for them. That's one thing they can't make us give up.*>

And just like that, I was forced to accept I'd lost this battle. After a round of deep inhales that did nothing to settle the unease churning inside me, I nodded into the darkness.

<*Yeah, okay. You're right. It's us against the world. So let's be us.*>

<*That's my girl,*> Griffin said, and his smile was so fucking sexy and gorgeous that he felt larger than life. Like no one could ever take him from me.

Griffin was passion and fire and intensity. He was broodiness and rough edges and power. Griffin was *everything*.

By the time we pulled up to where dozens of cars were parked on the shoulder of the two-lane country road, excitement had replaced my unease, and I buzzed with it.

"Looks like Rich got the word out," Layla said as Griffin pulled to a stop close to the front.

She exited first. Brady and Hunt filed out next, the three of them waiting for us.

I was pushing open my door when Griffin leaned over, his hand covering mine to pull it shut again.

<*Give us some cover, guys,*> Griffin said.

While I was still wondering what he meant by that, his hands gripped my waist and tugged me toward him. A surprised gasp slipped out of me. Half perched on the edge of my seat, half on his lap, with a gearshift digging into my outer thigh, Griffin's lips slammed against mine.

Instantly I was on fire, returning his kiss as if *carpe fucking diem* were inked across my forehead.

We picked up where we left off in my bedroom at the institute. His hands, my hands, they tried to be everywhere at once. I felt feverish with the need to explore his body the way only a lover could.

To claim him as mine.

All. Fucking. Mine.

When his mouth trailed down to my neck, I threw my head back and swallowed down a moan that was part panting whimper. "Griff..." I barely dared breathe, even now concerned with who might be listening and what it would mean if they realized Griffin and I were two hot seconds away from fucking right here in his car, spectators be damned.

He pulled me fully onto his lap, his lips dragging across my collarbones, a hand cupping my breast, rubbing across a nipple that strained to bust free of my bra so it could get where it belonged already—in his fucking mouth.

I heard voices outside that weren't our friends. Opening my eyes took real effort, but when I saw Brady, Hunt, and Layla positioned around Clyde to block as much of the view through the windows as possible, I didn't hesitate to straddle Griffin. The fit was tight, but ever so doable. I lowered myself onto Griffin's groin, his dick hard through his jeans, and had to bite my lip to keep in the wanton moan that wanted to escape. My eyes rolled back for a moment as I ground on him, and he grunted roughly, bringing both hands to my breasts, his thumbs rubbing my nipples over two layers of fabric that felt as unwelcome as two hundred.

My core throbbed as I rubbed it up and down the length of his erection. When I ran my fingers through his hair, I tugged and lowered my lips to his ear to whisper, "Screw waiting. I want you inside me right this fucking second."

This time, Griffin groaned louder than he probably should have. I had zero fucks to give.

He kissed my neck again, my ear, then sucked on my earlobe. There, his breath hot and tantalizing, he whispered, "You're everything to me, Joss. I want you. I want it all."

My core clenched. I brought my hand between us to his jeans, rubbing it over his hard dick.

He threw his head back onto the seat, his eyes clenched shut for a moment. A sweep of arriving headlights illuminated his face for several seconds, and I had to stop just to admire him—his full lips, his strong jawline, the dark scruff along it that made him look dangerous and entirely fucking edible.

<Keep looking at me like that and our first time won't be the special event I've been envisioning,> Griffin said inside my mind—and also into our friends' minds, *fuck me*.

<Git after it, bro,> Brady said, infiltrating what I was trying really hard to pretend was a private moment.

<At this point, I don't mind putting on a show,> I said. <Fuck it. Fuck it all.>

I lowered myself back onto his lap, rubbing myself against him.

<Don't tell me that. After all these years . . . .> His hands stilled my grinding hips, and with an infinitely gentle touch, he pulled my face down to his. With the barely-there lighting provided by headlights pointing away from us, his eyes were dark, glittering, possessive. "Later." He flattened his palm between my breasts and pressed his forehead to mine. "Just you and me," he breathed.

Both his hands moved to my ass. He squeezed, then slid them under my shirt and splayed his palms against my skin, pulling me close against his chest.

There, pressed together, with far too many clothes between us, we inhaled and exhaled, again and again and again, until our breathing slowed and calmed.

When his lips next found mine, their touch was gentle, a flutter. "You and me," he whispered against them.

Wanting that more than anything else in the world, I nodded against him, where our foreheads still met.

His hot hands slid down my back, across my waist, and beneath the waistband of my jeans to squeeze my ass—my cheeks bare around a string of lace.

I jerked my gaze up to his. His eyes were still dark, still glittering, still possessive.

He gave me a cheeky grin and a wink that made me melt all over again. "I have a race to win before I claim my prize."

As if I might not have understood what he was implying, after he pulled his hands free, he slapped my ass, then lifted me off him, guiding me to the passenger's seat.

My own eyes wide, my skin flushed so that even I could feel its heat, I stared at him.

Even knowing it wasn't the OG Clyde, he patted the steering wheel with open fondness, then winked at me again. "Come on, woman. Time to kick some ass."

He gave me a final kiss on the lips, then rapped his knuckles on the window, and when Brady cleared it, he opened his door.

Feeling as though a force of nature had swept through the car—as if *he* were a force to be reckoned with—and knowing I would follow him to the ends of the Earth and beyond, I opened my own door.

All at once, I realized music was thumping from the other end of the line of cars, and that several more had arrived since I'd last looked. A few sets of headlights illuminated bystanders—guys and a few smart girls wearing jeans and hoodies against the chill of early autumn, plus several not-so-smart girls in skimpy bodycon dresses and sky-high heels.

Layla walked over to me, nodding in their direction. "Sure, they look hot as fuck, but their tits have gotta be freezing off, am I right?"

I stuffed my hands into my own hoodie. "Totally glad we dressed for the weather."

Layla smirked knowingly. "Your jeans look painted on, your eye makeup is motherfucking smoky hawt, you're wearing fuck-me boots, and I'd bet the mother lode on you wearing matching lacy lingerie underneath it all."

I laughed, feeling so much lighter than I had when we first left the house. "You know me too well."

She shrugged. "Like you don't know I'm rocking the same. Never know when a girl's gonna get lucky around here."

She scanned our surroundings. Beyond our guys, others were busy checking us out. Appearing pleased by the attention we were drawing, Layla fluffed her hair and waggled her brows at Reed Carter.

I laughed at her antics, drawing Griffin's eyes just as Rich drove by slowly in the Aston Martin Valkyrie, a Slipstream Green that screamed of money. Before he passed us, he lowered his window and eyed Griffin.

"Ready to lose?"

Griffin chuffed. "Always trying for the clever lines and failing, aren't you, Rich? I'm ready to put you in your place."

"All right, then. Let's go."

With that, Rich rolled farther up the road and stopped to idle at the painted line. The county had tried to erase it several times over the last couple of years, but that never lasted.

Hunt, Brady, Layla, and I surrounded Griffin as he leaned against Clyde's door. He stared back at us, his gaze heating on me before nodding.

"I'll see you guys on the other side. Then, we'll celebrate."

Once more, his stare landed on me—and again heated.

Fuck yeah, we were going to celebrate.

"Give him hell," I told Griff.

He tipped his head at me, then the others. "Enough for all of us."

Before I was ready to say goodbye, or maybe good luck, he was inside the car, strapping on his seatbelt and revving the engine.

<See you guys in less than five,> he told us, rolling around the other cars to sidle up next to Rich at the starting line.

A girl in bodycon accepted a pair of flags from Tyler Houser, the organizer of these races. Born and raised in Ridgemore, and now in his late twenties, Tyler had never left town. We didn't know him well, just enough to understand he ran several shady ventures, including taking bets at these drag races.

"Hold up," I called out to both of them and hustled over.

Tyler turned fully my way with a question in the arch of his brows.

Across the few feet that still separated us, I called ahead, "I'll take those flags."

When I reached them, the girl hesitated, but Tyler didn't, taking them from her to hand them to me.

"Thanks," I said, handing him a bill. "And fifty on Griffin."

His brows arched again. "Even against an Aston fucking Martin?"

"Even then. Especially fucking then. Griff's gonna leave Rich's ass in the dust."

The finish line was a quarter mile out. Not long for cars going full-out, but long enough for a skilled driver to carve out a gap.

Tyler dipped his head to one side, scratching his pockmarked cheeks as he considered me, then pocketed the fifty as he nodded. "Shit, I guess I've seen the lot of you do crazier. Start it when you're ready, Joss."

While I'd been talking, Layla, Hunt, and Brady had drawn closer.

Layla pointed to the flags. "Since when do you wanna start the races?"

"Since I can't wait for it to be over." And because I wanted to have some part in this race, to feel like I was riding along with Griffin in some way.

The crowd around me quieted in anticipation. The music was turned down while Griff and Rich revved their engines.

I positioned myself between the two cars, my eyes on Griff for a moment I wanted to drag out forever, before I raised the red flags to either side of me.

<You've got this,> I told him.

<You know I do,> he answered.

Then I brought down both flags.

Griff was off a millisecond before Rich, who burned rubber as he pulled out.

I spun and held my breath against the smoke, watching the glow of taillights grow distant, knowing it would be over faster than seemed possible.

Brady, Hunt, and Layla joined me at the starting line.

"Looking tight," Brady commented as Griff and Rich seemed to be pacing each other.

"Come on, Griff," Layla urged though he wouldn't hear her. "You can do it!"

"'Course he can," Hunt said. "Griff's the man."

Griffin pulled ahead a few feet, and I laughed, suddenly buoyant.

He was going to do it. Of course he was.

Griffin could do anything—fucking anything—

A terrifying *BOOOOOOOOOOOOOOOOOOOM* clapped the night before rolling like thunder. The earth beneath our feet rattled—as Clyde erupted into a fireball.

Its back tires on fire, already smoking, the Aston Martin's body visibly shuddered as it raced past the burning Mustang.

I knew I was screaming but couldn't hear myself.

My ears were ringing.

My heart had stopped beating.

And the Mustang—with Griffin inside it—burned like a raging inferno.

Again, the Mustang exploded, the flames pushing higher, bigger, wider—deadlier.

My heart thudded back to beating, now too fast.

Pieces of Griffin's car rained down from the sky to the ground with horrifying clatters that were muffled by the incessant ringing.

I might have still been screaming when I took off at a flat sprint—fuck-me heels be damned.

Layla, Brady, and Hunt ran beside me.

Toward our friend.

Toward the man I loved.

The man we all loved.

Even when it was obviously too late. We'd find Griffin's beautiful body in charred, mangled pieces—a precise reflection of my heart.

About the Author

Lucía Ashta is the international-bestselling Argentinian American author of more than seventy young adult and adult fantasy and paranormal books including the Royals of Embermere, Smoky Mountain Pack, Witches of Gales Haven, Magical Creatures Academy, Witching World, and Six Shooter and a Shifter series. A former attorney and architect, Ashta lives in North Carolina's Smoky Mountains with her husband and three daughters. When she isn't writing, she's reading, painting, or adventuring.

Podium

DISCOVER MORE
STORIES UNBOUND

PodiumEntertainment.com